AMY LANE

Choose your Lane to love!
Readers love the
Romantic Suspense from AMY LANE

Fish on a Bicycle

"Jackson and Ellery have a huge place in my heart. Like, it's massive. And every time Amy Lane writes more about them and their many insane adventures, that piece of my grows and now it's taken over."

—Gay Book Reviews

"I knew better. I so knew better. You NEVER read an Amy book without tissues and oh my gah! You're killing me here."

—Love Bytes

"The problem for me with an author like Amy Lane is that she continues to exceed my expectations... Thank you, Amy, you're the best."

—Rainbow Book Reviews

Paint It Black

"*Paint it Black* had some very special moments and was a pretty compelling read overall. Amy Lane knows how to do angst and this book is full to the brim with it."

—Joyfully Jay

"Wow-o-wow, does Amy Lane orchestrate a symphony with *Paint It Black*... *Paint It Black* licks at our feelings, pushing them gently to the edge and back."

—Kimmers Erotic Book Reviews

By Amy Lane

An Amy Lane Christmas
Behind the Curtain
Bewitched by Bella's Brother
Bolt-hole
Christmas Kitsch
Christmas with Danny Fit
Clear Water
Do-over
Food for Thought
Freckles
Gambling Men
Going Up
Hammer & Air
Homebird
If I Must
Immortal
It's Not Shakespeare
Left on St. Truth-be-Well
The Locker Room
Mourning Heaven
Phonebook
Puppy, Car, and Snow
Racing for the Sun • Hiding the
Moon
Raising the Stakes
Regret Me Not
Shiny!
Shirt
Sidecar
String Boys
A Solid Core of Alpha
Three Fates
Truth in the Dark
Turkey in the Snow
Under the Rushes
Wishing on a Blue Star

BENEATH THE STAIN
Beneath the Stain • Paint It Black

BONFIRES
Bonfires • Crocus

CANDY MAN
Candy Man • Bitter Taffy
Lollipop • Tart and Sweet

DREAMSPUN DESIRES
THE MANNIES
The Virgin Manny
Manny Get Your Guy
Stand by Your Manny
A Fool and His Manny
SEARCH AND RESCUE
Warm Heart
Silent Heart

FAMILIAR LOVE
Familiar Angel • Familiar Demon

FISH OUT OF WATER
Fish Out of Water
Red Fish, Dead Fish
A Few Good Fish • Hiding the Moon
Fish on a Bicycle

FLOPHOUSE
Shades of Henry

Published by DREAMSPINNER PRESS
www.dreamspinnerpress.com

By AMY LANE

Published by DREAMSPINNER PRESS
www.dreamspinnerpress.com

SHADES
of HENRY

AMY
LANE

REAMSPINNER
PRESS

Published by

DREAMSPINNER PRESS

5032 Capital Circle SW, Suite 2, PMB# 279, Tallahassee, FL 32305-7886 USA
www.dreamspinnerpress.com

This is a work of fiction. Names, characters, places, and incidents either are the product of author imagination or are used fictitiously, and any resemblance to actual persons, living or dead, business establishments, events, or locales is entirely coincidental.

Shades of Henry
© 2020 Amy Lane

Cover Art
© 2020 L.C. Chase
http://www.lcchase.com
Cover content is for illustrative purposes only and any person depicted on the cover is a model.

All rights reserved. This book is licensed to the original purchaser only. Duplication or distribution via any means is illegal and a violation of international copyright law, subject to criminal prosecution and upon conviction, fines, and/or imprisonment. Any eBook format cannot be legally loaned or given to others. No part of this book may be reproduced or transmitted in any form or by any means, electronic or mechanical, including photocopying, recording, or by any information storage and retrieval system, without the written permission of the Publisher, except where permitted by law. To request permission and all other inquiries, contact Dreamspinner Press, 5032 Capital Circle SW, Suite 2, PMB# 279, Tallahassee, FL 32305-7886, USA, or www. dreamspinnerpress.com.

Trade Paperback ISBN: 978-1-64405-619-6
Digital ISBN: 978-1-64405-618-9
Library of Congress Control Number: 2019955263
Trade Paperback published March 2020
v. 1.0
Printed in the United States of America
∞
This paper meets the requirements of
ANSI/NISO Z39.48-1992 (Permanence of Paper).

This one is for Desi and Brenda and Mary of course—because everybody was as invested in Henry as I was, and that meant the world to me.

And also for Mate and the kids—because my house is just that nutballs sometimes, and Mate is my partner who looks at the chaos and then at me and goes, "O-kay... so we deal with this how?"

RUDE AWAKENINGS

HENRY KNEW what a cheap hotel bed felt like. With nine years in the military, he and Mal had gone on leave in a thousand different places. And the creak of the springs, the smell of sex, the chafing of cheap sheets?

It was all sickeningly familiar.

Except his face hurt, and his shoulder too, where someone had landed a blow, and his knuckles had that three-day ache from being clenched too hard.

Who'd he beaten up again?

His eyes shot open.

No. He hadn't landed any blows in that fight. And Malachi had effectively betrayed him and ripped his heart out. And his family had taken Mal's side.

Then why did he smell like sex?

He rolled over in the queen-sized bed and felt the warm spot—and the wet spot—and grimaced. Last night was so hazy. God. The bus had pulled in at, what? Ten thirty the night before? It had been raining, and he'd gotten a hotel nearby, and there'd been a guy... not bad-looking. Brown eyes, brown hair, a slick smile that showed all his teeth and a couple of dimples to boot.

He'd been a little tipsy. At first Henry had thought it was alcohol, but after the guy had come up to the hotel room, he'd popped open a little pharmacy bottle and offered Henry one. And it hadn't been vodka in there.

Usually drugs would have repelled the fuck out of Henry, but his face still hurt, and his heart still hurt, and he was alone in Sacramento—a place as strange to him as he was to it—and the only people he had to contact in the morning might just kick the door in his face.

He hadn't taken one, but he hadn't kicked Martin out of the room, either.

The shower turned off, and Henry swung his legs over the end of the creaky bed and rested his head in his hands. A burst of steam and hotel-scented shampoo blew Martin back into the room, and he grinned, the look so suggestive, so filthy, Henry felt his gorge rise.

"Ready for another round, soldier?"

"No, thank you," Henry muttered. "I need to shower and get out of here."

"That's a shame." Martin gave a patently fake pout. "You sure you don't want to stay around for... coffee?"

"Very." Henry stood up, keeping the sheet around his waist.

"Well, then, could you spare some money for a cab?" It was said with a raised eyebrow, and Henry's stomach churned. It wasn't even a one-night stand. Well, thank God for condoms *and* PrEP.

"Yeah, sure." Well, the guy could have taken his wallet and run while Henry was still sleeping; that was something. "Throw me my pants. My wallet's in—" Martin went straight for the wallet in the pocket. "—the side."

He wondered if he was going to have to chase his one-night trick naked down the Astroturf hallway of this shitty motel, but Martin froze as he was opening Henry's wallet.

"Henry?"

"That's me."

"Henry Matthew Worrall?"

Henry blinked and rubbed his eyes. "Martin Whoever-You-Are?"

Martin blinked and shoved the wallet back into Henry's pants, complete with the cash he'd been about to grab. "Sampson. But you can call me Martin About to Be Out of Your Hair," he said abruptly. "Thanks for the nice time, soldier. See you around."

He was dressing as he said it, the kind of quick, efficient movements of someone who was apparently used to getting in and out of his clothes a lot.

And then he was standing at the door before Henry could get awkward about not wanting to leave his wallet in the same room with the guy, even if Martin had just refused any payment for what had been about to be a business transaction.

"You said you're going to visit your brother?" Martin asked carefully, thin face expressionless.

"Yeah?"

"Good. I hope you both find your way home."

And then he was gone.

Henry groaned and banged his head silently on his fist. *Shit. Shit shit shit shit.* Sigh. Shit was a thing he had to get together in a paper bag right now or he was going to become one with this truly horrific bed.

Nine years in the Army. Nine years of learning how to pull himself up from his bootstraps and do the fucking job, and he was going to stop now?

He stood, back straight, and dropped the sheet, then grabbed the towels Martin had left on the floor. He had his brother's address in his phone and enough money for a cab and some breakfast. And he was damned if he was going to let a glitch in his plan like Martin No-Last-Name derail him from moving on with his life.

Funny how what fate planned and what we plan for ourselves are very rarely the same thing, right?

Right?

"Henry? Seriously. Is that you?"

Henry hefted his duffel bag over his shoulder and tried a smile. Davy, his brother, had always been the one with the charming grin. Henry had learned to keep his own features stoic and even in the last nine years.

"Davy?" Oh, this was harder than he'd thought.

His brother David lived in a cute little house in a nice residential area in the city proper. From Davy's letters years before, Henry knew that the property values in Sacramento were pretty high, and the yard was small and the house only had one full bathroom and a spare bedroom, but he hadn't expected it to be so... cute. The gutters and trim were painted green, the stucco painted a pale cream color, the fence recently stained, and from the looks of it over the fence, the backyard had some landscaping done.

The lawn was cut even with the driveway, and the shrubs in the front yard had been recently trimmed.

It wasn't some trashy den of iniquity, as his father had sneered about ever since Davy had come out—not just as gay, but as a former porn model. It was a home, right down to three sets of galoshes on the porch, one set a mud-covered and tiny pink color, with little umbrellas all over it....

Davy's boyfriend—husband, dammit, husband!—had a niece who they cared for. Henry had forgotten about that until he'd walked up onto their porch, and suddenly he couldn't decide who was dirtier, his brother for coming out to the family and walking away or Henry for getting kicked off the farm and dragging all his problems with him.

But then Davy opened the door, and Henry stopped asking himself stupid questions.

"Henry?"

Henry tried to give an ingratiating smile, but before it could even morph into a scowl, his brother—whom he had sneered at with their father for being a fag and a whore and a disgrace to the family—smiled at him with tears in his eyes and took Henry into the kind of embrace Henry had always dreamed of getting from his family, but never had.

An hour later—after Carlos, Davy's boy... erm... husband had taken his niece to school, all while giving Henry a lot of suspicious looks that Henry had more than earned—Henry sat at the breakfast table, eating pancakes and drinking coffee and feeling both happier and guiltier than he ever had in his life.

"Does Dad still call me names behind my back?" Davy asked. Something in his voice seemed to hurt, as if he hated himself for asking.

"Yeah," Henry said with a sigh, the pancakes suddenly tasting like tire rubber. "I… I have to admit, Davy. Until very recently I did too."

David had the family blond hair and blue eyes, with high cheekbones and a strong chin, a lush mouth, and a sort of innocence around his eyes that belied the fact that he'd readily admitted to putting himself through business school as a porn model.

Henry had a hard time reconciling his brother—the one who had always taken care of the younger kids, the nursemaid, the one who'd saved their youngest brother from drowning and who'd kept their sister from freaking all the boys out with her turbulent adolescence—had worked in porn. He *still* worked in it, if Davy's letters to their older brother were to be believed. Behind the camera or in front of it—porn. Not something Henry would have ever thought of. Even though Davy was beautiful, stunningly beautiful as few men could ever lay claim to, he seemed more suited to fatherhood and life at the office, the bulging muscles in his arms and chest notwithstanding.

And somehow that beauty made his look of understanding harder to bear.

Henry shoved at his plate and stood. "Look, you know, I should just go. You don't need me, with all of Dad's shitty attitude, crashing your life here. I should probably—"

"Sit down and finish your breakfast, Henry," Davy said quietly. Henry's knees actually buckled, he was so excited to obey that order. "You look like hell. Who did that to your face?"

Henry opened his mouth to lie, but he couldn't. And he couldn't meet his brother's eyes either.

"Dad," David said softly. "Well, I had Kane to protect me when he tried that shit. Who'd you have?" Kane. Sometimes Davy called his husband Kane, and Kane called Davy Dex—it really did mess with Henry's mind, and he didn't even want to think about the fact that the alternative name habit started when they'd fucked each other in porn.

Henry just shook his head. He hadn't been there when Davy had come out, Carlos by his side. He remembered that sick feeling, though, that terror, that if he ever had to do the same thing, nobody would speak up for him, because he hadn't spoken up for anybody else. Not in their family, where as far as Henry knew, only their oldest brother, Travis, had anything to do with Davy at all.

David nodded. "Do you want to tell me why?"

Henry shook his head. "No."

"Would you believe I could guess why?" David arched an eyebrow, and Henry's flush turned into an instant sweat, pouring down his armpits, stinging his eyes.

"God, Davy. I can't talk about it," he begged, wiping his eyes. His humiliation was palpable, so thick he could almost choke on it. "I... I can't even right now." Davy had been prepared to leave all he was behind—he'd practiced at it, probably from the moment he'd moved away from Montana. But Henry had worked his whole life to hang on to his family, and he just couldn't talk about what he'd left on the kitchen floor—along with not a little of his blood after his dad had beat the shit out of him, a military-trained adult, for being gay.

"I get that." Gah—Davy's eyes were still so earnest. "But you're going to have to someday. As for where to put you, why don't you stay here a couple of days? Shower, do your laundry. I'll get you a laptop, and we can work on your résumé."

"I can't live here," Henry said, looking around. There were pictures on the refrigerator of a turtle holding flowers, for God's sake, and a small shelf of children's books in the corner of the dining room. "This is your family." And Henry was unclean, whether he could tell his brother that or not.

"It's too small," David said grimly. "Frances has the other bedroom. All we've got for you is the couch. How you doing for money?"

Henry grimaced. "Not great. I... I was saving for college, but...." A dishonorable discharge didn't come with pay.

"You've got a little, but you don't think it'll go far," David said, nodding when Henry did.

"I can get a basic job," Henry told him. "Fast food, waiting tables—I just—"

"Need a place to start. I get it." David nodded, like he was making a decision. "Okay. I think I can get something lined up for you. It'll be sort of sporadic, odd jobs for me and John, my boss, mostly, but we've been talking about needing a gopher, and he's been pretty good about Kane holding lights and doing set production stuff for a salary."

"I wouldn't have to—" Henry's panic made his voice crack.

David let out a clearly negative snort. "No, you wouldn't have to film scenes. Jesus, Henry—I'm not going to whore you out on film when you're desperate. We only take the willing. Kane and I haven't been on film for two years, and the business has kept on growing. Don't worry. We'll find something. A place for you to live is what we need."

Henry's relief made sweat pop out on his back. "Good to know," he rasped.

David rolled his eyes some more and kept pondering. "There's a place…." He grimaced and looked at him directly. "You're not gonna like it. A bunch of the guys from Johnnies crash there. It's sort of a flophouse—two bedrooms and like five guys, and they're coming and going and shit. But they're babies, really. I mean, yeah, they're making their living doing porn, but some of them have never lived away from home. With the exception of the sex—and don't get me wrong, you can practically smell come rolling down the stairwell—it's like a boarding house for young men. They could use a grown man to help them out."

Henry stared at him, nonplussed. "So, you want a, uh, nanny for porn stars?"

Another expression from David that made Henry feel mean-minded. "I work with these guys—do me a favor and don't phrase it that way, all right? Like I said, they're good kids. But… you know. Coming out, girlfriends who don't know, parents who find out about the porn, boyfriends who don't understand. Most of these guys are eighteen, nineteen. I think the oldest is Lance; he's twenty-six or seven, and he does his best. It's all about the fuckin' drama with the other kids, and I…." He bit his lip like this hurt. "I've seen some *spectacular* flameouts. Friends. Friends who really needed a keeper so *somebody* could tell them they were worth the trouble and to please not do that thing that's about to hurt us all."

Henry caught his breath. Self-harm. Drugs. Dangerous behaviors. He could see all of that going down with young stupid people. Or stupid young people. Or just kids like he'd been, without the prop of the military and an out*standing* cover story to explain why he was spending so much extra time with Mal.

Henry was twenty-seven, trained in physical combat, and he'd let his father beat the shit out of him because he thought he deserved it. What would a teenager do if Daddy showed up at his door with an attitude?

He'd done so very little in his past to redeem himself. This was like… like protecting people, wasn't it? He'd wanted to serve his country, and while this wasn't anything close to that, it was something. Something that didn't make the world about Henry Matthew Worrall—liar, cheat, and potential homewrecker, dishonorably discharged from the job he'd loved.

"Sure," he said, wondering if this aching feeling would ever grow numb. "What do I have to lose?"

"Self-loathing," David said brutally. "Prejudice. All the bullshit Dad saddled us with that's going to kill you if you don't let it out. Feel free to put that shit in your rearview, little brother."

"Where'd you leave yours?" Henry asked bitterly, hating that his brother seemed happy, smug with it even, when Henry couldn't stand the fit of his own skin.

"Mom's kitchen floor, when Kane blocked his second punch."

Henry opened his mouth and closed it, not sure he had an answer to that, but David held his hand out to stop him.

"It's going to be harder for you, Henry. You didn't have anybody to block."

True enough. Because even before Henry had left his dignity on his mother's kitchen floor, he'd left his heart and his hope and his self-respect at Malachi's feet, and Mal had stomped on it all in combat boots. Well, fucking your brother-in-law was sort of an invitation for abuse, right?

He swallowed, the whole story pounding in his throat to get out, but at that moment, his brother jumped a little in that human gesture that said he had gotten a call but was determined to ignore it.

"Get it, Davy," Henry said gruffly. "I'll go shower and do my laundry and try to get my shit together, okay?"

David sighed. "This might be John about a car for you—Sacramento's sort of spread out. You'll need one. But Henry?"

Henry pulled his military mask in place. "Yeah?"

"I will talk about it. Anytime. Anything you want to say. I…." He grimaced. "There's some stuff that you can't keep secret, and it would kill you to try. I won't kick you out. I won't turn my back on you. Ever. Understand? I might not go to prison for you, but I'd write you every fucking day, okay?"

Henry swallowed hard and tried not to laugh at that idea. Straight-arrow Henry, go to prison? Daddy's favorite? Naw. "Roger that," he said, like the military speak could keep his emotions in check.

David touched his pocket again and sighed. "Hang tough, Henry. I'll get back to you with your living sitch, okay?"

"Yeah. Thanks, Davy."

"'Course. Washing machine's in the garage." David waved to a connecting door on the far side of the living room, and Henry took the hint and left him to his phone call.

As he emptied out his duffel of pretty much every scrap of civilian clothing he owned, he fought the burning in his eyes and the horrible conviction that facing his brother would have been a helluva lot easier if Davy had beaten the shit out of Henry like he deserved.

It was funny that Davy mentioned prison, though—Henry wondered if any of the troubled kids Davy had known had ended up there. It had seemed so random, but then Davy's life was a lot different from Henry's. Maybe his friends were targets for unfair prosecution.

Henry swallowed. They would have been, if they'd been in his barracks. He and Mal had known that right off. Maybe there was a reason for Davy's brain to go there.

And maybe it was just God, warning him of things to come.

DEN MOTHER

"LANCE! MAN, do you have any laxatives? I'm...." Randy's pink freckled nose scrunched up, making him look about twelve instead of barely nineteen. "I'm sort of... you know. Stopped up."

Galahad "Lance" Luna grimaced. "Randy, what have we talked about?"

Randy shifted uneasily. "Eating vegetables."

"What else?"

"But it's just so—"

"What else?"

"Gross!"

"Yes, but so is a bowel torsion. Stop douching every fucking day, Randy. Whoever you're fucking can deal with a blowjob. That shit kills the bacteria in your bowels that helps you crap. You are *literally* a constipated douchemonkey. Man, I get wanting to get some between your scenes, but you know one of the really outstanding things about using condoms?"

Randy swallowed. "Easy cleanup?"

Lance touched his nose. "Bingo. Now I've got some stool softeners in my bag. I'll get them. But man, stop trying to live on diet soda and come, okay? It's bad for you."

"Okay, Lance."

"At least drink some coffee with cream—it's a natural laxative."

Randy perked up. "Really? I did not know that!"

Lance restrained himself from ruffling the kid's hair. Randy was a fully functioning adult and hell-bent on proving that his private parts functioned better than all the rest of him put together—including his brain.

"Add it to your vices," he said graciously. "Diet soda *also* kills the good stuff in your stomach, so consider it a twofer."

Randy grinned, because that was his kind of humor, and Lance left the kitchen for the bed he'd marked as his.

God, these kids needed a nanny.

He fetched Randy his laxative and then went back to his textbooks, because in spite of the lovely late March day outside, he had to pass this damn exam in the morning, and then he had a shift to work for his residency at UC Davis Medical Center immediately after. God.... He'd wrapped up his postgraduate internship just a few months earlier, and now he had three more years of following Dr. Schearer through his residency in cardiac medicine before he could look for a fellowship or establish a practice.

So he could finish paying off his student loans.

He actually made a decent amount now that he was finally a resident. Not scads of money—but certainly better than a credentialed teacher after twenty years of tenure. But Lance had expenses, and he was paying off his debt, and secretly, in the place he never wanted to admit, Johnnies and the guys there had become his home—so much so that he fed their misunderstanding that he was still in school. It was just easier to stay in the flophouse if people thought it was because he needed the money.

He still did a porn scene every two months or so, not so much because he enjoyed them—although he did, because cutting loose his inner hedonist and fucking the shit out of somebody, no strings attached, was a voyeuristic *rush*—but because all the guys, with all their drama, made him feel wanted.

He wasn't above feeling wanted. Everybody needed validation, right?

But he didn't have to look at his finances to know that he could move somewhere, anywhere, even if it was another apartment in this complex where he could still watch over the guys.

One of the first things that had become apparent when he'd started this gig three years ago—when his school tuition had run out and his parents had stopped talking to him and he was so close to his internship, he could almost taste the steady income—was that most of the kids who started in the porn business really *were* kids. They were young, energetic, and could fuck like gods, but they were also rash, impulsive, and led by their hormones.

The first time Skylar—who had moved out to be exclusive with Rick nearly a year ago—had dropped his drawers in the living room and moaned, "Help me, Dr. Lance—what's wrong with my butthole?" Lance had realized that someone needed to offer nonjudgy, no-frills advice, even if it was just "Hemorrhoid cream, my brother, and maybe lay off bottoming until your next scene."

Dex tried.

Lance had seen that when Dex had told him about the flophouse in the first place. He remembered the way Dex's pretty blue eyes had studied Lance's face intently, like he was looking for something Lance wasn't sure was there.

"Yeah, the flophouse," he said thoughtfully. "Who told you about that?"

Lance had still been capable of blushing back then. "Uh, Skylar. We just did a scene together, and I mentioned I couldn't afford the dorm this year."

Dex had leaned forward over the desk in his office and steepled his fingers. "Medical school, right?"

It had occurred to Lance at that moment that Dex was maybe only three years older than he was, and he was studying Lance with the astuteness of a school counselor. "Yeah. I've got one more year to go, and then I'll be paying off my loans. But all my parents' assistance dried up—"

Dex raised his eyebrows, and Lance blew out a breath. "Yes, they found out I was gay and that college fund my father had saved for me was suddenly my little sister's." It hadn't been that much anyway, which was why he was helping Morgaine out with law school. Their *parents* might have decided not to speak to him, but Morgaine was still his biggest fan.

Dex nodded. "Would you believe it's not the first time I heard that?"

Lance felt his mouth twist. "No, really? Geez, mister, I thought I was the only one."

Dex let out a little laugh. "Not everybody who does porn here is gay," he said. It had been about six months before they'd started hiring women and diversifying, so Lance's eyebrows had climbed to his hairline. "No— seriously. Some of the guys are bi, and some of them are straight but not hung up on it. They have to do a lot of mental and physical gymnastics to get hard, though. We really do prefer the guys who are into it. But yeah. It's an issue. You seem to have dealt with it, but...."

Dex bit his full lip, and in spite of spending six hours having sex with the irrepressible Skylar, Lance felt his libido flutter. Dex had still been doing scenes at that point—*God, wouldn't it be great to do a scene with* Dex?

"But what?" Lance asked, feeling emotionally naked for the first time in the six months since he'd been kicked out of the house.

"But the flophouse, where Skylar gave you an invite to crash, is sort of… think of an unsupervised playroom where everyone is over eighteen and used to being naked."

Lance smirked, because he had this cartoon image of guys with boners just boinging around the house.

"Whatever you're thinking, it's worse," Dex confirmed. "I try not to recommend it to the guys who're making more money or have their shit together. There's drama—scads of it. It's naked high school with no girls to keep it sane. I break up a cat fight at least once a week. If I could afford to hire a gaybie-sitter, I totally would."

Lance shrugged. "Honestly, it sounds like the dorms, but nobody's saying, 'I only touched a penis 'cause I was drunk.' I start my internship in less than a year. How bad could it be?"

"Suit yourself." Dex stood up and shook his hand. "Now Kelsey will cut you a check for the scene today—but don't forget to check with her at the end of the month, because that's when the royalties come in, okay?"

Lance nodded, remembering that he got a flat fee for filming the scene and then a cut of the profits every time it was downloaded. The more popular the actors, the more they got paid, which was pretty cool, really. Kelsey, the receptionist, seemed a little disorganized but also pretty competent, and she'd been cheerfully normal about the fact that everybody entering the ordinary-looking office building was going in the back to have sex.

"Will do. Thanks, man."

Dex winked. "Thank you! Gotta tell you, you make really pretty porn."

Lance smiled, feeling the heat of the compliment way down to his toes. Dex had been behind the camera and had made him feel professional and respected for six hours, while Lance, in his birthday suit, did the thing with a pretty, flirty model who probably worked out with ben-wah balls six times a day to obtain that kind of control over his sphincter. Until this moment, right now, there hadn't been a single moment of connection or sexuality between them.

But now, with that pretty angel's mouth coming up in the corners and those blue eyes sparkling, Lance felt the hint of possibility. And part of the attraction was that Dex was watching out for him, making sure he was happy.

Lance had admired that sort of responsibility, even then. It was the thing that had driven him through medical school, the idea that if everybody helped their neighbor, the world would be a better place.

Now, three years later, he was really glad he and Dex had gotten to film that scene together—but he totally regretted not moving on that spark of attraction outside the office. Dex had started dating Scott not long after that, even though everybody knew Scott was a douchebag. And when that imploded, Kane had apparently been waiting to move in. The two of them were married now, and both off-screen but still working the business. Lance had watched Dex organize medical watch for a model who'd tried to hurt himself, prepare Christmas for the guys who weren't allowed to go home, and find apartments for guys who got kicked out. He'd found lawyers, helped place siblings who needed mental health care, and with the help of John Carey, the founder of Johnnies, he'd started a job-placement project for guys who wanted life after porn.

Dex was more than just a boss for Lance's part-time gig—he was a role model for anyone in the sex industry who wanted to see how to be an adult *and* an adult-film star.

Unfortunately, Lance had been too focused on his endgame to even see where that attraction would have gone.

He sighed and dug into his medical journals, trying not to pine for something that never was. The thought kept haunting him, though, that it wasn't that he had missed out on *Dex*, but that he was missing out on something bigger.

Here in apartment 126C, he pretty much had sex on tap—but he hadn't been interested in anyone for over a year. And even then, it had been Reg and Bobby, who were better together than they'd ever been with him. He'd been their pity fuck, both of them, and other than that?

Well, it was a good thing he filmed scenes once every six weeks, wasn't it?

He was officially too old for this shit. But he had no intention of growing up in the near future, and that was depressing the hell out of him. Jesus, was it so hard to fix his life so he could find a guy of his own?

He had just settled down *finally* when a knock on the door jerked him out of his concentration. He looked up to see Randy lying on the bed across from his, Billy sitting naked on his face. Billy—small, compactly built, with dark hair and big sloe eyes, was returning the rim job by sucking Randy's surprisingly thick cock, their sex sounds muffled in each other's flesh.

Damn—he really *had* gotten used to blocking things out.

"Lance!" Dex called from the landing. "Lance! I've got someone here for you to meet. Could you make sure nobody's naked in the living room?"

Lance looked at Billy and Randy again, his libido waking up in a big way. He probably wouldn't have participated—he'd been avoiding sleeping with the flophouse guys because God, who needed the drama?—but voyeurism was very *very* acceptable here, and he could have given himself a big favor watching that.

As it was, he grunted, stood up, and left the bedroom, then padded out into the living room and checked the door to the other bedroom. He heard very specific noises coming from there, too, and sighed. What, was sex in the afternoon a thing now and nobody had passed him the memo?

"Coming," he called, opening the door. "I mean, on my way. But I can't make promises about the nak—" It wasn't just Dex out there. "—ed?" Standing next to Dex, who was rangy and blond and tall and built and constantly flashing dimples because he liked to smile, was a shorter, stockier version of Dex. This guy had the same color hair and the same color eyes, but his jawline was squarer, he had slightly less neck, narrower shoulders, and more attitude. He was built too, but his muscles looked like they'd seen some hard use.

Everything about this not-Dex screamed military, and Lance wrinkled his nose in distaste.

He really wasn't that great with authority.

"Hi, Dex. Uh… hi, Dex's twin brother?"

The newcomer rolled his eyes. "Hi, porn star," he sneered.

Lance recoiled, surprised, and Dex smacked the guy on the back of the head. "Dammit, Henry—it's this or living in our garage. Take your pick."

"Sorry," Henry muttered, rubbing the back of his head. Then, to his credit, he met Lance's eyes and managed to look a little ashamed. "Sorry. I'm an asshole. This is a bad idea all around. I've got a little bit of savings—"

"Did I show you the cost of living around here?" Dex said sweetly. "We spent a couple of hours on it, remember? If you could manage not to piss Kane off with every sentence, the garage might actually work, but you can't, so mind your mouth. Remember—five guys besides Lance live here. They're all gay, and they all do the same thing for a living. You may be built, but I'm pretty sure if they all gang up, you'd be history and I could help them hide the body."

Lance held his hand up in front of his mouth so Dex's little brother—it *had* to be a little brother—wouldn't see him smirking.

Henry closed his eyes and opened them again, and this time when he looked at Lance, he seemed to see a human being. "I really am sorry," he said. "I'm… I'm afraid I'm not very… what's the word?" He looked at his brother in earnest supplication.

"Progressive?" Dex offered.

"Yeah. I'm not very progressive. I'm going to try not to be an asshole and likely fail a lot. If you could… I don't know, don't kill me in my sleep and maybe give me some pointers, I'd be grateful."

Lance put everything they were saying together. "Wait—don't kill you in your sleep? Does that mean you're going to be sleeping *here*?"

"Please?" Dex said, pinching the bridge of his nose. "He'll pitch in for the rent, and in spite of being an asshole of the first order, he'll be helpful. Kane, John, and I can lend him our cars so he can help you guys out, because I know only, like, one of you has a car, and he can help with the plumbing and help the guys fill out their student loan applications—"

"Oh God," Lance muttered. "That deadline is coming." It was practically the reason the kitchen table was invented. The last three years, they'd made a party out of it, inviting the other students they knew from

Johnnies, with everybody bringing their shit and their laptops and their forms. One of the most interesting things that had happened was Lance had learned everybody's real names—which was another reason he'd stopped having sex with his roommates.

He knew them as people now.

Dex nodded. "See? He *can* be useful, and he'll be running errands for John and me until he can get his shit together."

"Understood," Lance said. A loud groan issued from his room, and he grimaced—Randy and Billy were apparently reaching a, uh, climax. There was a stack of shoes in the entryway because it was wet outside and nobody wanted to track mud in. Lance slid his feet into a pair of loafers that were probably his and reached for the coat hook for a hoodie that was definitely not.

"Here, Henry? Is that your stuff?"

Henry slid the military duffel off his shoulder. "Yeah, uh, should we come in?"

"No. Definitely not. Give me that, and you and me can take a walk around the apartment complex, and I can explain shit, okay?"

"Yes! Yes! Yes!" And that came from the room next to them, where Curtis and Zeppelin—at least Lance assumed it was Zeppelin—were. The fact was, the Johnnies guys got tested regularly, and they knew one another. There was a lot of fucking around in-house because they could trust that their partner had a clear health screen, the other guy definitely knew the score so no strings attached meant no strings attached, and they tended to be friends before, during, and after.

So who knew who was naked in the other room?

Which was sort of what Lance needed to talk to Henry about.

Henry's blue eyes—the same shade as his brother's but not as guileless or as innocent—had opened wide. "Are there, uh… is anybody, uh—"

"Yes, yes, and yes," Lance said bluntly. "Now give me your duffel, say goodbye to your brother, and you and me need to have a little talk."

Lance grabbed the duffel and threw it directly onto the couch, checked the pocket of his sweats to make sure his keys were in there, and shut the door behind them. Together, the three of them clattered down the stairs, Dex apologizing the whole time.

"Lance, I'm so sorry. This shouldn't last long, man. I really appreciate—"

"Stop!" Lance laughed as they got to the bottom of the stairs. "It's all good, brother. You'd do the same for any one of us—and you *have*."

Dex shrugged. "Yeah, but he's no Bobby."

Ah, gods. Bobby, the big young country boy with the solid heart. That pity fuck Lance had given him had left a lasting impression, actually. When Bobby and Reg had gotten their shit sorted, Lance had needed to stomp hard on his own regret. Sort of like with Dex, he'd been so focused on his future, he hadn't moved in on a possible here and now.

"Well, Bobby still stops by to check on the guys," Lance said. "Gives them piecework with his construction firm if they need it." He looked briefly at Henry. "You could probably take some of those jobs to tide you over."

Henry looked interested. "Thanks. I appreciate it."

Oh, this question was a little personal. "I, uh, take it you won't be filming scenes?"

The horror on Henry's square-jawed face spoke volumes, and Lance tried hard not to be hurt. Well, Dex was buckets full of awesome—he was allowed to have a redneck family member who wore his ass for a hat.

Dex let out an amused sound. "No scenes for Henry." Unexpectedly, he put his hand on his brother's shoulder and squeezed. "And probably no relationships until he gets himself sorted out." Henry shifted uncomfortably, and then broke Lance's heart a little by biting his lip, the expression making him look about fifteen years younger and vulnerable as hell.

"No," Henry said gruffly. "Probably not."

Lance nodded, hopefully *looking* confident, but inside he was a little confused. He'd assumed Henry was straight. His posture, his judgy sneer, his horror when he'd realized what was going on inside the apartment—all of it had pointed to a straight guy thrown into his worst nightmare.

But this? This sadness, this discomfort—this wasn't the judgment of someone who didn't want to join the party. This was the judgment of someone who'd assumed the party wasn't for them.

Looking at Henry's extreme unhappiness and the self-loathing that seemed to radiate off him like sound waves, Lance thought he might be only a little right. Maybe *this* party wasn't for Henry, but there might be some guy out there who'd throw him a hell of a happily ever after.

"I'll take over from here," Lance said softly. They stood at the bottom of the stairwell now, and Lance could see Dex's SUV parked in the visitor's spot near them, Kane in the front seat, fiddling with his phone.

Dex looked over at his husband and waved gamely, and Kane smiled. Then he shot Henry a glare that should have thrown a bolt of lightning through his chest.

Lance swallowed. He'd never seen Kane really pissed off, but given Kane's size—the width of his shoulders, the thickly muscled thighs, the pure no-bullshit way he carried himself when he wasn't goofing off—he'd never really wanted to.

Poor Henry. Whatever this guy had done to earn that glare, it must have been truly heinous. But not, apparently, unforgivable.

"You should go," Lance said because Henry wasn't backing down from that glare. He was matching Kane scowl for scowl, probably out of sheer cussedness.

Dex pulled his brother into a hug. "Text me tonight and let me know how you're settling in."

"That's not really nece—" Henry argued.

"It is. It's completely necessary," Dex told him. "You don't just spend two nights on my couch and get to disappear out of my life again." Dex's angel's mouth made a funny little wobble. "I… you could be the only family I get to hold on to, Henry. I'm not going to let you go."

Dex hugged his brother again, tighter, his windbreaker rustling against his brother's denim jacket, then pulled away and turned toward the SUV before Lance got a look at his face.

He didn't need to.

"C'mon," he said to Henry, pulling him in the direction of the super's office on general principle. Behind them, the SUV started up and backed out, but neither Henry nor Lance looked at Henry's retreating brother.

"Where we going?"

"I'll show you the super's office, the vending machines, the laundry room, and then we're going to borrow Billy's car—" He jangled the pocket of the sweatshirt, where Billy's keys sat. "—and go get pizza."

Henry let out a bark of laughter. "Pizza?"

"Yeah. Mountain Mike's—it's right down the street. I'm a paid resident now, and I'm not going back to Little Caesar's, no way, no how."

"Resident?" Henry said, and Lance didn't let the surprise bother him. "As in med school?"

"Yup. Student loans only get you so far. But, uh…." Oh, how embarrassing, secrets already. "Don't tell the rest of the flophouse, okay? They think I'm still a student. I just get tired of explaining first-year intern and residency and student loans—this way they don't get all weird because I'm a real doctor." Lance wasn't going into the rest of the happy psychological porn dance he did, not with Henry—not now, when he still remembered Henry's palpable disdain.

"Yeah." Henry let out a sigh and his shoulders slumped. "I've got some savings from the Army, and in the Midwest, it would have set me up for a couple of years. Not so much here."

"And your brother didn't want you to be alone."

Henry grimaced. "No, sir, he did not."

Lance let that one hang as they walked down the damp sidewalk. As a whole, the grounds were kept nicely—the shrubs were clean of litter and the grass neatly trimmed. The complex itself was, well, complex. Lance had lived here for three years, and he hadn't figured out the rhyme or reason to the numbers on the different buildings.

The super's office faced the street, with a buffer of a wide lawn, a fence, and a sidewalk. Across the parking lot were the dumpsters, and Lance told Henry that they kept the key on the peg by the door. The rule was supposed to be the first person who saw the trash was full took it out.

"How's that work for you?" Henry asked, wrinkling his nose, as if he knew what to expect from a houseful of post-adolescent men.

"Not as well as you'd think," Lance said, quirking his mouth in a smile, inviting Henry to laugh with him.

Henry rolled his eyes. "Sure. Do you keep a chore chart or anything?"

Lance wrinkled his nose back. "Uhm...."

And now Henry assumed a patient look. "Does the toilet need to be donated to science?"

"No respectable lab would take it," Lance said, feeling embarrassment for the first time in ever.

Henry shrugged. "I can do that shit. I...." He sighed. "It's why I joined the military. I like order."

"How far'd you get?" Lance asked. "In the Army, I mean."

"Staff sergeant," Henry said, and Lance heard the faint ring of pride in his voice before his shoulders curled forward even more. "I miss it."

"What happened?" Boy, was Lance curious—but not surprised when Henry shook his head.

"Can we not talk about this?" he asked plaintively. "Please?"

Lance took a breath and gestured. "Super's office. By the way, avoid him if you can. He's this sort of creepy asshole who likes to leer. Anyway, we usually pitch cash into the kitty and get a cashier's check to give to him. Due on the first, late on the fifth."

Henry nodded shortly. "Everybody pay the same?"

"People with actual beds in the bedrooms pay twenty bucks more a month than people on the couch and the air mattress."

Henry grimaced. "How's the couch?"

"Not bad. We actually replaced it last year, because it gets a workout." Lance watched Henry's eyes get big, and backtracked quickly. "Not like that! No! Seriously. We just like to be social. So, you know, movie nights, game nights, 'sit on the couch and eat ice cream and bitch about our lives' nights—the couch and the recliner and the kitchen chairs and the air mattress. Works for us."

"So if I'm sleeping on the couch, who gets the air mattress?"

"Well, it's been sort of like musical chairs. Randy, Billy, and I all pay for a bed, but the master bedroom has a queen and a single. So Cotton, Curtis, and Zeppelin all go random when it's time to sleep. Zeppelin's prone to bring home Johnnies guys to get busy, so he usually gets the queen-sized, 'cause it's practically the guest bedroom. Curtis has the single unless Zep brings home more than one guy, and Cotton takes the couch or the air mattress, depending."

Henry shook his head. "Oh my God. It really *is* porn-o-topia in there!"

Lance let out a breath, not sure if he could explain. "Yes and no?"

Henry just regarded him steadily as Lance turned around and took him back through the quad so he could see the gym, the clubhouse, and the pool, all of which were in fairly decent shape, although the gym was small.

"Your brother can get you a membership at the one up the street," Lance told him. "They've got rocking equipment and a personal trainer that'll blow your socks off. She's straight, in her fifties, and doesn't grab your ass—all of which are pluses. But she knows what she's doing with nutrition too, and we'd die for her."

Henry let a smile slip. "I may be working out a lot," he admitted. "But yes and no on the pornotopia?"

"Zeppelin's a very happy little slut," Lance conceded. "And Randy will literally go down on you before you say hello. But Billy has a girlfriend and only takes a pity fuck when they're on the outs. Curtis is pretty job-monogamous. He only films scenes and does the occasional roommate; he doesn't really have his own lovers. Same here. Cotton is…." Lance let out a sigh. "Cotton's the one I worry about most because he keeps looking for Mr. Right and he keeps getting Mr. 'I hear you have a nine-inch dick.' So we see him making these dates, and then he gets his heart broken. It happens about once a week. There's a difference between filming a scene and sleeping around. And some of the guys do both and some of them don't, but finding a guy outside of Johnnies who doesn't assume we all do it all isn't easy."

Henry grunted.

"What?" Lance asked.

"I'm going to have to take your word on it," he said.

And while part of Lance prickled—because what a dick!—a part of him appreciated the straightforwardness. "What? Every guy you've ever boned has been true love forever?" Lance asked acerbically.

Henry made a hurt sound then, almost like Lance had kicked him, and for a moment Lance was actually afraid. Was the guy going to deck him for assuming Henry was gay when every vibe he gave off said he was trying not to be? Was he going to protest?

Was he going to tell the truth?

"You said something about pizza?" Henry asked, his voice curiously devoid of any emotion at all.

"Yeah," Lance said. "But first, look. I don't care what you think of me, or of sex work, or of the damned apartment, but you need to listen. Because if I can't get you to agree on this one thing, I'm calling your brother and kicking you out on your ear."

Henry nodded at him to go on.

"Those kids in there currently buying stock in Kleenex are like my little brothers. They don't always do the right thing, and they don't always make me proud, but I love them, and I don't want them hurt. Don't say anything that hurts their feelings or makes them feel like crap because they can get that shit at home and that's why they moved here. Do you understand?"

And then—oh God—the most intense thing happened. Henry's blue eyes, each one with a faint bruising underneath, like from an old fight, grew bright and red-rimmed and shiny.

"I won't hurt your little brothers," he said after a moment, swallowing hard. "David has always done right by me. That's the least I can do to repay him."

"David?" *Who?* "You mean Dex?"

Henry scrubbed at his face with his palm. "I'm not calling him by his porn name," he said, and Lance blinked.

"Oh my God. Yeah. Right. David."

"Pizza," Henry said almost desperately.

"Sure. Pizza."

THERE WERE, in fact, two cars owned by Johnnies guys. Lance owned one, but he'd managed to find a guest parking spot and he didn't want to lose it because those were like gold. Billy had the other, and it was in the actual numbered spot with the overhang, and nobody could take that away from him.

Besides, Lance had grabbed Billy's keys, and since Billy was currently on the outs with his girlfriend and getting laid in Lance's room, Lance had no problem with stealing his dented Kia and heading for Mountain Mike's.

Henry looked around the car, at the schoolbooks in the back and the waiter aprons and spare clothes, and grimaced.

"Busy guy."

"Well, porn only pays well if you're famous at it," Lance said. "If you're in Johnnies' top twenty, it pays the bills and more. But if you're one of their workhorse guys, it's a nice income boost, but it's not living-on money unless all you do is fuck."

"Hunh," Henry said musingly. "I never thought of it that way. So, uh, my brother…."

"Was a fucking superstar," Lance confirmed. "So was Kane. Usually people don't last long in the business, though. Maybe a year, sometimes two. It's a young man's game, really."

"You, uh…." Henry shifted uncomfortably. "You don't look old, but, uh, med school—"

"Student loans, not just mine," Lance told him, still not wanting to get into the other reasons, the personal reasons, that made porn so seductive, so easy to continue. "And I'm twenty-seven."

"So am I," Henry said, like that depressed him. "I thought… I thought I'd have my life together by now."

"Hey, mine's just starting out," Lance said. "I make no judgments."

"I do." Henry let out a big breath. "My father taught me to judge and judge hard and judge mean. And I learned that lesson so well, I judged myself right into a fucking corner."

"And then what?" Lance asked.

"I gnawed off my own leg to get out of it." Henry let out a broken laugh. "I'm making no goddamned sense. Pizza. Meet the kids. One thing at a time, right?"

"Right." Lance figured there'd be more than that; there *had* to be more than that. But unlike his brother, who had "Den Mother" written all over him, Henry seemed to be a much tougher nut to crack. A handsome nut— hard mouth, flat eyes, soldier's bearing and all—but a tough one. In truth, Lance was expecting Henry's first meeting with the guys to be a disaster.

He was pleasantly surprised.

The guys—he'd been right, Zeppelin had been in Curtis's room, along with Fisher, who didn't live at the apartment but had just sort of come along for the come—were all gathered in the living room, Cotton included, watching some sort of Hallmark romance movie and eating popcorn.

Lance walked in, followed by Henry carrying two XL pizzas, and they were suddenly the heroes of the hour.

"Oh my God!" Randy stood up, his obviously still growing frame showing ribs in spite of the almost continuous working out he did. "Is that food? Real food? Can I have some?"

"My treat," Lance said dryly. "We've got a vegetarian and an all-meat."

Cotton sighed, his brown-velvet eyes—surrounded by black lashes and black hair—were huge in his fair-skinned face. God, this kid looked fragile. Who let him turn eighteen and get naked with strangers? "No vegan?" he asked pitifully.

"Ta-da!" Lance pulled out a small gluten-free, vegan cheese and spinach special that he'd been holding in his free hand. "Vegan it is!"

"Woo-hoo!" That suddenly bright look on Cotton's face was all Lance needed. Yay! He'd made this kid happy. "You love me."

"Yes, little brother, I do."

"Plates?" Henry said, setting the boxes down and opening them up, then setting the bag with the napkins and parmesan cheese down next to it.

"Who needs plates?" Billy asked. "There's napkins." Billy was in his early twenties, short, muscular, Latino, and quiet. He was one of the few guys who'd been there for over a year, and he and Lance… well, they weren't exactly brothers, but they had some of the same damage. Some of the same damage they didn't share with anyone else.

"What's a plate?" Zeppelin asked, shaking his sandy blond hair out of his puppy-dog brown eyes. He wore it down to his shoulders, and it was practically all he wore, almost all year round. Right now, his outfit consisted of a pair of holey blue briefs, and Lance rolled his eyes.

"A plate is a thing I'm going to make you hold in front of your balls unless you go put some shorts on. Guys, this is Henry. He doesn't do scenes, and if you want to know if he does guys, ask him, but look at his muscles and his scowl first."

He looked over his shoulder and gave Henry a game smile, and Henry scowled theatrically for his benefit.

And then he winked.

Lance saw it, but the rest of the guys couldn't, and so when he turned that scowl on the rest of the household and they all straightened their posture and stared at him with a little bit of fear, Lance had to contain a smirk.

"Plates," Henry reiterated, and then he gave Zeppelin a particularly hard stare. "And pants."

And for all they were supposed to be adults, Lance hadn't seen such scrambling to obey an authority figure since the second grade.

In three minutes there were six young men wearing clothes, gathered around the table with garage-sale dinnerware, getting out cups and gallons of milk.

Henry sat down at the table, but as he did, he told them, "A table's a luxury on deployment. By all means, sit where you want—this is just me."

The guys all nodded respectfully and reassembled, draping themselves over the couch, the recliner, and the inflatable mattress that had apparently been brought out to accommodate sheer numbers.

But they didn't leave Henry alone.

"Deployment?" Billy asked. "When'd you get back?"

Henry finished chewing his first bite of meat-lover's special and swallowed. "About two weeks ago."

"You turn in your papers?" Billy grimaced. "I tried to enlist, but I failed the physical."

Lance arched an eyebrow, and Billy gave him a barely perceptible nod. Oh, sweetheart. No. The weight of their shared secret seemed to press on Lance's chest—or his stomach, which was where most of the pizza they ate would *not* be by the end of the night.

"That's too bad," Henry said, and his sincerity made Lance dizzy with relief. And then, blessed, blessed Henry… he didn't pry. "It's hard when you want to serve but they won't let you."

"Is that what happened to you?" Lance asked and then had to not clap his hand over his mouth.

Henry gave him an inscrutable look. "What happened to me was… complicated. And in the long run, it wasn't something I did so much as something I had coming." He twitched his lips at Lance.

"And it's something you don't want to talk about. I'm sorry."

"No worries." Henry munched doggedly on his pizza. "What are you aiming for now?" he asked Billy.

Billy bit his lip in what looked like hope. "A degree in engineering. I've got another year—"

"He's been head-hunted," Cotton blurted, wide-eyed.

"Dude, that doesn't mean nearly what you think it does," Zeppelin said with a smirk, and Cotton flat-out ignored him.

"No—two firms, right, Billy?"

Billy nodded. "Yeah. I may get to do a paid internship next semester."

"And then you'll move out of this dump and we can visit you in a real house?" Curtis asked hopefully. Curtis—African American, skin of pale bronze, as clean-cut as an ROTC cadet—was going to school to study kinesiology so he could get into sports medicine, and he seemed to need examples of guys who got out of porn and moved on to other things. He volunteered his spare time at a children's shelter, and while Lance wanted to point out that if he waited tables with that time instead he might be able to afford a different living situation, he got the feeling Curtis was there for the same reason Lance was. And it had less to do with money than with not being able to buy family.

"Absolutely," Billy said, his voice ringing in sincerity. Sometimes guys meant that. They kept up with their buddies at Johnnies, made friendships. Sometimes guys were in and out. Lance recognized that this was probably like a lot of jobs, a lot of living situations, but still, it gave him hope to think of Billy becoming like Reg and Bobby. Reg's house was a dump—that was a given—but damned if every two weeks or so, somebody didn't go visit them and end up having a beer and some dinner and TV in a different living room. Of course, they might also get co-opted into helping Bobby restore Reg's beloved dump, but it seemed a small price to pay.

"Engineering," Henry said with respect. "Those are tough courses. I looked into that." He knocked his skull with his knuckles. "Too thick."

Billy laughed, but he looked pleased. Well, yeah. They were *all* pretty here. Being praised for your brains, your drive—that was unusual, and Lance felt a teeny bit of relaxation seep into his stomach. Henry had promised, and apparently he was going to live up to his word. Lance was relieved.

"Anybody else got a surprising major?" Henry asked, and he seemed to have relaxed as well. "Rocket science? Economics of underdeveloped countries?"

"Personal trainer, dude!" Zeppelin hammed. "The better to surf when the surfing's good!"

"You live in a valley, Zeppelin," Fisher said patiently. "This isn't the place to be a surfer bum."

"Cheaper here," Zeppelin said, nodding, as if he could get the rest of them to believe him. "And this way I can go surfing on the weekends."

"He spends his weekends as a yoga instructor," Fisher told Henry. "I know this because we both work in the same gym. Asshole hasn't taken me surfing once."

Zeppelin grinned at the guy he'd been fucking not more than an hour ago, and Lance looked at them both curiously. Fisher was a recent addition to the Johnnies stable, and while he seemed undecided about porn, he'd been Zeppelin's guest more than once, and that was unheard of. "You haven't asked me to take you."

"That's not how it works," Fisher explained, a note in his voice telling Lance that he was pretty sure Zep didn't know this already. "You say, 'Hey, Fisher! I'm all fucked-out this weekend. How about we go surfing instead!' and I say, 'Yeah, Zep, it would be great to know you liked more about me than my cock!' See how that works?"

Zeppelin looked abashed. "I don't got a car, dude. Neither do you."

"Oh God," Billy muttered. "*I* have a car. And a week off school. Let's go."

"Or a wetsuit," Zeppelin said, looking embarrassed. "Or a surfboard. You guys, I'm all talk about surfing, and you know it."

"We can still go," Billy said. "I'm sure there's places to rent."

"Yeah?" Zep perked up. "Let's plan!"

"Good for you, guys," Randy huffed. "Can we see the end of the movie first?"

"You can come too," Fisher offered.

Randy arched his almost transparently ginger eyebrows at him. "I go poof in the sun," he said. "That's sweet, but I prefer pasty and sad to surfing and peeling. Really."

Henry let out the most amazing sound, but Lance was the only one to notice. The guys went back to their movie, with the addition of pizza, of course, but Lance couldn't help staring at Henry, wondering if he could get him to laugh again. Just once. Just for real. Because that had been like rain after a long dry summer, and Lance yearned to feel it over his body again.

OLD HABITS

SOMEONE WAS having sex again.

Henry rolled over on the couch and covered his head with the pillow, thinking he could probably manage another hour of sleep if they finished in the next five minutes.

When he'd first heard the idea—him, crashing with a bunch of oversexed porn stars—of course he'd been outraged and morally horrified. Because his *father* would have been outraged and morally horrified. But after that first night, eating pizza with all those sweet young men, he'd gone to sleep with memories of his first leave after basic training. He and Mal had ended up with a bunch of their fellow sufferers in a bar in Georgia—because there was seriously nothing else to do—and they'd bullshitted and played pool and swapped life stories and given one another a ration of crap. Even though he and Mal had been hoping for some time together, the camaraderie had made him so happy. It was almost more important than friendship—it had been the knowledge that he could fuck up and somebody would have his back.

To a point, of course. Because if anybody had known about him and Mal, well... well, he would have ended up on somebody's couch anyway, except now he was twenty-seven and not nineteen.

But at the time, that sense of belonging had empowered him, and he'd reveled in it. Watching those young men drape themselves over the furniture, over one another, and talk about their futures with such hope, he'd remembered his promise to Lance that he'd be kind to his "little brothers," and he remembered his own brother's kindness and had been determined to make good on it.

It was the least he could do.

And as for the sex?

Sometime after the third night, when he'd been sleepless and as on edge as a traumatized cat, he had a flashback to his first week in the barracks, when everybody had been waiting for the guy next to him to stop snoring so he could jerk off. Mal had been the first to pretend to snore, and then Henry, and then they'd been surrounded by relieved privates, doing the private under the covers. Henry and Mal had caught each other's eyes and giggled, then shivered, and then nursed their own hard-ons, quietly, waiting for the noise around them to subside.

The minute it did, they'd closed their eyes and came, and it had been just the two of them in spite of the twenty other men and the overwhelming smell of spunk.

Yes, they'd been surrounded by guys getting off.

None of it was for them.

And in spite of the absolutely open sexuality of every guy in the apartment except him and Lance, this was the same situation.

From the bedroom with the queen-sized, he heard Zeppelin's low moan and Fisher's strangled cry, and the banging of the headboard slowed down, then stopped. Henry gave a sigh of relief, until he heard another sound, this one from the air mattress next to him, where Cotton curled up in a tight, defensive little ball.

For a moment, Henry groaned, thinking he was going to have to wait for Cotton to get his rocks off before he got to sleep, but then he heard the actual sounds Cotton was making.

Tiny sobs, the kind that sputtered because the body wanted to do more but the mind was trying to do you in. Cotton was *crying*.

Oh shit. Oh shit oh shit oh shit.

Henry got up, not sure what he was going to do—he was *not* cuddly— but knowing that he had to do something.

Lance. Lance would know. Lance deftly managed these hyperemotional, high-strung post-adolescent hormone bundles with the sweet touch of a mother—except Henry's mother would have turned her kids over to his father for the strap, when all the poor kids needed was a hug.

Henry stood up quietly and leaned over to squeeze Cotton's shoulder, as if to say, "Help is coming," and Cotton seized his hand, hard enough to overbalance Henry and pull him onto the air mattress. Henry ended up on top of him, wriggling around and trying to escape, while Cotton just clung to his shoulders, sobbing on his chest.

Oh Jesus. They were both sleeping in their briefs, and he was almost naked with another man for the first time since the time he wasn't going to think about.

"Cotton... uh, buddy...."

The kid was warm and smooth-skinned, stringy with muscle, and hysterical. He looped his arms around Henry's neck and held on so tight, Henry couldn't breathe—and Henry's libido started tugging on his shirt.

Uh, Henry. Buddy. 'Sup. Been a while, right?

No! He's a freaked-out kid. Chill! Dammit!

Cotton felt it—of course he felt it—and he started to grind, his sobbing easing infinitesimally, his hips apparently doing what came as natural to him as breathing.

"No no no no," Henry mumbled, scooching to get away. The mattress was pretty well constructed, but Henry was a solid guy, and Cotton followed him across. When Henry got to the end, the side collapsed just enough to send him tumbling to the ground, bumping the cheap coffee table and sending it over on its side. A still hysterical, mostly naked Cotton landed on top of him, and Henry couldn't seem to wiggle away without making things worse.

"Cotton, man, c'mon. Let's go get… coffee. Or ice cream…. Buddy, you've got to get off me. Come—" Oh God. Cotton's groin caught Henry's right where things counted, and the stroke against his shaft was unmistakably arousing. "*On.* Oh Jesus, dude, this isn't what either of us wants!"

Henry tried to sit up, pushing his arms behind him, and suddenly Cotton's mouth, his briny, wet, sobbing mouth, was on his neck, and it was all Henry could do not to tilt his head back and yield.

God, he'd been here for a month, and it felt like a year, and his body was whining that it had been *so long.*

"Cotton!" he barked. "No!"

Cotton pulled back, the hurt etched clearly on his face. "But you want it," he said, hiccupping and palming Henry's aching erection without shame.

Henry caught his hand. "Even if I did, you don't. Not really. Man, let me get Lance, okay? You're a mess."

Cotton's lower lip started to wobble again, and Henry let out a groan of frustration. "You can hug me," he muttered, needing that face with the eyes and the chin and all the sad things to stop. "But no sex."

"O…o…okaaaaaayyy…."

And then they were back to square one, except Henry was leaning uncomfortably against the shambles of the coffee table while Cotton lost his shit.

Eventually he fell asleep on Henry's chest, and Henry managed to get him situated on the air mattress again. He was picking up the coffee table groggily, wishing for actual coffee, when Lance wandered in, dressed for rounds.

"What happened?" he asked, frowning.

Henry squinted at him. God, he looked good, his tawny skin aglow, black hair water-combed, full lips quirking up. Did he know how beautiful he was? Well, he apparently bared that beautiful body to the camera every so often, let people stroke it and invade it and kiss it for money—so maybe he did. But he was so pretty. Even at gawdawful a.m.

"There was crying," Henry mumbled. "There was crying, and then there was groping, and then there was 'no, Cotton,' and then there was crying." He closed his eyes and opened them again and shoved his hands through his hair. "I never got to the why there was crying. But there was crying."

Lance quirked his mouth in sympathy. "You can sleep in my bed if you want. Randy's alone for once, thank God, and I think Zep and Fisher are finally quiet."

Henry shook his head. "No. I need to get Galen to the airport in an hour. Need to get up and coffee and bus."

Davy had made good on helping him find work, and part of that promise led to Henry driving for Galen. Galen was John's boyfriend—John being the owner of Johnnies—and he'd been injured badly in a motorcycle accident a few years back. He *could* drive, but it hurt, and he'd confided to Henry in a rare moment of vulnerability that he lived in fear of his legs going out when he was behind the wheel. Since Galen was mostly a sarcastic asshole whose every word dripped with disdain, it had been a rare moment indeed.

"I can drive you," Lance said easily. "Go shower. What are you doing after airport duty?"

"Mm… since I have John's car, I think I'm on for taking Frances to school. It's a little late for before-school day care and apparently her second-grade teacher is a real bear about tardies. Kane was writing a paper last night, and Davy said he was leaving early so he could go talk to his professor." Kane apparently had learning difficulties, and part of Henry—the part that was like his father—wanted to sneer at him for being a big dumb gorilla. But the part that watched Kane play with his niece or work until the small hours of the morning trying to read and write way above his education level, thought that maybe he should have a little fucking compassion.

God. Learning. Henry certainly needed more of it.

"You mind nanny bus duty?" Lance asked with a smirk.

Henry shrugged, embarrassed. "I like kids," he mumbled. "My brother Travis's kids are sort of fun, and Mal—" He swallowed. This had never been so hard to say before. "Mal and Debbie's baby was super cute."

Lance tilted his head. "I keep forgetting—was Mal your brother?"

Henry shook his head vehemently. "No. He's my sister's husband. Me and him were in the service together." God, he wanted to clap his hand over his mouth. He wasn't going to talk about that—no matter what Davy said about them needing that conversation.

Lance must have sensed something was up. He straightened his shoulders and frowned. "There's a story th—" At that moment, the coffee maker started hissing, and Henry backed away.

"I've got to get ready. I don't want to make you late. Back in a few."

"Hey, Henry—"

He ignored Lance's softly called entreaty and hustled for his duffel bag of clean clothes and the bathroom. He thought rather wistfully that he wished he had something besides jeans, a T-shirt, and a hooded sweatshirt and denim jacket, but as he soaped his hair with Lance's shampoo—because the guy had offered, dammit, and not because he loved the scent—he couldn't imagine what else he'd wear. He'd seen the guys go out clubbing in slickly cut trousers and button-downs, tight cashmere sweaters and low-waisted jeans, but he'd never actually stopped to think about what he'd wear outside the military when he'd been in it.

He and Mal had never dressed to impress each other, just in case people noticed who they were trying to impress. Hell, everybody had given Henry shit for being Mal's babysitter, keeping him on the straight and narrow. Having a club shirt would have blown Henry's cover.

But now, as he got ready for his day of running errands and trying to pick up a shift waiting tables at a local restaurant, the idea was a low-key rumble in his gut.

Who *was* Henry Matthew Worrall without Malachi Daniels and the U.S. Armed Forces behind him?

Well, apparently, he was a guy who'd hug a stressed-out kid in his sleep and not take advantage of the poor kid even when he offered him a sobbing hand job. At least, that was a place to start.

He and Lance got situated in Lance's car—a used CR-V, colored silver like every other car on the road—and Henry sipped his coffee appreciatively from a Johnnies travel mug. He could admit to himself privately that he rather loved the stylized line drawing on the side.

Then he asked the real question of the morning. "So... Cotton."

The boy had been sleeping when they'd left, but Henry hadn't been able to resist pulling the blanket up to his chin and tousling his hair before he'd walked out the door. Cotton had smiled a little in his sleep and snuggled in deeper, and Henry's heart had broken.

God, he looked about twelve.

Who said this kid got to fuck on camera for a living?

Henry couldn't help thinking about him now as Lance made his way down Howe Avenue toward J Street.

"Yeah?" Lance said, turning the radio down.

"Cotton," Henry said again. "What's his deal?"

Lance made a sound. "It's bad, Henry. Do you really want to know?"

"He's fragile. He's... I don't know if he should be making porn. I don't know why his parents let him out of the house."

"His mother *kicked* him out of the house," Lance said, and Henry grunted.

"Of course."

"His first boyfriend was three years older than he was—he was seventeen at the time. She had the guy arrested. The charges didn't stick, but the guy didn't want anything to do with him after that. I guess he slept on people's couches through high school, but eventually he ended up on the streets. He was hustling in front of one of the clubs our guys go to for promotions. He hit on Reg—"

"The promotions guy?"

"Yeah. Reg did scenes before that. But Cotton hit on Reg, and Reg let him sleep on his couch for a night before taking him to John. Reg would probably have let him move in period, but his sister was living with him at the time, and that sitch was no good. Anyway, John was going to have him do lights and sound, sort of like Kane, but Cotton had been street hustling for a month by then and was like, 'Hey, I can whore my ass and earn my keep,' so John gave him a shot. Turns out, he's dynamite on film. It's just, you know, off camera...."

"He's looking for love," Henry said with a sigh. "We... we need to talk to him. I mean, we're not going to kick him out, but he's... he's going to fall apart."

Lance made a hurt sound. "We can't save all of them, Henry. I mean, yeah, we'll help Cotton, but you gotta know that right now. This flophouse thing, it's not permanent. I mean, *porn* isn't permanent. Some people stay in it for a while—they get houses, they get cars, they treat it like a profession. Some of these kids started porn because they wanted a new tattoo. Either way, for most of the guys who go through the flophouse, it's like you. Not meant to last."

Henry ruminated. "Look, it's like when I was on deployment. You see a civilian on the road in a war zone—you help get them out of the way. Yeah, it's a war zone. You don't know what's going to happen to them tomorrow. But for *today*, you get to be the good guy. I'll talk to him tonight. That kid needs a good guy." He took a sip of his coffee and brooded, because he'd gotten proficient at that. "How often do you really get to be the good guy in life, you think?"

Lance's voice was sort of hurt. "Well, you know. I try to do it every day."

Henry felt a laugh burble up, and he was caught off guard so he let it out.

"What?" Lance asked, and as Henry watched, a warm red crept up his cheeks. "Why's that funny?"

"I don't know!" Henry's own cheeks felt warm. "I mean, you're a doctor. It's like you're going to school for an incredibly long time so you *can* be the good guy every day. I think that's awesome, by the way. But I'm just a grunt. Closest thing I ever get to being a hero is moving some poor family out of the road."

"Or making sure Cotton's okay," Lance finished softly.

Henry let out a sigh. "Yeah, well, there's that."

Maybe.

Lance dropped him off at John's house, and Henry thought for the umpteenth time that if Davy's business partner and boss was going to be a porn mogul, he should live in a bigger, better place.

The tiny one-bedroom, one-bath structure apparently boasted a pool in the backyard, and the flowers in the front were already blooming. It looked so… ordinary. As Henry knocked on the solid oak door, he caught a scent of jasmine from the backyard and wondered if he would ever get his head screwed on straight about these people.

Cotton the porn star was like a puppy left in the rain.

John the porn mogul was a nice guy, and his boyfriend was giving Henry a job.

Lance, the med student, was treating porn like any other profession— waiting tables, working retail—and Henry was starting to agree with him.

Henry's brother was a businessman, a good parent, and he shot and edited porn for a living.

And Henry, who had lied to his family and to himself for the past ten years, was in the middle of all of this, pretending to be straight.

Aces.

"Henry. So good to see you on time."

Henry smiled grimly at Galen.

Galen had probably been the prettiest man in any room, once upon a time. A brutal motorcycle accident—and a few years addicted to painkillers—had left him a little thinner, with a scar he tried to hide behind tousled hair and scruff on his chin. Henry privately admitted that the guy was still stunning—his brown eyes and lazy-eyed smile would have appealed very much to Henry once upon a time.

But Galen was a dry, sarcastic bastard who seemed to sense Henry's general judgment of all matters porn, and he was really good at leaving little verbal slices just under Henry's skin.

"Lance gave me a ride," he said, giving credit.

"Ah, Lancelot—even helping out the dragon."

Henry smiled thinly. "Not all of us dragons have our own chariots," he said, and Galen's lazily lifted eyebrow should have warned him.

"What a good vocabulary word, Henry. A few more of those and you can go out and get your own job."

"I could go now," Henry said sweetly. "But then you'd have to take an Uber to the airport, and that would piss all sorts of people off."

Including Davy, dammit. And Henry was trying so hard to do right by his brother.

"Galen…." John looked at Galen expectantly, and Galen glanced away, backing from the door and letting Henry in. John didn't *appear* to be a force of nature. Five-foot-nine, maybe, with red hair and freckles, and perpetually ten pounds underweight with bony ankles and Opie ears, John was neither handsome nor powerful. But he seemed to have good ideas—and the kids in the flophouse talked about him like he was their favorite teacher.

Henry had to admit that they'd all been paid regularly and treated well as employees. He'd heard the boys talking—they got robes before and after scenes. They were tested often and counseled well on how to avoid disease and how to stay safe in general if they were going to do other gigs besides just porn. They were even given a chance to go to clubs and be celebrities, promoting their faces, their personalities, and their videos. It wasn't a job Henry would have chosen, but he could tell that John was trying to run a respectable outfit and give his boys every chance possible.

And he seemed to owe Davy some sort of blood bond, because he was constantly reminding Galen not to be an asshole.

"I apologize, Henry," Galen said, glaring at John through slitted eyes. "If you can get my carry-on bag, we can proceed."

"Travel safe," John said, putting a casual hand on his lover's hip. "Play nice with the other lawyers. Don't eat anybody for breakfast."

Galen bit his lip almost shyly and leaned in for a kiss, and Henry had to look away. Not because he was disgusted—although he remembered the body language, the quiet huff, the rolled eyes—but because he was touched. There was a tenderness there. Galen could be a bastard with a dagger for a tongue, but he seemed to melt when this scrawny redheaded porn-pervert said nice things to him. And Henry wasn't iron or stone. He was as susceptible to romance as the next guy—if the next guy had been yearning for his lover to be that kind, that open about his feelings for his entire life.

Henry grabbed the practical carry-on and the less practical garment bag, and passed the two of them, engaged in their goodbye kiss, on the way out the door that led from the kitchen to the garage. John had property in Florida, and Galen had old contacts he was trying to break away from, cleanly and legally. He'd made this trip twice before since Henry had shown up on Davy's door, and this was supposed to be the last time for a while.

Henry situated the luggage in John's newest acquisition, a Buick LeSabre, as old-fashioned as it was luxurious. He turned toward the connecting door to the kitchen and walked to the steps, ready and waiting to help Galen down. Galen took them by himself, eyes narrowed in concentration, cane wielded with sheer force of will. The accident that had scarred his face had nearly cleaved his foot in half, and while he could walk without the cane most of the time, when he was stiff or there were stairs involved, he seemed to really need it.

Henry could respect a guy who tried to work past an injury, and he tried to be a gentleman.

Galen was just crap at accepting help was all.

Still, Henry waited by the car door and made sure Galen was belted in before closing it and opening the garage door to the bright spring day beyond. The dismal rain hadn't lasted long. They were in the first week of May and it was almost hot, and Henry was wondering what the summer would hold. As Henry made his way down the tree-lined streets of what he privately admitted was a very pretty city, he couldn't stop himself from commenting on the weather.

"It's gorgeous today. When do you think the rain will come back?"

The soft snort behind him wasn't reassuring. "October if we're lucky."

Henry took in the green lawns and the leafy canopy overhead. "No, seriously."

"No, seriously. This part of the country is in the tail-end of a drought, Henry. John won't even flush the toilet after a piss—none of the locals will."

Henry blinked as several moments from the past month in the flophouse came into focus. "Oh my God! I thought those assholes had been born in a barn!"

For once Galen's dry laugh was not aimed at him. "No, sir—that was a concerted community effort to not flush away a precious resource. You're welcome."

"It's hard, getting used to a different place," Henry confessed. The Army was the Army, barracks were barracks, and everywhere else felt like traveling. But to live somewhere, let it thrum through your blood—Sacramento wasn't the rest of the world.

"It is that," Galen agreed softly. "Do you have any idea what you want to do yet?"

"Besides strain my brother's good graces and be at your beck and call? Not a clue. God, I wish I did."

"Have you looked into online classes?" Galen asked, and when his voice was gentle like that, Henry could see the charm that apparently had John wrapped around his little finger.

"Yessir," Henry replied crisply. Traffic was starting to pick up, but he made the right turn onto the freeway with relatively few obstacles. "I have. I've even applied. I just don't know what I want to take. I was thinking computers but then, that's what everybody says."

"Mm." Galen appeared to be thinking about this sincerely. "Maybe don't decide at first. Maybe simply survey classes to start with. Most young people make the mistake of thinking they have to know exactly what they want the minute they hit the boards. School was originally a time to explore so you could figure out what you wanted. Maybe approach it that way."

Henry let out a breath. "That's a really nice idea," he said, almost surprised. "Thank you, Galen. I'll keep that in mind." His father's voice said, *"Computers are practical!"* and he didn't want to go that direction, but it was nice to have Galen in his head, for once not being an asshole.

"Well, Henry, you are punctual, you are efficient, and you are, within certain boundaries, as courteous as you can be. These qualities can get you far if you apply them right. You need not be a chauffeur forever."

It was Henry's turn to snort. *As courteous as you can be?* What the hell did that even mean? "But Galen! My life would be empty if I couldn't lick your loafers."

Galen tilted his head back and emitted a soft laugh. "And there's the little asshole I've come to expect. Forget everything I just said. I've heard fast food is hiring—perhaps you'll find your vocation there."

"I'd be sure to deliver the extras to your door," Henry replied sweetly, "but I understand you people aren't fond of carbs." There was no mistaking the "you people" snideness in his tone, but then Henry had done it on purpose. The bitchfest was on.

As nasty as they got to each other—and Henry didn't flatter himself; he gave as good as he got—he still got out of the car to assist Galen to his feet and set his luggage up for easy transport. Galen watched him impassively until Henry handed him the roll-aboard and his briefcase, the garment bag secured firmly on top of the suitcase.

"Thank you, Henry."

"You're welcome, Galen."

Galen took a deep breath and shook his head. "Henry, I can be a vicious bastard—and you are no sacrificial lamb. But do take my advice about looking into exploring the world. I know you *think* you've seen a lot with the military, but very often, when you're traveling as a soldier, you only see the world as a bullet. Do you take my meaning?"

Henry grimaced. "I do. Thank you." He had to admit this, or he really would be as ugly on the inside as the entire car ride would show him to be. "It's kind of you to take an interest."

Galen's mouth twisted, and he winked. "Well, for better or for worse, you are one of the few people who can bitch right back in my face. John's the other one. We assholes have to stick together." And with that, Galen seized his luggage and hung his cane from the handle, using the works to balance his way into the arrivals wing so he could check in.

Henry swung back into the car and left for Sacramento, so he could help his brother with child care, and the very odd world he found himself in now.

A WORLD that felt no less odd that night as he pulled Cotton aside to talk after dinner.

"Take my bed," Lance offered under the murmur of roommates eating spaghetti and sausage. Henry had instituted an "everybody cooks for one night a week" rule, complete with a chart on the refrigerator. And while that meant they ate chicken on whole wheat with sprouts when Zeppelin cooked, and tofu lettuce wraps when Lance cooked, the result was everybody got at least one home-cooked meal a day. And even when the guys were fasting for a scene, they had company as they nibbled celery and drank seltzer water.

Tonight had been Cotton's night to cook, which meant everybody else did cleanup, and it was the perfect time to take the kid aside and mess with his head. Of course, that wasn't what Henry *meant* to do, but he had no doubt he was going to fuck this up somehow.

But he couldn't get over those broken sobs against his chest, and the way Cotton had morphed so seamlessly from despair to sex.

There had to be a different way to approach life, one that didn't seem to break him quite so much.

"You want to come with?" Henry asked a little desperately, and Lance shook his head.

"Sometimes it's Mom's job, sometimes it's Dad's," Lance said primly.

"My dad used a strap," Henry muttered. "I think we need a better Dad."

"You're what we've got," Lance told him, but not before Henry saw the little wrinkle between his eyes that spoke of pity. "Unless you want to turn the job over to Dex and John—"

"I've got it." Galen's pointed remarks had apparently left little puncture wounds in his psyche. He *could* pull his weight, dammit, he really could.

So after dinner, he shoulder-bumped Cotton and dragged him to Lance's bed, grateful for the offer. Lance didn't have sex outside of scenes—not that Henry could see, anyway. And he hadn't filmed anything since Henry had arrived, which Henry found… comforting, for reasons he couldn't name. It would have to happen eventually, he knew. Lance had said something about checking the schedule.

But Henry wasn't worried about that right now. Right now, he was worried about the kid who was currently taking off his shirt and unbuttoning his jeans, right in front of Lance's bed.

"Zzzzomigod!" Henry burst out. "What are you doing? Stop! No! Put your clothes back on! We're not doing that here! That's not what this is about!"

Cotton stopped and frowned. "Then what are we doing here?"

His chest was a thing of alabaster beauty. Pale skin, riding the muscle groups so tight, Henry could mark the places you'd shade the shadows in with a pencil. His shoulders were wide and his elbows had been moisturized, a curiously vain, vulnerable gesture that hit Henry more in the solar plexus than the groin. He had giant fucking Bambi eyes, luminous and brown and vulnerable—dammit, couldn't this kid stay out of the goddamned rain?

"You are getting dressed first," Henry said. "Then we're sitting on opposite ends of the bed, and we're going to talk like people."

Cotton grabbed his T-shirt—a Johnnies promotional one, with the model on the front and everything—and curled up in the far corner of the bed, his back against the corner of the walls. He looked, if anything, more naked now.

Henry sat down on the end of the bed with a sigh. "Cotton, son—"

"I'm not your son."

"No, but you're too young to be my boyfriend, so we're going to roll with that, okay?"

Cotton swallowed. "Too young?" he asked. "I've fucked guys way older than you—"

"And shame on them. I mean, I get—sort of—why the people you do on set may be older than you. That's a professional relationship, and those cross age boundaries sometimes."

"Most of them aren't much older than you or Lance. You're sort of, you know… old."

At twenty-seven. Fantastic. Henry couldn't control his glee. "Thank God," he muttered, wishing for Galen's dagger-like dryness. "Anyway, if I'm so old, why are you looking to hook up with me?"

Cotton started to pluck at Lance's comforter, which looked like a homemade thing in vibrant magentas and blues. Henry wanted to touch it too. "I dunno," Cotton muttered. "You were… warm. And safe. It feels good when it's safe."

Oh. "Well, yeah. It should feel good. It should be safe. But—and this isn't for work, mind you—but maybe you should have some action… some *agency*, when you pick your warm and safe. You were going to sleep with me because I was there, Cotton. Maybe don't sleep with guys because they're *there*. Sleep with them because you *want* to."

"But how will I get anybody to like me if I don't put out?"

Henry's swallow was audible.

Mal, can't we just, I don't know, hang out?

C'mon, Henry—I wouldn't have asked you over to my folks' house if I didn't want to fool around.

A thousand years ago. That had been a thousand years ago. And Henry had bought that line and bought it until what he was doing wasn't wrong because it was with Mal—it was wrong because Mal was married to his sister, and she'd had Mal's baby.

"You can't do that," Henry said, his throat so tight, he almost couldn't talk. "You putting out—that's not a condition of a relationship, Cotton. That's…." What did he want it to be? "That's like, your *reward* for letting the rest of the relationship work. I mean, I get it. Some people hook up and they walk away and that's okay for them." Martin—wasn't that his name? Martin had been a prime example. "But not everyone is built like that. I don't think *you're* built like that. I just…." Henry blew out a breath, because God knows, his adult decisions hadn't been any more awesome than this kid's. "I just think it would be kinder to yourself if you kept the sex on set for a while, and decided what you wanted for yourself when you're not there."

Cotton swallowed, looking smaller and smaller in his corner. Oh Jesus. Once again, he wanted to call Lance, and then he saw the kid wipe his face with his sleeve.

"Look, Cotton—if I come sit next to you, do you promise not to come on to me?"

The kid took one of those deep shuddering sob breaths and nodded, and Henry did what he promised. Sat next to him. Warm and safe.

Cotton put his head on Henry's shoulder and cried. Not racking sobs—silent, cleansing tears. Eventually, he slid down Henry's arm, falling asleep, his head on the pillow, and Henry covered him with the yellow-and-green crocheted blanket at the foot of Lance's bed. He emerged from the room to find the dishes done—he'd insisted *somebody* do them after dinner, because yuck!—and the living room surprisingly empty. Lance was reading under the lamp at the end of the couch.

"Where is everybody?" Henry asked, looking around.

"Well, Zep and Fisher were going to sleep, for once," Lance said, "so Randy asked if he could spoon with them. Curtis is in there doing homework. Billy is staying at a friend's house—"

"A friend?"

"Apparently so. There was nothing about a hookup in his voice. Old high school buddy. And you sort of took my bed."

Henry made a sad-clown-horn sort of sound. "And the answer to whether or not Lance gets his bed back is…."

"No!" Lance filled in, laughing softly. "I get it."

"You can sleep on Randy's bed," Henry offered blandly, and Lance's look of horror reassured him.

"Only if I'm into pain. His sheets are so stiff, they'd cut my skin."

"God, that kid's lucky he doesn't get scabs on his penis. For God's sake, that thing's like the Energizer Bunny of dicks!"

Lance had to hold his hand in front of his mouth, he was laughing so hard. When he calmed down, he dropped his hand and said, "You shit! All the kids are asleep for once and nobody's having sex! God, don't make me wake anybody up!"

Henry gave one more chuckle. "Sure. You can have the air mattress. Do you have to be anywhere tomorrow?" Lance had classes sometimes—in-services, Henry supposed, not knowing what the doctor term for it was—and meetings all the time. It was hard for Henry to keep them all straight.

"Well, yes, but only because I want to," Lance said cheerfully. "Have you met Reg yet?"

Henry nodded. He'd been to the Johnnies main office several times. He'd never been invited to the back suites, where the offices were made to look like bedrooms and the filming happened during business hours, but he'd been back there on occasion to make repairs. And he *had* dropped Galen or Davy off in the front on several occasions. That's when he'd met John's shy promotions director.

And had wondered about him, a lot.

Reg wasn't pretty, or at least as pretty as the other guys. He was, in fact, pretty average, although his body looked like he took care of it. His hair was getting a little thin on top, so he kept it buzzed short, and his cheekbones weren't razor perfection. He had an amazingly sweet smile, and while Henry had noticed that he wasn't quick on the uptake—he'd needed to be reminded of who Henry was more than once—he was very good about asking questions from the people around him. Reg wouldn't have made it in the military, he was just not quick enough, and from what he'd let drop, he'd spent several years in porn.

Until this night, right now, Henry had been sort of pissed off about that. Who had let this guy—this not-so-bright, super sweet guy—spend his twenties giving it up for anyone who looked good on camera?

But Reg talked about trying to fix a house and trying to keep a car, and about how any job he could have gotten out of high school wouldn't have let him do that. And Cotton—that kid couldn't work six days a week in food service, with people yelling at him. He'd be a wreck.

Sure, there were better ideas—but you usually needed connections to get you that job, and these guys were barely connected to their own shoes.

Henry was beginning to get a picture of a very different world than the one he'd assumed existed, where gay men were the same as sex perverts and porn stars were degenerate drug abusers. These were his father's ideas— these were the thing he'd said loudly about Davy the minute Davy left. These were the ideas Henry had littering his brain from the minute Mal had kissed him, laughed in his ear, and shoved his hand down Henry's pants, when they were sixteen.

But he was starting to see that sex was very different than he'd been raised to believe. He was almost as horrified as he was surprised.

That didn't stop a part of him from thinking sex should be sacred.

"Have you met Reg's boyfriend, Bobby?" Lance asked, breaking into his thoughts.

"No, not yet, but Reg said he was looking to hook me up with a construction job."

"Well, he's about six-three, and built like a tank. Like maybe three-hundred pounds of chest with a thirty-inch waist. It's *insane*."

Suddenly Henry remembered one pertinent bit of information that Reg *had* dropped about his boyfriend, and he *knew* a brilliant shade of magenta was washing up from his neck.

Lance chortled. "Reg told you Bobby's got a ten-inch dick, didn't he?"

Henry buried his face in his hands. "Yes!" he wailed. "Why did I have to know that?"

"Because, my brother, you would have wondered, and now you don't have to. Reg is doing you a service. I've filmed scenes with him—it might even be eleven inches, but the kid doesn't like to brag."

Henry felt his grin break free before the full import of what Lance said hit. "Scenes…," he choked, and Lance looked away, obviously embarrassed.

"I'm sorry. I… we've been trying not to mention that in front of you. You get all weird, and the guys get weird, and… you know. You seem to be fitting in okay. And now I had to go—"

"Forget about it," Henry said, waving his hand and ignoring the hollowness in his chest. "It's just… weird. To think you were… whatever. Why are you telling me about Reg and Bobby?" His throat ached, like it did when he was trying not to cry, and he was a little appalled. What was wrong with him? Why did the thought of Lance with some Panzer tank with an eleven-inch johnson freak him out so badly?

"Oh!" Lance sounded as desperate for a different subject as Henry was. "Yeah! Because Bobby's foreman has a boat. The guy offered to take Bobby and some friends out on the river, and Bobby picked Reg of course, but I got the invite too, so, well, it's my day off and I'm not spending it catching up on my med journals, and that's pretty damned exciting."

Henry was genuinely happy for him. "You work too hard," he said, leaning sideways against the couch and wrapping his arms around his knees. "You totally deserve it."

Lance put down his medical journal and turned to mirror Henry's pose. They were facing each other from across the couch, and Henry suddenly realized how intimate this conversation was, in the living room at night, the only two people awake in the house.

"Well, you deserve a medal for falling on the Cotton grenade tonight," Lance said with admiration, and then he sobered. "Did your dad really take a strap to you and Dex when you were kids?"

"Yeah," Henry said, not sure when that had become a secret. "But, you know, not randomly. Only when we were dumbasses. Didn't your parents spank you when you were a kid?"

"Only when we wandered into traffic," Lance said, his brow still furrowed. "And that's the truth. Only time I saw my little sister get spanked was when she jerked away from my mom's hand to get something in the street. Mom must have been terrified, but Morgaine never did it again."

"My youngest brother, Sean, fell in a creek on a family hike once." Henry remembered that day, him being the good little soldier, just behind his mom, thinking that Davy was going to get in trouble. "Dad wasn't even there. If Davy hadn't done that thing he does, running around in back to check on everybody in line, Sean would have drowned. So we get back from the hike, and Davy and Sean are wet and covered in mud, and he's got blisters because he carried Sean back the whole way. And what does Dad do? He gives Sean a solid ass-spanking for poking around in the creek and not being where he should be."

"Harsh," Lance murmured.

"You think so?" Henry shook his head. "'Cause Davy got the belt for wrecking the new leather boots he'd worn when Mom had told him to wear the crappy ones he'd grown out of."

Lance made a hurt sound. "That's not a lot of incentive to do the right thing."

Henry nodded, his throat tight. "That's why I joined the Army," he said, wishing this didn't hurt so much. "Because I thought, hey, being a soldier, all you gotta do to do the right thing is follow orders."

"Mm. How'd that work for you?"

Henry tried a tight smile, but judging by Lance's continued wide-eyed sober look, it didn't work that well. "Not so much."

"Why not?"

Henry took a deep breath, one that shuddered on its way out. "Would you like a beer? I'd like a beer—"

"C'mon, Henry, who's it going to hurt?"

Henry closed his eyes and stopped trying to get off the couch. "Me."

"Can it feel any worse telling me than keeping it inside?"

"I didn't even tell David." That hurt. He'd been there for more than a month. It was what? Mid-May? He'd had dinner with his brother at least once a week, played with Frances, pretended not to enjoy the assortment of snakes, turtles, and iguanas that lived in their house and backyard, and rolled his eyes at Kane every chance he got so he could feel just a little bit like the person he was hadn't been left behind completely. But he hadn't talked about why he was there, and Davy hadn't asked. Maybe Travis had called him—their older brother still got Christmas cards and called Davy every month or so, and he didn't care if Mom and Dad knew it. But David was still waiting for Henry, and Henry appreciated that, but it also got scarier every day he stayed.

"Tell me," Lance urged. "If things go south, you can pick up and leave again, but we'd miss you. And if I keep this confidential, just you and me, and we keep going, every day, like we've been, you'll be one step closer to knowing it's okay."

Henry regarded him soberly for a moment. "You already know about me," he said, his chest contracting. "You know my brother, you know the Army kicked me out, which means I failed at life. What about you? You appear to be winning at life, but I don't understand…." Oh hell. *No, Henry, don't open up that cup of porn worms!*

"Because," Lance said, not flinching. "Because my whole life, I was told I was important. I could be anything. I could fly. But I wasn't stupid. I knew how my parents voted. They didn't go to church often, but I knew what the church said about people like me. So I was twelve, and I realized exactly who I was, and I was pretty sure Mom and Dad weren't going to be so excited about that. They'd given money to the local pray-the-gay-away place."

Henry closed his eyes. "My dad actually said he should have sent Davy there when he was a kid. He thought him and the neighbor kid were too close."

"Well, they were super excited about this place in Nevada—said it was God's answer to all the bad homosexuality in the world."

"I wish," Henry muttered, *really* wishing this wasn't a part of him.

"I don't," Lance said, and his voice grew low, vicious, and gleeful. "I had to hide it—I *had* to hide it. I buried myself in schoolwork, hid my porn, beat off like a motherfucker. I probably gave Randy a run for his money in my senior year. I'm not even ashamed. And I held it. I held it through my first seven years of school. God, I was so close to my internship, it was like I could smell a paycheck."

"What happened?" Henry asked, fascinated. He never saw Lance like this—never saw him angry, or bitter, or impassioned. The man he'd learned to appreciate was usually smiling, always compassionate, gentle as a… well, a doctor, with the hormonally insane adult children they were sharing an apartment with.

"I had a boyfriend at the time—a doctor. Nice guy. My…." Lance swallowed. "My first, really. First lover, first love. And we were out for dinner, good restaurant, wine. He put his hand on top of mine and told me he was already married but he'd like to put me up in an apartment so he could pay my way through med school."

Henry shot bolt upright. "What. An. *Asshole!*"

Lance gave a bitter laugh. "You think? So did I. I stormed out—and ran right into my parents, who were there with some work friends of my father. And there was Teddy, right behind me, yelling, 'Galahad, I hate to lose you!'"

Henry's brain trainwrecked. "Galahad?"

Lance's cheeks colored. "Swear to Christ, it's my real name."

Galahad, Lancelot—Henry got it, and he managed a grin in full bloom. "Suits you."

Lance snorted. "So would Gawain, but nobody can pronounce it."

But that's not what the story was about. "What did your parents do?" Henry asked, and even though he had a pretty good idea, given where Lance was now, he wanted it to be a happy ending. Lance was such a good guy, a good person.

"They looked at me, and their faces grew shock white, I swear to God, even my mother, who's Filipino. And they looked at Teddy's hand on my arm, and then at me. And my father says, 'We'll discuss this at home tonight.' I was living on the other side of town in a dorm, so I knew that was bad." He let out a sigh. "Gotta hand it to Teddy, though. I mean, we were broken up—that was over. But he followed me to my folks' house and helped me get all my stuff after the throw down."

"How bad was the throw down?" Henry was dying to know. He'd carried his bruises for weeks.

Lance caught his eyes directly. "Not nearly as bad as yours. They yelled, they cried, and I just stood there. I wasn't even surprised. I...." He swallowed and looked away, some of his composure slipping. "I didn't think so anyway. I... me and Teddy moved all my shit out to our cars, so we could get it to the dorms, anyway, and I cried all the way back."

"Have you talked to them since?" Henry asked, and Lance shook his head, killing a hope Henry hadn't known he'd had.

"My sister—she's in law school. We still talk, have lunch sometimes, text once a week. She says...." He shrugged. "They don't say my name."

There was a silence, and Henry couldn't seem to swallow past the lump in his throat. "Were they paying for the dorm?" he asked finally, because he needed the end of the story.

"Well, not after that." Lance's mouth twisted. "I had about a month to find new digs, find a job that would work around my hours. I'd been watching Johnnies porn for years, thought it was great that they were in my hometown. I'd even met some of the guys for non-penis-related injuries, and they seemed... fine. Nice. A little cocky, you know, because obviously they can fuck on camera and good for them, but not awful. And I'd just broken up with a guy who wanted me to be a dirty little secret. I was my class valedictorian, in med school for Christ's sake, and my parents wanted to forget they'd ever had me. I… it was very *fulfilling*, if you know what I mean. To wave my gay penis around and say, 'Hide this, motherfuckers! Hide *this*!'"

Henry smirked, because sweet revenge was something he got. "Well done," he said gruffly, meaning it. "You're braver than I ever was."

Lance's hand on his ankle wasn't sexual, exactly, but it was tender. Kind, gentle—things Henry had never asked for, had never been given. That kindness was like a solvent, dissolving the last of the shell that held Henry's words back in his throat.

"How'd your coming out go?" Lance said softly.

"It's still going." And wasn't that the truth. "I'm not even sure how you know."

"Because I looked at your eyes when you looked away."

"Do the other guys?"

Lance considered. "They're pretty comfortable with you—maybe. But that's what this is about."

So much for putting things off. "I… my best friend married my sister, right out of high school."

"So?" Lance cocked an eyebrow.

"So, his bachelor party was me and him with a fifth of jack, an open field where nobody could see us, and his dick in my ass, no lube, because that was the one thing we hadn't done yet and he wanted to do it before he got married and we'd have less time to hook up."

Lance sucked in a breath of what sounded like horror. "Fucking. Ouch."

Henry let out a little laugh. "Yeah. We were going into the Army in two months anyway. I figured…." He shrugged. "Figured it was the last hurrah for Mal and me. Some people give up their virginity on prom, so what was the big deal?"

"Was it? The last hurrah?"

Henry swallowed, and the bitterness didn't go away. "No. I mean, next time I made him use lube, believe you me, because it took me a week to stop bleeding—but there was always a next time. After basic training, there was still a next time. Every time we got leave, there was a next time. And… and every time I'd get like, 'Mal, dude, you're married. This is wrong,' he'd be like, 'Just guys fooling around, right? I mean, it can't be sex if there ain't a girl involved.'" He left out parts, parts with Mal's lightning-quick hands and bruises Henry had brushed off as being part of training or sparring, but that wasn't important, was it?

Lance blinked slowly. "Well, *that's* some fucked-up logic right there."

And he still couldn't swallow the bile in his throat. In fact, it rose up and threatened to choke him. "You think? And… and I listened to him. I fucking listened to him, because the alternative was to… to just stop. And he may have thought that I was like… like a human Fleshlight he could use when my sister wasn't there, but…." This was the worst part.

"You loved him," Lance said, and that made it easier.

"I did." Henry had to breathe then. His chest was tight, his throat was swollen, his head ached. If he could only breathe, breathe, breathe… maybe that ache could go away.

"But being gay isn't illegal in the military anymore," Lance said, starting to stroke along Henry's leg under his jeans. It helped to ease the ache a little.

"It is not," Henry said. "But… coercing men you're promoted over is."

Lance frowned. "Did he—"

Henry shook his head. "I got a promotion. For nine years we managed to get promoted at the same time." Some bitterness slipped out, and it tasted like old come. "He told me I should fake my test scores because otherwise, I would have been about three ranks ahead. And we wanted to stay together, right?"

"Of course," Lance muttered. His eyes were shiny in the lamplight, but Henry couldn't think about that right now. If he could get this out, tell the story, maybe he could keep the ache, the bitter, bilious ache inside.

"But I couldn't do it. Not one more time. Dammit, I loved the Army. I… I wanted to shine. My CO came to me one night and asked me why I was holding myself back. He told me Mal would never be more than a hometown guy, and friendship and loyalty were one thing, but Mal didn't have the promise I did. And a part of me was angry, you know? I wanted to show him that I *did* do shit right and I *didn't* fuck around. So I took the test, and I got the promotion, and I told Mal, hey, we had a reason not to do the thing anymore. Because it could ruin us both."

"What did he say?" Lance asked.

And Henry shook his head, because he thought, hey, that should cover it, right? Things didn't work out—obviously.

"Henry, what did he say?"

"He was… he was pissed. And he… you know. Always liked a rough fuck when he was pissed…."

"He *raped* you?" Lance's voice came out as a squeak. "Is that what you're telling me?"

"Well, seduced," Henry said, because it had dignity. Lance's hand clamped around his ankle then, not gentle.

"Define seduced."

Seduced. Seduction was a hand over his mouth, bent over the bed of his new private barracks, cold tile hard against his knees, in pain.

Without lube.

"Coerced, then," Henry managed to admit, but his face was wet, and he wasn't sure how it happened. He tried wiping his eyes on his T-shirt, and it came back soaked.

"Henry," Lance murmured, and his touch grew softer again. "C'mon, man. Say it. Just to me. I won't tell a soul."

Henry shook his head. "Don't make me say the word."

"Henry—"

No. "I wish that was the worst part," Henry choked, because he couldn't get the rest of the story out if he said the word.

"There's something worse?"

"For me, yeah. He threatened me. He threatened to tell our CO, have me court-martialed, have the entire affair blow up in our faces, if I didn't keep… doing what we'd been doing."

C'mon, Henry. I don't like doing it this way. Just keep being sweet. It'll all be okay.

"Oh, honey—"

"My sister has a baby, and she's pregnant again. If it blew up, and she found out, her life would be over. But I… I thought we were doing it because we were…." God. "At least friends," he said bitterly.

"You were in love with him, and he betrayed your trust," Lance said.

"Is that what love feels like?" Henry rubbed his chest, and then shook his head. "I'm the bad guy here. I was fucking my sister's husband. I mean, there's no sugarcoating that."

"People aren't all black and white, Henry." Lance gave him a game smile. "I mean, my dad's Russian and my mom's Filipino—living proof, right?"

"That they should bottle that gene pool?" Henry said, smiling a little.

"Damned straight." God, he was beautiful.

"No flirting in confessional," Lance said, and he dropped Henry's one ankle, so Henry could bend his knee again—and then started to stroke the other one.

"Understood," Henry said.

"So what did you do? I mean, you're here."

"I went to my CO and confessed the whole thing," Henry said. He closed his eyes, remembering the man's sorrow, his disappointment. "He was… kinder than I'd expected. Told me that I had two choices. I could take the dishonorable discharge, and Malachi could keep his job, or it could come down to a court-martial, and it would be my word against his. He said…." Henry swallowed. "He said now that I had rank, it was likely they'd find in Mal's favor."

"And both your careers would be ruined."

Henry let out a breath. "It's… I was fucking my sister's husband," he said again, as if Lance hadn't gotten the enormity of that sin. "It just seemed better for her. She and my nephew and the baby in her stomach are innocent. I thought…." He couldn't go on.

"How'd Mal take that?"

"I don't know. I took my walking papers the next day and… disappeared from his life. But he must have said something, told my sister something. Because I showed up at my parents' house to tell them… I don't know. I was gay. Something. And Dad was there. With his fists, I guess. Mom sat and cried and said, 'Not another one!'"

"Oh, dear God."

Henry shrugged and wiped his face on his shirt again. "But you saw that. I lived." He wasn't a complete pussy.

"I'm not so sure," Lance said with a little laugh. "When was the last time you took a day off?"

Henry snorted, sputtered tears, and tried to get his shit together. "Jesus, Lance, when was the last time I *worked*?"

"You call how you spent your day not working? You did nothing but run errands for twelve hours—and trust me, if you weren't here, John would have tapped another porn kid and paid him a fair wage, just like he's paying you."

Henry shook his head again and tried to still his breathing. "Just… just enough. Is there something on television? 'Cause God, it's been a—"

Lance stood up and moved over to Henry's side of the couch. "Scoot over," he murmured.

Henry rolled to his side wordlessly, giving Lance enough room to lie down. Lance did, his body warm and smelling spicy and a little sweaty, but safe. Henry laid his head on Lance's arm and said, "Why are we doing this?"

"C'mon, Henry. Haven't you ever needed a hug?"

"Yeah," Henry whispered, laying his cheek against Lance's chest. "Yeah."

The apartment was so quiet, so peaceful, and for this moment, Henry was too weary to think of being anywhere else.

IT'S NOT WHAT IT LOOKS LIKE

LANCE DIDN'T get many opportunities to sleep in—and that morning was no exception. He remembered Henry rolling off the couch, and then that subtle relaxation that came when the other body with you gave you some space.

There was a blanket, though, Lance thought, snuggling. And someone had taken his cargo shorts off, leaving him in his boxers and T-shirt. He snuggled deeper into the blankets as the morning apartment ritual started, with coffee and banter and "Hey, do we have any bacon, I might try keto." He dimly remembered Henry asking if he could help with the shorts.

"Sure, but don't go," Lance had mumbled, and Henry had crawled in next to him, on the outside this time, and they'd slept, cuddled, safe.

A persistent buzzing interrupted Lance's rosy glow, and someone— Cotton?—poked his arm. "Lance, man, wake up. Your phone's buzzing."

"What time is it?" he mumbled.

"Almost eight. You said you wanted the shower after Henry, remember?"

Oh yeah. Shit. Lance sat up and checked his phone, unsurprised when he saw six texts from Reg, asking if he was up yet.

Gotta shower. Will be out in five.

Okay. We're almost there.

Lance took that to mean "Hurry!" and grabbed his shorts and sneakers and headed to get his stuff from the bedroom.

"Where's Henry?" he called before ducking in to start the shower.

"Taking out the trash. Every morning. Like clockwork!" Cotton replied, and Lance nodded before jumping in.

Unless there was something special going on, like there had been the day before, Henry woke up at eight, took out the trash, did basic chores around the house, and then buzzed John and Dex to see what they needed him to do. Bobby had told Reg they might need someone to work construction a couple of days a week starting next week, but Henry really had been filling in his time—driving people around, buying supplies, doing odd jobs at the set. Not while there were models, of course, but Henry had gone in and fixed the plumbing in the girls' shower and on more than one occasion repaired furniture broken in the scene rooms. In general, he'd made himself useful, Johnnies own little handyman, guy Friday to the hormonally insane in the flophouse.

None of which could explain the swelling in Lance's chest as he remembered the night before.

Vulnerability didn't come easily to Henry Worrall. Watching him come undone as he'd told that painful story…. Lance's throat ached thinking about it. Henry had limitations—that was obvious. He didn't roll his eyes anymore when the guys talked about scenes or boyfriends or scoring a hookup—but that sense of solid Midwestern farm-boy disapproval was never far from the surface.

But he kept his mouth shut about it, and Lance could respect that. Lance got the sense Henry was trying to reserve judgment about things he didn't understand—and even when he did understand, to not be like his father about things that weren't necessarily in his life experience.

The fact that he'd wanted to talk to Cotton and not yell at him already made Henry a better person than 70 percent of the parents Lance knew.

Maybe eighty or ninety. Bobby's mother was the Johnnies' receptionist, and she mommed as much as the boys would let her—she'd started to matter more on a basic math level. She *was* that good 30 percent; Lance was sure of it.

But she hadn't been the one holding Lance during the second half of the night. Sure, they'd started out with Henry resting his cheek on Lance's chest, crying softly, until he'd fallen asleep like a child. But after Henry had gotten up to use the bathroom, he'd spent some time making Lance more comfortable, helping him undress, getting him a blanket, and then had crawled in next to him and held him tight, even though they had a perfectly good inflatable mattress, complete with sheets and blankets, made up next to them.

But Henry had chosen Lance instead.

Lance wasn't sure what it meant, but there was a pleasant tingling in his stomach, a hope. It was stupid, of course. Henry still couldn't talk about the guys filming scenes, or porn, or even about all the hookups that happened in the bedrooms while Henry slept in the front. Lance really *could* sleep while Randy was going down on whoever got bored, but he wasn't sure how Henry was taking it in his fortress of solitude on the couch. Sure, he'd laughed when Lance had talked about waving his gay penis around, but had he thought it was funny enough to date someone who was doing that?

Still, having those arms around his shoulders, the way being held by Henry had felt like he was holding an equal, someone who would shoulder Lance's burdens and lay his own down for Lance to carry—that had been pretty damned intoxicating.

Lance was so lost in thought, he likely wouldn't have caught the excitement going on downstairs if Zeppelin hadn't stuck his head into the bathroom.

"There's some guy downstairs screaming at Reg. And Henry's gonna beat the shit out of him!"

The fucking *hell*?

Lance got dressed so fast, he was halfway down the stairs before he wondered if he was wearing his own shoes. He got there just in time to catch the tableau—Johnnies guys lined up on the stairs, watching a cop thriller down by the dumpster.

Lance wasn't sure what had been said before he got there—all he knew was that things had devolved into a total shitshow now.

Bobby—the sandy-haired Panzer tank Lance knew and loved—was standing in front of Reg, his face red with anger as he faced down a stringy, vaguely familiar-looking young man wearing a khaki duster.

"C'mon, Reg, ya fuckin' retard—don't tell me you don't want some! Your sister's a fucking basket case. I'd want to get away from that too!"

"Get the fuck away from him, Scott!" Bobby snarled. "I've got no beef with you—fuck!"

Because Henry hadn't waited for Scott to back down. As Lance watched, he dragged the guy away from Reg and Bobby and frog-marched him to the dumpster, maybe thinking to pin him there while somebody called the cops.

"Martin Sampson, you hustling piece of shit. You should have just stolen my wallet when you had the chance!"

"So now I'm a hustling piece of shit?" Scott snapped, but he didn't sound surprised or even angry. Just sad.

"What are you even doing here? Reg doesn't want any fucking pills!"

Scott gave a sheepish smile. "Everybody likes candy, Henry."

Lance had no idea who Martin Sampson was—he'd always known the guy as Scott. And even when he'd worked at Johnnies, Scott had been an asshole. John usually weeded out the guys who were violent or too self-centered to shoot good porn—often before the come had dried in their audition video. But Scott had hung around. He'd even dated Dex for a while, and then Dex had the good sense to break up with him, and Scott had moved on to Kelsey the receptionist, and from there, Lance had heard he'd gone to jail. He'd been well known as the local coke dealer, but judging from the little packets sliding from his pockets now, Scott had apparently moved on to pills.

"Get the fuck out of here," Henry ordered, his hands fisting in Scott's button-down shirt. "These boys don't want what you're selling!"

"Lookit you, Henry," Scott murmured, and the sorrow on his face was shockingly sincere. "Being the hero and shit. Just like your brother."

Henry's fighting stance eased up a little, and he lowered his fists. "My brother?"

Scott gave him a sheepish grin, his eyes peeking out from under his lashes, and for a moment, Lance almost saw that he could be charming. "You know… your brother?"

Then he realized what that grin could mean.

"Henry!" Lance called, hustling down the steps. "Henry, no!"

"*Fuck!*" Henry swung and clocked Scott in the jaw before grabbing his duster again, lifting him bodily, and shoving him into the dumpster. It was pretty impressive as an act of strength, and absolutely horrifying as an act of violence. "These are *my* kids. Don't you *ever* come back here selling your filth again!"

"Damn," Zeppelin muttered, following Lance down. "I was hoping he'd have some P-Top with him. All this cooking at night is making me fat."

"P-Top?" Henry asked, apparently hearing the most irrelevant detail in the midst of chaos.

"Diet pills," Lance snapped. "And they fuck up your metabolism, Zep, so back off. Jesus, Henry, are you all right?"

"Coke keeps you skinny," Scott mumbled, trying to push himself out of the dumpster. Henry turned to him with a snarl, and he settled back down against the trash bags and closed his eyes.

"Fine," Henry muttered tightly. He turned toward Bobby and Reg, making an obvious effort to relax his shoulders and his expression. "Reg, you okay?"

Reg peeked out from behind Bobby's shoulders. "Yeah, fine, Henry." Reg's arms crept around Bobby's trim waist. "Thanks for doing that. Bobby was trying to keep his temper, but—"

Bobby clasped Reg's hands at his middle. "I'm still on probation," he admitted grimly. "Which means *we* should probably get scarce. Lance?"

Lance looked at Reg and Bobby, remembering Bobby's misdemeanor conviction for assault. "Yeah. You guys go get in the car. I'll be right there." He checked his pockets for his phone and his wallet, relieved to find he'd brought them with him. "Let me go talk to Henry."

Henry was herding the rest of the guys up the stairs, and Lance ran by the dumpster, giving it a check inside.

Scott—who was apparently Martin Sampson—was muttering to himself and trying to clamber out over the piles of trash. Good for him. Lance could see the little plastic baggies of pills falling out of his pockets and littering the ground in front of the dumpster. He was unimpressed by drug dealers, particularly ones who badgered guys like Reg.

But Henry had some explaining to do.

"Henry?" he called from the base of the stairs. "Can we talk a sec?"

Henry nodded to Curtis, who was dragging the rear, and came back down to where he stood.

"What?"

"Who the hell is Martin Sampson?" Lance hissed.

Henry grimaced. "Who the hell is Scott?"

"Scott is your brother's ex-boyfriend—the guy he was dating before Kane, who stalked him and tried to sell coke and… fucking Jesus, he's a sleazeball."

Henry scrubbed his face with both hands. "He's the sleazeball who was hanging around the bus station the night I got in." His voice rose at the end, like he was wishing it wasn't true.

Lance groaned. "No."

"Dude, I hadn't seen my brother yet, my face looked like hamburger, and…." He let out a groan. "I'm a fucking idiot."

"What are you going to tell Dex?" Lance demanded.

"Nothing!" Henry dropped his hands and stared at Lance in horror. "Oh my God! With all of the other shit I've got to tell him, does he really need the cherry on the shit sundae? I'm telling him nothing!"

"How could you do that?" Lance demanded, the irrational anger kicking in. "Pick up a stranger like that?"

"I don't know. How can you have sex on camera for cash?" Henry lashed out. "We all have our lines, Lance." He grunted. "Mine just happens to be trying to get out of the fucking dumpster."

Lance let out a slow breath. "I was an asshole," he admitted, and then glared at Henry, expecting the same thing in return.

"And I'm white trash with all the wrong answers," Henry snapped, obviously not giving in. "Look, man, one thing at a fucking time here, okay?"

And there was the disdain Lance had been expecting. He'd known it was there, waiting to jump out and bite him. "Whatever," Lance muttered. "I'm going out for a day off with the other whores. You have a nice fucking day."

"Whatever," Henry snapped behind him. "Make sure Reg is okay, wouldya? You're the one who knows what to say."

Lance drew up short, suddenly realizing that was a compliment and Henry was trying to be an adult. He turned around, but Henry had already made it up the stairs, and all he saw was the door slamming behind him.

"WHAT'S WRONG?" Bobby asked quietly as the boat knifed through the Sacramento River like a machete through butter. Reg was still in the front, looking out excitedly, and Bobby had literally wrapped a rope around his waist to keep him from going nose first over the side. Lance had hung out in back thoughtfully while Bobby's boss and his wife took turns piloting the thing, talking loudly between themselves. Gruff and homely, in their midfifties, they'd made Lance feel welcome when he'd arrived at the dock. Like with most boating trips, conversation wasn't going to get good until they arrived at their destination for the planned picnic at Discovery Park, where the Sacramento River and the American River joined.

Lance looked out at the water and then smiled briefly. "Henry surprised me, that's all," he said. The trip to the dock had been a lot of Lance and Bobby calming Reg down and making sure he felt safe after Scott had gotten in his face. "I didn't realize he knew Scott, you know?"

Bobby raised his eyebrows. "A lot of us did. He was in one of my first scenes. But, you know, there's hookups that matter and hookups that don't. You taught me that. Which one do you think it was?"

Lance swallowed and remembered Henry's painful confession. Wouldn't Scott have come up in their discussion the night before if he'd mattered? "I know," he muttered. "I *know*. But it... I mean, his brother's ex-boyfriend. That's just so...."

"Twisted," Bobby agreed, turning his tanned face toward the sun. Lance thought fondly that the only reason Bobby and Reg weren't true rednecks was that they *were* in porn, and they *had* been conditioned to take care of their skin. Bobby had a long, strong face with a bold nose and no-bullshit green eyes. He was one of those people who would rather rebuild your porch than sit and watch TV with you, which was good, because Reg needed some looking after. Bobby didn't mind being busy, and Reg didn't mind being looked after.

"Wasn't his fault," Lance said after a moment. "But...." *Dammit.*

"You were starting to like him?" Bobby asked delicately.

"He has unexpected depth," Lance said with dignity.

"Then he'll forgive you for being an asshole," Bobby told him, lips twitching.

"But will he forgive me for being in porn?" Because as soon as Lance had wounded him, that's where Henry had gone.

"Remember that one time you and me hooked up?" Bobby asked him softly.

"Yeah." Lance closed his eyes. Reg, Bobby—he'd done them both, on and off camera.

"That was special to me, even though I was breaking my heart over Reg. Sex is complicated—you taught me that. Love is simple. It's where the two meet that shit becomes a tangled mess."

Lance laced his fingers behind his head and tilted his face up to the sun. "It's not that tangled yet," he admitted. "There's been no sex."

Bobby let out a laugh. "And he's lived in the flophouse for how long?"

Oh God. "Since late March?" Lance was really asking if that was bad.

Bobby's out-and-out guffaw told him it was. Really bad. "Oh my God, Lance. You've managed to tangle this mess without a penis in sight. You realize that, right?"

Lance buried his face in his hands. "Oh, for sweet fuck's sake…."

"Yeah. I'd say you and this guy are more fucked-up without the sex than him and his brother's ex were with it. Fun shit right there. I hope you survive."

Lance glared at him. "You. Asshole."

"We've met," Bobby said evenly. At that moment Bobby's foreman shifted the boat into a lower gear, and they all looked in anticipation of the dock at Discovery Park. Picnic time. Time for Lance to be fun and charming, for Bobby's boss to be a neat old geezer who didn't mind a bunch of porn kids in his construction company, and Lance to put his worry on hold.

HE GOT home that night, happy, a little buzzed from the beer Bobby's boss had so generously provided, and full from the picnic. He hated feeling full—and he hated himself for what he was about to do about it, but he figured he'd turn on the shower to cover the sound, the way he always did.

But first, he had to deal with the aftermath of that morning.

He opened the door to find Henry in the corner of the couch, his knees drawn to his chest, watching an action flick, with the guys gathered around him, hooting at the screen. There was a big bowl of popcorn on the table—unsalted, unbuttered—and a smaller bowl of carrot sticks. Snack time for porn models.

Lance closed the door behind him and looked meaningfully at the spot on the couch next to Henry, currently occupied by Cotton.

Cotton looked back at him, his eyes wide and innocent, and Lance narrowed his in return.

"Scoot, junior, or I'll break your arm," he said softly, and Cotton laughed.

But he retreated, moving to the air mattress with Curtis, Zep, and Fisher.

Lance wriggled in and very casually leaned against Henry in a way Cotton had seemed too scared to do.

"Good day?" Henry asked, his voice careful and civil.

"Sunshine, wind," Lance said, smiling pleasantly. "Beer."

Henry gave a soft laugh. "Well, good. You needed it."

"Anything fun happen while I was gone?" *Did you suddenly realize how much I like you and decide that porn didn't make me a completely unsuitable candidate and human being?*

"Nope. Fixed shit for John, shuttled Frances to child care and back. Davy wanted me to ask you to dinner next week, so, you've been asked."

"That's nice." Lance regarded Henry through half-masted eyes. "Was there any more trouble?"

Henry shook his head grimly. "Nope. I don't think he'll be back."

Lance nodded. "Good." Was he forgiven? He couldn't tell. "Scoot over a little," he murmured. "I need to lean on something."

He waited until Henry had turned and lowered his feet to the floor before he laid his head on Henry's shoulder and made himself comfortable in the sprawl. Henry's arm wrapping around his shoulders made him smile, relieved. Good choice.

He felt Henry drop his head and breathe softly in Lance's hair. "You smell like river," he murmured, so low Lance could barely hear him. "And sun and wind."

"Mm…." Henry smelled like shower, and it was really turning Lance's key, but he wasn't going to say that.

Henry took another deep breath. "Freedom," he said.

Lance closed his eyes then. *Someday, Henry, you can be free.*

But he didn't say anything. Instead he ate lots and lots of popcorn and made sure Henry was fast asleep before he threw it up.

EVERYTHING WAS the same after that, but not.

Work—the insanity of the hospital was hard to quantify, but at the same time, it was a job like any other. Lance liked working with people. He'd been raised to give back to the world, and for all his parents' flaws, that was one of the good things that had stuck.

As for family, Lance still saw his sister once a month, listened to her stories of law school, and told her about his residency. She never asked about his living situation—he was pretty sure their parents had made her afraid to, which was too bad. He wanted to tell her about home.

He wanted to tell her about Henry.

Coming home was… well, nice, as bizarre and sex-saturated as it was. Apartment 126C made him feel grounded. And coming home to Henry—

Until that day with Martin Sampson, when he thought he'd lost Henry Worrall's good opinion forever, he hadn't realized how much he valued it.

Which made him dread what was on the schedule for the end of May.

"Not eating?" Henry asked that night at dinner, and Lance grimaced.

"Scene the day after tomorrow," he said briefly. Sure, there were other alternatives to fasting, but that tended to leave his breath shiny bright, as Reg called it, and gum left his mouth pasty.

Henry grunted. "You kids—it kills me. I… I mean, I was raised where you got loved with chow. I feel like you're depriving yourselves, you know?"

Lance regarded him, surprised. "Nothing shitty to say about filming the scene?"

Henry rolled his eyes. "Have I said that to anybody else?"

And Lance felt a little ashamed. "We can feel your disapproval," he said, regarding Henry over his can of seltzer water.

"Well, that's not my fault." Henry glared mulishly, and Lance's heart melted a little more. "I just…." He grunted. "Sex isn't… sanitary," he said after a moment. "I… it's one of the magic things about it. Or it was. Or it should have been. You wanted it so bad the… uh, sanitation didn't matter." He shrugged and fidgeted with the spaghetti on his plate, looking at Lance under his lashes. "You break out a washcloth and a towel and get on with it, you know?"

Lance wanted to ruffle that pretty blond hair. "That's what, uh, sex *should* be. But in sex fantasy, there is no washcloth."

Henry blinked slowly. "You're a sexual fantasy?" The strangest things happened then. His eyes narrowed, like he was trying to be sarcastic, but his voice… his voice got rough and smoky, and real, like Lance was *his* sexual fantasy and he'd only now realized it.

"To some people," Lance said calmly. "To some people, I'm the roommate who's becoming emotionally invested in watching you eat spaghetti."

And those narrowed eyes suddenly widened with mischief. "Emotionally invested? Or… you know, *physically* invested?" He took a little bit of meatball on his fork and nibbled it. "Mm… like, are you *emotionally* invested in this meatball? Do you *want* this meatball?" He swallowed and grinned. "Are you *feeling* this meatball?"

Lance's stomach gave a vicious cramp, and he was tempted—so tempted—to devour an entire plate of spaghetti and spend ten unpleasant minutes in the bathroom with his fingers down his throat. God knows, he'd done that before.

But Henry was having such innocent fun there—and Lance had kept his little bulimic secret for the last two months. He didn't want Henry to feel bad, oddly enough. The eating and binging thing was his little problem. He couldn't make it something Henry would hate about himself.

And he really wanted to see Henry smile. God, he was too grim most days.

"I am *so* feeling that meatball," Lance said, saturating his voice with all of the sexiness he probably would *not* be putting into it when he went in to film in two days. "Oh, Henry, eat that fuckin' meatball!"

Henry waggled his eyebrows and took another bit of meat on his fork. "Like this? Do you want me to eat it again?"

"Oh yes! Yes! Eat that meat some more!"

"With sauce this time, Lance? You want some sauce on that?"

"Give me all your sauce! And noodles! Oh God, slurp my fuckin' noodles!"

Henry did, sucking on them slowly, making sure the sauce dripped temptingly down his chin. When he was done, he stuck out a surprisingly long pink tongue and caught the last drop before it drizzled too far, and that was as far as Lance could take the joke before he kissed him, straddled him, took his grim mouth and made it swollen and ripe with kisses. Before he worshipped the strong column of Henry's neck, nibbled on his collarbone, showed him what sex could be like with someone who didn't just know what he was doing but who believed sex was magic to boot….

Or, uhm, cracked up.

Lance covered his mouth with his hand, closed his eyes, and laughed. Because that other vision had been so close, so tantalizing, so real, and if he didn't laugh, he'd reach out his hands to touch the thing that would burn him the worst.

"Hey, wait, is that spaghetti?" Zeppelin was coming out of his bedroom, Fisher at his heels.

"Forget spaghetti," Fisher said, wrinkling his nose in confusion. "Was that *sex*? I could have sworn I heard sex!"

Henry grinned and winked at Lance. "Nope," he said, taking another bite. "The only noodle getting slurped here was spaghetti."

The guys cracked up too, and Henry invited them to dish up and come sit down to eat before asking about their day. Behind them, Lance lowered his forehead to bang it repeatedly on the table when Henry couldn't see, because never before had spaghetti gotten so close to getting out of hand.

"LANCE!" DEX called, effectively ending the scene. "What are you doing?"

Lance had to think a minute, and then Kent, his partner in the scene, thrust his cock into Lance's mouth, and Lance was suddenly in the present.

"Gimminf m bwwmb?"

Kent withdrew and tagged him playfully on the back of the head. "Nice guess, but no cigar and no blowjob. No dick either. Jesus, Lance, it's like your eyes rolled back in your head and you went somewhere else."

Lance sat up in bed, feeling suddenly naked and wrong about it, when it hadn't ever bothered him before. "Sorry, guys. Not sure where my brain went." He smiled greenly at Kent. "I was sort of looking forward to this too." God, he'd needed to get laid in the worst way—because his sexual fantasies about Henry Worrall were consuming his every waking minute.

But Kent didn't know that. Kent was a giant blond tank of a guy, with thick muscular thighs, a chest almost as wide as Bobby's, and a seven-inch cock the width of a soda can.

If you were into sex-for-pay, Kent was a wet dream—or at least a wet workday.

Kent ruffled his hair. "You're probably hungry," he declared practically. "I know I'm starving. Here—we only just started. Go think the dirty, do what you gotta, we can regroup in five, 'kay?"

Dex cleared his throat, and Lance had to laugh.

"Is he taking your job, Dex?"

Dex checked the camera and set it down on a nearby desk put there mostly for that very reason. This set only *looked* like a bedroom.

"He is, sort of, but it's good advice."

"You gonna fluff for me, Dex?" Kent asked with a wink.

Dex rolled his eyes. "Not my job anymore, you horny bastard. Don't you have a boyfriend watching?"

Conrad was a sweet guy, with thinning hair, fish lips, and a wicked sense of humor. Kent adored him, and Conrad? Conrad watched his boyfriend fuck on set all day and apparently went home and got his rocks off with style.

Lance was all for whatever turned guys on.

Sensual, consensual, healthy—sex could be *such* a good thing.

Or at least it could be in a controlled environment, with partners who agreed to the same terms. If there weren't any emotions involved.

Without warning, his thoughts turned toward his breakup. He'd thought Teddy had loved him, but he'd just been really excited by the "rent boy on the side" idea.

And then they turned toward *Henry's* breakup, and the look on Henry's face when he'd mumbled, "Don't make me say that word."

With a groan, Lance rolled over to his front and buried his face in the rumpled sheets of the bed.

"Lance!" Dex moved to sit on the bed and started to rub his back. "Buddy, what's wrong?"

Oh God. This was the wrong person to talk to.

Lance looked at Henry's brother and heard the way Henry called him Davy, and the shame of having not treated Davy better, and the half-worshipful way he felt about his brother now.

"Oh Jesus," he mumbled. "I have got to pull my shit together."

He wasn't surprised when Dex draped the robe over his shoulders, but he was disappointed.

"No sex today?" he mumbled.

"Not for you, buddy." Dex ruffled his hair. "Conrad? You do test stuff with Kent to keep him company. You want to film a scene with him?"

Conrad looked up from where Kent was kissing his neck and tried to focus. "But I'm homely as a potato," he said in honest surprise.

Lance chortled into the sheets, and Dex contained a snort. "Only to the blind. Kent thinks you're beautiful, and I think his fans will too. Trust me—you'll give the average guys something to shoot for."

"He's hung like a donkey," Kent mumbled, sliding his hands down the back of Conrad's pants.

"Down boy," Dex barked, and both of them pulled in a deep breath, like they were *both* turned on.

Dex sat a little straighter. "O…kay. I've got an idea. You two, different sides of the bed. I'm going to go make a call. I've got a guy—new, a little dominant—and all he's gonna do is tell you two lovebirds how to fuck each other silly. How's that sound?"

Conrad moaned a little, and his hand snuck toward the button of his jeans.

"Stop!" Dex barked, and before their eyes, Conrad's dick unfurled under the denim.

"Wow," Lance whispered.

"Like a frickin' donkey," Kent breathed. "Can you hurry it up, Dex? This is the greatest thing to ever happen to me."

"Glory hallelujah," Dex said dryly. "Now you two, across the room from each other." He made eye contact with Lance, who nodded, because both of them were apparently subby as hell. "And don't come."

They gave a matched pair of delighted whimpers, and Kent dragged himself away from his lover, practically stumbling naked to the opposite wall.

"I'm going to go make a call and get John to take over the camera," Dex said. "Lance, go shower, then meet me in my office, okay?"

"Half an hour?" Lance said.

Dex looked at the guys. "Can you wait that long?"

They were apparently eye-fucking, because they both nodded dreamily, like edging with just their gazes was a real thing.

Lance wrapped his robe tight around himself, grabbed his clothes from the cubby on the edge of the wall, and left the sex-saturated room. A part of him was aroused—because that yearning between Kent and Conrad had been damned hot—but part of him was perplexed.

This used to be so easy.

When had walking into the room, getting an erection, and getting off gotten to be a problem?

He had, in fact, felt sexier, more excited, when he and Henry had been doing their thing with the spaghetti.

A HALF an hour later, he was fresh and clean, hair washed, body loose and unsatisfied. He walked down the hall from the showers to the office, pausing by the scene room. The door was open, which happened sometimes to give the cameraman room. Dex and John were absolutely adamant that nobody not *in the business* be allowed to walk past the door from the reception area during business hours, for exactly that reason.

Kent was facedown on the comforter, his ripe, muscular ass thrust into the air, while Conrad buried his face between Kent's cheeks and licked.

Behind Conrad, naked and willing, was a tall kid, maybe nineteen, with deeply tanned or bronzed skin and black hair down to his shoulders. He was fully erect, and decently sized, but that wasn't the sexiest thing about him. What caught Lance's attention was the way he was standing—two fingers in Conrad's asshole, one hand wrapped around his cock, while Conrad gave Kent the rim job.

"Good," the newcomer whispered in Conrad's ear. "Now finger him. Slowly. Not fast like I'm doing to you. Not two fingers—oooh, wait, three—like I'm doing to you. One. Slow. Because I fucking said so."

Lance swallowed and managed to keep his groan—and his hard-on—
to himself. Oh *fine*. Now his cock was working.

But you'd rather watch this scene than participate, right?

The voice shocked him.

Sure, he hadn't watched a lot of porn since he'd become a model. But
then, he'd really only indulged in the low-key, in-house relationships since
then too.

Bobby, Reg—yeah, sure, there was the chance there'd be some regret
when the person moved on, but in the meantime, it was all safe, sensual, and
consensual. What was bad about that?

Except Lance's body was now on full-on alert, and his heart knew only
one thing for certain: he did not want to be the guy in the room. Not today.

He swallowed and kept walking, unwilling to even contemplate what
that could mean.

"So," Dex said as Lance entered the office. "How're they doing in there?"

Lance gave him a full smile. "It's gonna be some damned hot porn, sir."

Dex laughed a little. "Yeah, sometimes shit just falls in your lap,
you know?"

"Yeah. I'm sorry it had to, though. I mean, I showed up ready to work."

Dex (Davy? Dammit, Lance kept thinking of him as Davy. *Damn*
Henry Worrall, anyway!) smiled slightly. "You did, but your heart wasn't in
it. That happens sometimes. We… you know… don't ever want this to be
a place where you feel like you *have* to work." He reached under his desk
and came out with a small packet of whole-wheat wafers, no flavoring, and
some vitamin water. "Here. You've got to be starving. This'll tide you over
until you can get to the nearest buffet."

Lance took the packet of wafers, absurdly touched. Healthy with
some easy-on-the-stomach carbs, because obviously Dex knew his fasting
comedown food. He remembered Henry talking about his brother as a
caretaker, and his stomach knotted again, and not because it was empty.
Henry's brother was a good guy.

So was Henry.

"I'm sure it's a onetime thing," Lance said hopefully, trying to overcome
that weird little gap in his head when he wanted to call Dex by his real name.
"I mean, you know, the last three years I've been down to fuck—"

Dex held up his hand. "You've been really professional, and you've
been fun, and you've made some glorious porn. And you are always
welcome here. I, you know… want you to know that it's never mandatory."

Lance chewed his lip. "Well, no, it's always been—"

Dex shook his head. "Lance, you still get to come to the company picnic if you're not doing the wild thing with someone on set."

Lance swallowed hard. "We having another one of those?" he asked weakly, not wanting to admit how much that thought moved him.

"Yeah, it's during the buttcrack of July, because John is really fucking demented that way. Of course you can come. You can still go out with your friends, you can still live in the flophouse—although when you move, I suggest you burn all your clothes, because just hearing 'flophouse' makes me smell come. Sort of like work. But yeah. Lance, your family doesn't leave you because you don't work on the farm anymore, you know?"

It flew out before he could censor it. "Yours did. Henry's did. Mine did."

Dex's eyes opened really wide, and Lance could really see him as a little kid.

And seeing him, he could see Henry, and his heart practically fell out of his chest.

"I'm sorry. That was rude and intrusive and uncalled for. I'll go. I'll quit and I'll go and I'm—"

"Lance! Sit down!" Dex blinked a couple of times. "Man, did Henry really tell you why he got kicked out of the house?"

Lance sagged in his seat and gnawed on his lip. "It was personal. I never should have—"

"I know," Dex said, letting out a shuddering breath. "I've known since before he showed up on my doorstep. Our older brother, Travis, he's like the family liaison to the gay. He sends me letters from Sean and Joey, our younger brothers, and pictures of his kids. He hit me up a couple of hours before Henry showed up on the doorstep and told me about the discharge and Dad, but not how bad it was. I've known about... the situation for a while. It was bound to explode. I... I've been waiting, you know? Been waiting for Henry to tell me about it. And he just looks at me, like he's mad he had to ask for help. So he told you, and...." Dex swallowed. "God. I'm just so glad he told somebody."

Lance took a deep breath, his eyes burning. "I don't know... I don't know if your brother really understands how bad it was, himself," he said softly, feeling like a traitor. "His... your brother-in-law... he did a number on him. When Henry picked his promotion over...."

"Over Malachi." And Dex's face—it closed down. Suddenly he looked like he could kill a man, and Lance normally would have put that in Kane's court. "Explain what you mean by number."

Lance looked away. "Don't make me betray a confidence, David."

"Don't make me beg, Galahad. I am worried for my brother. He won't talk to me. And I don't know why."

"He's ashamed!" Lance burst out. "He… he did what he had to, you know? To pass? To live up to your father's expectations? And… and in the end, he was trying to pick the honorable thing—and he lost it all."

"He didn't lose me," Dex said. "I am still in his court. I am *always* in his court. Make sure he knows that, okay?"

Lance nodded, still not able to look Dex in the eyes. "I will. I—he just wants to do something useful. He's so lost. And he's so betrayed. I…. Malachi was a rat bastard, you know that, right?"

Dex's eyes sharpened. "What do you mean?"

"Henry took a promotion so he could feel like he could say no." Well, shit. "It didn't work."

Dex sucked in a breath. "I'll kill him. I'll tell Travis. Travis will beat him until he has pulp for a face. They have thirty-thousand acres in the middle of bumfuck, USA. *They will never find the fucking body*!"

Lance had trouble finding his balance. On one hand, he wanted to tell his friend to calm down. But on the other, the look on Henry's face, the way he'd been trying so hard to be strong….

The utter devastation.

"I'd help you," Lance said, voice rusty. "But it's not going to help him. Not right now."

It was Dex's turn to nod, and then he scrubbed at his face with his hands. He took a few deep breaths and peeked out at Lance with some semblance of the Dex that Lance knew.

"Sorry," he said automatically. "Sorry. This went from me telling you that we wouldn't abandon you, to you wanting to run away screaming. I didn't mean for that to—"

Lance shook his head, and the burning in his eyes spilled over. "I was worried, you know," he said, swallowing. "I don't know if this is the end for me at Johnnies. I'm still not sure what happened today. But I… you know. I fit here."

"You didn't want to lose your family," Dex said. "It's… it's the hard part about making this a good place to work. I…. Reg didn't have a plan after porn, you know? We had to give him one, because he was ready to stop but he didn't… didn't have a plan. You've got a plan—you walked in here with one. But that doesn't mean we want you to just walk away."

Lance wiped his eyes again with the back of his hand. "Sorry. I don't know why…." He gestured to his face. "I'm having the weirdest month."

Dex cocked his head. "Why? What happened, besides meeting my stupid brother?"

Lance raised his eyes to meet Dex's, and Dex made an "ooh" face.

They both laughed wretchedly.

"God. This business." Dex pulled in another one of those ragged breaths. "I used to think, 'Show up, do a guy, have some fun, day over.' It gets harder than that."

"I… I don't know why he's got me so nutted up," Lance said. "I don't even know if he wants to kiss me."

Dex let out a brief bark of laughter. "*That* is probably the least of your problems."

Lance made to stand up and then frowned. "Oh, hey, since Henry's being a closed-mouthed bastard, I was wondering, did Reg tell you about Scott?"

Dex's surprise would have been comical—if his horror hadn't been so palpable. "Scott?"

Oh God. Lance was *not* going to tell him all of this one. Just no. "He showed up at the flophouse—trying to deal. He sort of scared the shit out of Reg." Lance had to smile a little. "Henry threw him in the dumpster. It was very caveman-like, and a little hot, I'm not going to lie."

Dex let out a strained chuckle. "God. Scott. That's a name I haven't heard in a while. Okay. I'll keep an eye out for him and let the guys here know. We run a clean house—we've got help if guys get hooked, but God. Drugs—" Dex shuddered. "—do not make good porn."

"You're a purist," Lance said affectionately.

"It's only worth making if it gets people off." They seemed to have shaken their worry—and their *fury*—over Henry, and Lance stood, grateful for the wafers, for the talk.

For the kindness.

"Henry said I'm coming over for dinner sometime next week."

Dex shook out his hand. "Yeah. I was going to say he just wanted a buffer so Kane would stop glaring at him, but…." Dex bit his lip. "Maybe he also wanted a… friend?"

Lance nodded. "A friend. Sure. We'll call it a friend."

"We'll call it a… *hope*?" Dex's sideways look would have been a devastating punch to the solar plexus, if Lance hadn't been looking at Henry's scowl for the past two months.

Somehow Henry's scowl held more power. Who knew that was possible?

"Okay." Lance was game. "What am I hoping for?"

Dex gave him a mild gaze that showed he wasn't fooled. "We'll hope my brother can sort out his ass from a hole in the ground and realize that you're ready to be more than a friend."

Lance wiped at his eyes some more. "Goddammit. If nobody said it, I could pretend it wasn't happening."

"Galahad, you wandered away from a sex scene when you had a guy's cock in your mouth. It's cute that you think you're fooling anybody but yourself."

"Not even my mother called me Galahad," he muttered.

"What did she call you?"

Lance couldn't even meet his eyes. "Gally."

Dex's snort of laughter was somehow reassuring. "I'll call you Lance for the rest of your life if you like. But it's not going to change the fact that your head wasn't in the game today." He sighed, some of the playfulness fading. "Do you really want it to be?"

Lance looked away. "I'm on the schedule in six weeks," he said. "Can I think about it?"

"It may take Henry longer than that to find himself."

Lance finally glanced up and saw nothing in Dex's eyes but compassion. "Yeah, but by then, I can at least know if he even sees me."

"Fair enough." Dex flashed a tight grin and stood, then walked around the desk. "You still get a check for showing up. You're doing direct deposit these days?"

"Yeah."

"Good. Mrs. Roberts will send that out tomorrow. Now go find yourself something to eat. You look like you need it."

Lance stuck his hand out to shake, but got pulled into a hug instead. He stood immobile for a moment, surprised, and Dex said, "You guys could be good for each other, but be careful, okay?"

"Yeah."

And with that Dex swung around to leave the office, and Lance was left to go home.

CONTRARY TO Dex's directions, he didn't stop anywhere for food. He'd always enjoyed that clean, hollowed-out feeling he had from knowing his digestive system was empty and void, and he was just a vessel. He was missing the thrum under his skin that usually came from sex and a good workout, but it was replaced with another odd buzzing, something he didn't want to quantify.

When he walked into the apartment and saw Henry, alone in a quiet *clean* apartment, surfing the web on his laptop, the emptiness and buzzing stilled inside him, and he practically gasped.

Dammit.

Oh, this was worse than he thought.

Henry looked up as he walked in and gave a strained smile. "You're done already? Usually the guys spend all day doing… uh, scenes."

Lance grimaced. "I, uh, well, I wasn't focusing. Happens sometimes. My scene partner got to do something new and kinky, and I got to go home."

Henry's smile did an odd, fluttering thing. It was like his mouth didn't change shape, but suddenly the smile wasn't tight anymore—it was real. "That's… well, I hope you didn't need the money."

He didn't sound disappointed at all that Lance hadn't spent all day having sex with someone else. Go figure.

Lance allowed himself to squeeze Henry's shoulder before he sat down kitty-corner and looked over Henry's shoulder.

"Looking for work?"

"I should be, but I'm looking through community college courses. I filled out the apps, and I've been planning on computers, but nothing's appealing to me." He shrugged. "It does help to have residency."

"Yeah, it does. So, uh, I haven't eaten in two days. You wanna take me out for a burger or something?" Oh God, he was so nervous. A burger was actually the *last* thing he wanted.

Henry grinned, though. "Absofuckin'lutely."

Well. Awesome. Lance bit his lip and thought that maybe, just maybe, he might be able to keep food down for once.

LANCE DROVE, and they found a bistro in midtown. He parked near McKinley Park, and they took their food to go to eat in the shade. McKinley wasn't the best of areas, but nobody bothered them as they sat on a park bench in the shade of the palm trees, looked out over the duck pond, and told random stories from their youth.

Lance had been an honors student—Henry wasn't surprised.

Henry had been a football star—Lance was unshocked.

But underneath their stories, a picture started to emerge of Henry as a boy denied.

"Oh my God," Henry said, laughing. "No you had to be there. Because cow-tipping—it's the dumbest fucking thing. And I was, like, 'Mal, you crazy stupid asshole, there's nothing funny about how sad they are when they fall and how much they can get hurt. This is my family's livelihood!', right?"

"Yes, and I find it a little bit sexy that you don't approve of random cruelty," Lance said, wrapping half his burger up and putting it carefully in the brown takeout bag.

Henry gave him a quick grin and a sideways look that punched Lance in the stomach *way* harder than Dex's, and continued with his story.

"So Mal, he decides he's going to push the cow anyway, and the poor old thing goes down—*on me*. She wakes up and goes 'Moo!' and wiggles her bony spine all over my leg, which snaps like a twig. We're, like, in the eighth grade, and thank God it was after Pop Warner or my life would have been over. Anyway, I'm pinned. Mal took one look at me and ran off. I'm just lying there, yelling my damned head off, and Davy and Travis come out of the house because I guess they're the only ones who were still awake and heard me. They pull me out—I so puked all over myself too, because God, I cannot take pain like that, it's embarrassing—and they set me up on my side. Davy gives me his jacket to keep me warm—it's Montana in November, you people here don't even fucking know what cold is—and Trav runs to go get Dad. And there I am, whimpering like a weenie, and Davy says, 'Look, Henry, you got two choices here. You either tell Dad who pushed the fucking cow on top of you, or you keep silent and suck it up.'"

Lance let out a strained chuckle. "Your brother's not stupid."

Henry shook his head. "No, but Dad was. 'Cause I picked option B, and Dad bought it. I was not only laid up with the broken leg, I had no TV and no video games and Mal couldn't come over for two months."

"Good," Lance said viciously. "Fucker should have stayed away. But your dad actually bought it? That you tipped the cow on top of yourself?"

"Yeah." Henry chuckled a little. "Dad's got lots of convictions, but Travis doesn't think much of his smarts."

Lance grunted. "I don't either."

Henry stood. "Time to get back," he said, not meeting Lance's eyes. "I told Davy I'd go in afterhours tonight and fix some cabinets in the back." He wrinkled his nose, completely naturally, and completely Henry. "God, you think the apartment smells like jizz. I would really like to live someplace that potpourri doesn't smell like cedar shavings on a spunk-puddle, you know what I mean?"

Lance laughed. "Yeah, yeah I do." They headed back to the car, the shade adding a layer of oppressiveness to the early June heat. Tomorrow was going to be a scorcher.

"Why do you stay?" Henry asked, and Lance swallowed.

"I don't have anywhere else to be," he said, voice remote.

Henry let out a sigh. "That's going around."

Lance let out a sigh, and it was time to go.

They took off back toward the apartment, and while the conversation was quiet, Lance felt hope. He hadn't understood why he'd walked off that porn set that morning, but he was starting to see why it was a fair move.

That night, he and Henry and the guys stayed up playing board games that Henry had borrowed from Dex. It was a fun night, really, but not particularly intimate.

That was okay. Lance had gotten a lunch and a frank conversation. There was hope for more—there must have been. Because Lance couldn't help lingering, sitting on the arm of the couch after the others had gone to bed.

"What?" Henry asked, sitting on the corner of the couch and hugging his knees. "Was there not enough soul baring at lunch?"

Lance snorted. "We barely scratched the surface."

Henry gave him a hard look, and Lance did some fast backtracking.

"Okay—nothing hard. Just, I'm having trouble with the timeline. You and Mal were in eighth grade during the great cow-tipping incident. Were you… you know. Fooling around?"

"No!" Henry shook his head. "Jesus, we didn't get like that until after he started dating my sister, about two years later. We didn't start fooling around until our junior year."

"So, uh, can I ask?"

Henry didn't look at him. "He was dating my sister, they'd started fooling around, but it wasn't doing much for him. One day I was at his house and…." Henry moved his shoulders, like it was no big deal. "He was all over me. And I'd been faking it with girls—all those gross objectifying posters in my room, whacking off every night. I said all the appropriate redneck shit about boobs and ass and pussy and putting out."

"But…?" Lance knew the answer to this—but it was hard, watching Henry trying to find words. He moved to sit on the couch, and to his surprise, Henry kicked off the covers and sat next to him. Not across from—next to. It was like an invitation.

"But," Henry said slowly, "I dreamed about Malachi every night. He was all over me, and I barely put up a 'This isn't right for Debbie' struggle, and he said…." That shrug—that hunch of shoulders, the way he wouldn't look at Lance when he said it—it hurt more every time. "He said it was just us, fooling around. But it felt like more."

"Yeah," Lance said softly. "I'll bet."

Deliberately, Lance scooted an inch or two over, so their thighs were brushing. Henry cast him one of those sideways glances. "Just fooling around?"

Lance swallowed. "I walked out on a job today because of you," he said softly. "I don't know if I told you that."

"Why'd you do that?" Henry's voice sounded rusty, like he was having trouble getting air through his throat.

And God, Lance had to be honest. "There's something about your eyes. I didn't want to look at you and think 'I just had sex for money.' So, whatever it is I'm doing here, it's not just fooling around."

"Talking," Henry said gruffly. "Talking with a friend." And Lance's heart might have fallen, dropped right to his knees through his stomach, but Henry leaned a little, up against him.

Then he put a tentative hand on Lance's knee.

Lance put his hand over Henry's and squeezed, and then held his breath when Henry leaned his head on Lance's shoulder.

They sat like that for quiet moments, and Lance watched as Henry's breaths grew slower, evened out.

"Night, Henry," Lance murmured, nuzzling the top of his head. Henry startled and Lance stood. They both had to be up early, and it was already later than was comfortable for either of them.

That was okay—they'd made progress. There'd been talking. There'd been honesty.

And a lean. There was definitely a lean, and a squeezed hand.

Couldn't forget the squeezed hand.

Because that was what Lance went to sleep dreaming of—Henry's hand on his, those bright Montana farm-boy eyes looking at him softly, and that sweet curve of his lips that meant a smile was coming.

He dreamed of hope for a kiss.

HE WOKE up to Zeppelin, wide-eyed and panicked.

"Dude! Lance! My man! You gotta join us here!"

Lance frowned. "My shift doesn't start until ten," he moaned, turning toward the wall. He'd been in the middle of a dream—lots and lots of dreams about Henry. Lots of *feverish* dreams about Henry.

"Yeah, but man, there's bad shit going down. Henry found a *body* in the trash, man! And we know the guy!"

Lance shot upright at the word *body*. "We know the guy? Holy fucknuggets, Zep. Who's dead!"

"Dex's ex, man! Scott's dead in the dumpster, with his head smashed in!"

Oh shit. Oh hell. There would be cops—cops who'd think Henry was a prime suspect!

Lance went charging out the door, with the guys behind him, not thinking about what it would look like. When he got halfway down the stairs, he saw Henry, surrounded by policemen. Henry looked up and saw Lance and the guys—in their tighties, to a one, because fuck everything— and clapped his hand over his eyes.

Fuck.

Lance pulled to a screeching halt and turned around to Curtis, who was right behind him. "Okay, guys, someone go inside and call John and tell him we need Galen, stat." Lance swallowed and looked out at the steaming pavement where Henry was being grilled like a trout. "Our boy's gonna need some help."

YE GODS AND BATTERED FISHES

HENRY COULD barely drag himself up the porch.

God, what a day, and it wasn't over yet. From hiring him a lawyer and a PI to help him with his case, to driving the PI all over the city looking into the facts, to seeing Martin Sampson's body in the morgue—God, that moment sucked—to the fight he'd had with his private investigator because Henry was just that fucked-up and needy and he and Jackson Rivers, the PI, had started off on the wrong foot.

All of it had sucked. And right now, every ache, every bruise, every cut, was secondary to his dread of telling his brother why he was suspect number one in a murder investigation—because Henry had slept with Davy's ex.

Henry knocked on their door after a day of holding back stupid, useless tears and feeling that awful helplessness that had been building since he'd shown up on David's door. What was he supposed to do now? He had no purpose—except maybe to hang a murder rap on, because that was apparently what the universe wanted.

He had to rub his chest against a burning desire to see Lance, to see his eyes crinkle at the corners and that kind, patient look he got when the kids— erm, other residents of the apartment—were being particularly young and hormone-driven.

He wanted Lance to put his hand on the back of Henry's neck, to squeeze his shoulder, to lower his lips to Henry's own and….

Oh God. Oh hell. Not this now. Why would Lance even look at the guy who was about to be arrested for murder? Falsely arrested, yes. But Henry knew it was coming. His *lawyers* knew it was coming. And his lawyer's private investigator would probably just as soon kick him in the balls as make sure he was proven innocent. Henry couldn't say he blamed the guy.

It was like all of the emotional bullshit Henry had been putting off since he'd gotten there had dropped on his head that morning when he'd looked into the dumpster and seen one of his most painful mistakes.

And he had to talk to David *now*?

He could catch an Uber home. He was supposed to drop off Galen's car and get a ride when Davy and Kane went to pick up Frances, but screw this! Henry pulled his hand back from the door and went to do an about-face, but Davy got there first. He flung the door open and grabbed Henry's shoulders to shake him like an anxious parent.

"Are you okay?"

Henry swallowed hard and shook his head. "I'm sorry," he said rustily. "I'm so sorry." Because he had to have heard, right?

"Sorry about what?" Davy took a step back but kept a hand on his shoulder.

"Martin Sampson. Your ex-boyfriend. Sleeping with your ex-boyfriend."

Davy's eyes went wide, and then he shocked Henry by letting out a deep belly-laugh. "Really? You little rascal you. When did that happen?"

Henry scowled. "My first night. I was stupid—"

Davy sighed. "And scared and alone." He stepped outside onto the porch, where the shade from the trees and the green of the lawn gave an illusion of coolness in what was really a miserable scorcher of a day. "Here," he said, sitting down on the top porch step and patting the spot by his side. "Sit."

Henry did, a little surprised, because inside the house was cool and comfortable—and it was the last place Henry wanted to be right now. It was like his big brother sensed this. He let the silence grow comfortable as they sat next to each other before Davy draped his arm over Henry's shoulder.

Kane stepped out at that moment. "Oh, I'll be inside—"

"Nope." Davy looked over his shoulder, and what followed was this weird eyeball-conversation thing that Henry used to do with Malachi whenever they had a chance to have sex when they were on leave. Except this wasn't about sex or deception. This read more like…

Kane: *Are you sure you want me?*

David: *Yeah, he needs to know it's both of us.*

Kane: *But Dexter!*

David: *He's family, and we're all he has.*

Kane: *Fine, but he's still an asshole.*

David: *Yes, but he's ours and I love him.*

When it was over, Kane let out a sigh like a big guard dog who wasn't going to get to eat anybody today, and hopped off the porch without using the stairs. Then he flopped down, cross-legged on the lawn. "It's fuckin' hot," he said to Henry. "I hope you appreciate this."

Henry stared at him for a moment, this hulking kid who the family blamed for stealing Davy away.

This good man who had taken care of Henry's brother when nobody had even seen who he was.

"I do," he said in a small voice. "I know you think I'm an asshole of the first order, and I am, but… but you'll never fucking know."

"Know what?" Davy asked.

"How much I appreciate this," Henry said, a big lump in his throat. "Like… never. Like… like, you know why Dad kicked me out, went to town on my face—I know you gotta know." Oh God, the fucking humiliation.

"Sh…." Davy kissed his temple. "I know Mal told Debbie that you were caught having an affair with a junior officer. He never admitted it was him."

Henry's chest was so tight. "But… but you know?"

"God, Henry, Kane and I saw right through you when we went back that Christmas. It took us ten minutes."

"I tried to get out," he mewled, feeling pathetic. "I tried. I took the test and got the promotion and told him we couldn't… 'cause my sister had a baby…." Oh God, he couldn't breathe. This was worse, somehow, than telling Lance. Lance was kind to everybody. Lance was kind to Randy, who was going to rip his dick off one of these days. But this was his family, and they didn't forgive you, and you got what was fucking coming to you for fucking up the way Henry had.

"What'd he say?" Davy asked softly, that arm, that big brother part of him, never going away.

And Henry hadn't been planning to say it. Lance knew. Wasn't it enough that Lance knew? "He forced me," Henry whispered. "And then I really *was* having sex with a junior officer." He felt Davy stiffen next to him, and thought, *Good. I know where the line is. That's what it takes to lose my brother's love.*

And then Davy wrapped his arms so tight around Henry that he shouldn't have been able to breathe—but suddenly he could. And after a moment, Kane was all over both of them, in the heat of the afternoon, holding him while he lost his shit for maybe the second time in his adult life.

They couldn't stay like that. It was too damned hot. Davy pulled him up and told him they were walking to the corner to get a cold soda, and Kane trailed behind them while they talked briefly about the case, about Henry's altercation with Martin Sampson at the end of May, and how he'd found the body that morning. It wasn't even until they got back to the house that Kane asked the obvious question.

"What in the hell happened to you, by the way?"

Henry just laughed. He'd forgotten all about the dusty hospital scrubs he was wearing, and his regular clothes in the bag he'd left on the porch. He'd even forgotten about his knuckles and the stinging cut above his eye and his cheek and the fact that he looked like he'd been through a meat grinder.

"That," he said weakly, "is a long fucking story."

Kane actually looked unhappy about this. "I would seriously love to hear it, but…." He had one of those eyeball convos with Davy again.

"You're late!" Henry said, his sense of time suddenly coming back to him. "Oh my God! You're late. We need to go so you can get Frances from day care. Oh Jesus, I'm so sorry!" He'd picked the little girl up from her after-school day care often enough to know what a big deal this was.

"It's okay," Davy said with a shrug. "We called up Ethan and talked to her. We told her we were helping Uncle Henry today. She wants to see you sometime this week. She seems to think you need the attention."

Henry's tears had finally dried, his eyes finally felt normal, but he couldn't stop the lump in his throat.

"Thanks," he said gruffly. "If you guys can drop me off, you can go get her. Tell her I'll see her soon."

They didn't say much during the drive—Henry couldn't have pinned a thought down with a lawn dart at that point anyway. When they dropped him off in front of the apartment, he was expecting Kane to pretty much drive off before his feet hit the ground, but that's not what happened. Instead, Kane put the SUV in Park, and Davy got out for one last hug.

"I'll keep you posted," Henry told him, because God, didn't he owe David that much after all this?

Davy nodded and kissed his forehead, like he had when Henry had been lying on the ground with a broken ankle because Malachi had dropped a cow on him.

But now Henry knew how precious this was. "Thanks, Davy."

"Call us tomorrow—"

"I might be brought in for questioning tomorrow," Henry told him, swallowing painfully, because after talking to his lawyer and PI and Galen, he knew it was likely. "Those guys Galen found—"

"Are those guys okay?" Davy asked quickly. "Reg and John seemed to think they were okay."

Henry grimaced. "They're actually very good," he said, but Davy's eyebrow arched because Henry didn't look like things were "very good."

"Dexter!" Kane urged from the car, and Henry waved them on.

"Go," he said. "I'll tell you later."

"Let us know when you're brought in for questioning," Davy told him, and he nodded, thinking that Ellery Cramer and Jackson Rivers—his lawyer and the PI who worked for him—had told him to talk to his lawyer first, family second. He sort of agreed with them. He didn't want to burden Davy and Kane with anything more.

Not after what they'd done for him that evening.

He waved goodbye to them and then started up the stairs again, his plastic bag of dirty clothes swinging by his thighs as he let himself in.

Lance was already home, in his scrubs, which meant he'd worked a short shift that day, and Henry's heart gave a gentle throb, just knowing he was there.

"Holy fucking gods," Lance muttered. "What in the hell happened to you?"

"I don't want to talk about it," Henry told him, trying not to meet his eyes. He was still so raw. "Davy and Kane dropped me off. I told them... well, stuff." The rest of the apartment was quiet. "Are you the first one home?"

Lance shook his head. "The guys are in their rooms, chilling. We were all worried about you. Go jump in the shower, and we'll talk about it while I'm tending to that cut above your eye."

"It's got a butterfly on it," Henry said defensively, then sighed, the weight of his fight with Jackson Rivers catching up with him. Davy had barely asked about that—maybe because there was so much other stuff to talk about. And maybe because he was merciful and knew that sometimes you aired the oldest hurts first. But now Henry was feeling his day, every hellishly long bit of it, and he shook out his wrist and grimaced. "That's gonna need some ice, though." He held up his battered knuckles and ducked from Lance's killing look.

"What in the hell—"

"I don't want to talk about it!" Henry muttered, wishing for Davy's wise silence on the matter. "Here, I'm going to go jump in the shower, so *I don't have to talk about it*!"

"How about you jump in the shower and plan about how we're going to *talk about it*!" Lance snapped.

Henry stalked to the bathroom and stripped without thinking about bringing a change of clothes with him. He just jumped under the pounding water, not caring that it was cold at first.

He *really* didn't want to talk about it.

That talk with Davy had distracted him from the events of that morning. For a minute there, he'd actually been glad to see John and Galen. Galen had taken charge of the police inquiry, and John had begged a ride from Lance back to his house so he could get his own car. The last Henry had seen of Lance had been a rather troubled wave as Lance hopped into his

CR-V in his hospital scrubs. And after that, Henry's day had been something of a roller coaster.

The minute the cops had let him go, Galen had chivvied Henry into the car with barely enough time to have one of the guys (Cotton, *still in his briefs*!) run up and grab his wallet and cell phone. They'd driven then—do not pass go, don't catch your breath—to a criminal defense attorney, while Galen nitpicked every last ounce of the story from Henry.

Sort of.

Because Henry was *not* going to tell Galen about sleeping with his brother's ex-boyfriend. As far as he was concerned, nobody had to know about that but Lance.

Gah! And now Davy and Kane. And his lawyer, and that goddamned PI. The best laid plans....

"Henry, you can't hide in there," Lance said from the doorway.

"You wanna make a bet?" The water had grown hot and then cold again, and Henry's bruises were starting to cramp up. Reluctantly, he turned the shower off and was taken aback when Lance presented him with Henry's own towel—soft and fluffy from the laundry, a giant blue-striped beach towel that covered all the things—through the gap in the shower curtain.

"Thanks," he mumbled, feeling stupid. He dried his face and his hair, and then toweled off enough to wrap the terrycloth around his ribs so it could drop to his knees. He peeked around the corner and found Lance there in his scrubs, his black bag clutched in one hand and the other hand on his hip.

"Are we going to come out and get checked over like a big boy?" Lance asked, lips pursed in disapproval.

Oh for fuck's sake. "I've been looked over," he said mutinously even as he took a step out of the shower.

"By whom?"

"By the forensic specialist in the morgue where they took the body?"

"Toe-Tag?" Lance said, gaping. "You met Toe-Tag?"

"Dr. Tagliare?" Henry had liked the guy—he'd been no-nonsense, kind, and informative. Unlike some *other* people Henry could mention. "Little guy, with lots of ear-hair? A very zen sort of approach to the world? Yeah. That was him."

Lance's eyes raked over his body. "You are bruised *everywhere*! Now sit down and let me take care of the eyebrow and those knuckles. And for God's sake, tell me what—"

"I don't want to talk about it!" Henry said almost desperately.

"*I don't care!*" Lance roared, and Henry was so surprised, he sat flop-bott on the lid of the porcelain throne.

"Okay." He wrapped his hands around his knees. "What do you want to know?"

Lance scrubbed at his face with his free hand before setting up his bag on the small counter by the sink. Carefully, he took out a little silver tray and set up some stitching equipment and some bandages and ointment on it.

"Let's start with who hit you?"

Henry grimaced. "That would be the private investigator who came with the lawyer Galen hired."

Lance paused, frowning. "Isn't Galen a lawyer?"

Henry let out a breath. "Yes, but as he was so careful to inform me, he's a corporate attorney. He said I needed a criminal defense attorney, and he'd read up about a guy who took… I don't know. Underdog cases. So we drive to the offices, and they, like, just moved there. They were still painting when we walked in."

"They?"

"Well, the actual lawyer guy, Cramer, he's in the back, doing lawyer stuff, I guess. But he's got this guy named Rivers, wearing, like, beat-up cargo shorts and no shirt. When he finally *did* put on a shirt, it was so ragged, you guys wouldn't use it to sop up jizz. Anyway, he's the PI who works for Cramer, and he's a fuckin' piece of work."

Lance snorted and slid his gloves on. "Define 'fuckin' piece of work.'"

Henry blew out a breath, trying to describe Jackson Rivers. "Well, I guess he and Cramer are boning—"

Lance pulled back and looked at him. "Are you trying to sound offensive, or are you just pissed off?"

Henry regarded him unhappily. God, trying to explain what happened—the way Rivers had insisted on the whole truth, nothing but the truth, and anyone who didn't play it his way wasn't worth his time…. That rankled.

"I just—why's everybody got to know the big gay secret?" he asked almost tearfully, his conversation with his brother still raw in his soul. "Why does anybody have to know I slept with the guy in the fucking dumpster? Why's that important? What does that prove to anybody?"

Lance leaned over closely and began to apply ointment to the cut over his eyebrow, then to the one on his cheek.

"It proves you're human, Henry," Lance said quietly, his breath fanning Henry's cheek in a way Henry had hungered for since that strangely intimate night on the couch two weeks ago. Since the other interlude the night before. "What did Rivers think it proved?"

Henry swallowed, remembering their confrontation. The first thing Rivers had done, besides been kind and funny and try to be his friend, was to go talk to Reg about the confrontation two weeks earlier. Reg wasn't stupid—he'd heard Henry call Scott "Martin Sampson," and the truth had come out. But not before Henry had stepped on Jackson Rivers's last nerve.

"He knew I was lying," Henry said. "And he just kept at it and kept at it, and then I told him but…." God, he sounded like a little kid. "I pissed him off. He's… I guess he's got his own issues. He's got scars all over his body, Lance. I mean, I've seen guys scarred up from deployment who didn't have anything on this guy. So I yelled, and he asked me to let him out of the car, and I got mad because…." God.

"Because…?" Lance put the butterfly bandage over his eyebrow with such tenderness, Henry almost didn't feel the ping when the edges of the skin were drawn together.

"Because he was like you. Not like you, exactly…." Henry grimaced. He was so tired. That conversation with his brother had been his last straw. He knew all his yearning shone through in his eyes, the way he liked Lance's almond-shaped eyes, his decisive eyebrows, the kind twist to his full lips. "Not as pretty," he finished weakly. "Not as… as sweet. But he wanted to be my friend, and I drove him away because apparently I don't know how to act around nice people. Anyway, he got out of the car, and I lost it, and…." And this was the really humiliating part.

"You decked him?" Lance asked, horrified.

"I'm so stupid." Henry wanted to bury his face in his hands.

"Oh my God. You hit your lawyer." Lance's eyes were as round as his mouth.

"I hit my private investigator!" Henry protested. And then, glumly, because apparently he'd already proven his maturity level hadn't improved much since he'd gone cow-tipping on a cold November, he said, "But my lawyer knows about the fight. After we… finished fighting and did the bro-bullshit-make-up thing, we went to look at Martin Sampson's body, and Cramer was waiting at the hospital with Dr. Tagliare." Henry sighed. "It was obvious Rivers had wiped the floor with me. God. Everybody knows I had a one-nighter with the dead guy, and now *you* know I got my ass kicked by a guy I outweigh by about thirty pounds. *I* should have been the one in the dumpster and saved everybody the fucking trouble."

Lance flicked him on the forehead, which was probably the one spot on his face not injured. "Shut up," he said thickly. "You have no idea how worried I was about you."

Henry swallowed against his need to grab Lance and never let him go. "I'm sorry I worried you," he said softly. "I... it's been sort of a fucking day."

They stared at each other for a fraught moment before Lance turned his attention to Henry's battered body again.

"You have gravel in your shoulder!" Lance exclaimed. "I thought you said you'd been treated!"

"Tagliare cleaned me up enough and gave me some hospital scrubs so I could look at the corpse," Henry said, exhausted. "I don't think he saw the shoulder thing—it was covered by the scrubs."

"Oh dear God!" Lance's horror was eloquent as he carefully pulled out the last of the parking lot gravel from Henry's shoulder. "Is there any other part that stings?"

"My knees?" Henry looked down and saw that the pebbles had sliced him open. One of the cuts was trickling blood again. "My pride," he mumbled, because that was the worst part.

"It could not have been that bad." But it was obvious Lance was only asking to make sure.

"So bad." Henry shuddered. "Twice. I... oh my God. He's not that much older than I am, but once he got the drop on me and grabbed my ear, and the other time—" Jesus. "—I swung first and he took me apart."

"Poor baby," Lance said, kneeling at his feet and working gently on those cuts on his knees. "And he still took you to the autopsy?"

Henry let out a sigh. "We seemed to have reached... I dunno. Détente. I... him and Cramer, they were pretty up-front. They told me I'd probably be brought in for questioning tomorrow, and my one and only answer needs to be 'Talk to my lawyer.' They seemed pretty on top of it. But... I don't know." He closed his eyes and tilted his head back. "I... I wanted him to think I was worth it, that was all."

Lance grunted. "That sounds sort of... stalky."

Henry opened his eyes and let his mouth soften. "I want you to think I'm worth it more," he said. "Besides, it's not a sex thing. We'd kill each other. It's more... this guy? This guy was... you know how everybody wants a hero? You want somebody to be like, somebody who is worthwhile to emulate?"

Lance nodded. "My attending physician—Dr. Schearer. He's a really good guy. Decent. Kind. Enjoys the money, but that's not why he's there. I watched him treat this woman with schizophrenia today. He was the best. He made her feel valued, like she was important, and explained to her why she needed to take her medication. It was… you know, why people go into healing."

"Any crushing going on there?" Henry asked. And while part of him was afraid of the answer, most of him knew.

"No," Lance told him. "I've got… other prospects."

Henry let out a breath and rested his hand briefly in Lance's hair. "I know the feeling," he confessed.

"We just have to clear *my* guy for a murder he didn't commit," Lance said dryly, standing up. "And it would be *great* if he didn't piss off his lawyer while he was at it."

Henry groaned. "Dude, if only." Cramer had hardly looked at Henry, though. It had been all Henry and Rivers.

"You think this guy will forgive you for being a complete assbucket?" Lance asked. "I mean… it sounds like you need him on your side."

Henry tilted his head back and squeezed his eyes shut. "God. I have no idea."

Lance put a large gauze pad on each knee. "Wait, you said Galen looked him up? When we're done in here, we can look him up too."

Henry nodded docilely. "You know," he muttered, "the cops are going to pick me up tomorrow probably. We need to tell the guys to call Galen and Cramer when that happens. I…." He took a deep breath. "Everybody remembered me throwing Sampson in the dumpster. And there he is again. It's just too coincidental. I'm spot-on for it."

Lance stretched his shoulders and began to remove his gloves, but he didn't back up, and Henry drew some comfort from his nearness. "Any idea who did it?"

Henry felt a small thrill at the next part. Yes, the day had sucked, but the investigation—watching the way Jackson Rivers's mind worked as he tried to figure out what happened to prove Henry *couldn't* have killed Martin Sampson—*that* had been fascinating.

"Not yet," Henry said thoughtfully. "But the autopsy revealed a puncture wound on his hip. Tagliare was going to get a tox screen, even though the blunt force head trauma is what did him in." Henry shuddered. He hadn't seen his one-night lover, not really, not when he'd been on the slab. But when Dr. Tagliare had shown him the guy's liver—scarred and sickly brown from drug dependency instead of healthy and blue-red—Henry had suffered a terrible realization. That guy who'd picked him up, sweet-talking, funny, and yes, a monster in bed, had sore parts, parts that nobody could see.

Wounds nobody had healed.

Like the porn models Henry had been dealing with over the last few months. He'd known Cotton was lost, that Lance had his damage, that Curtis seemed just too cool and too all over it to be real. But seeing that… that wrecked body—a boy who was dying before he was dead—had shocked Henry.

Was that who *he* was too?

His disdain—the disdain he used to cover that *he* was the guy his father had hated, whether his father had known it or not—was that covering up his rotting parts?

Rivers seemed to think so. Maybe that's why he'd been so pissed when he'd realized Henry had been lying. Maybe he knew about things that festered. He'd been shirtless when Henry and Galen had walked in—the scars on his body were an assortment of old and new. How much wounding could a person take and still come back whole?

"You okay?" Lance asked softly, probably because Henry's brain was chasing its own tail and the silence had stretched on too long.

"Sure." God, it was a lie.

Lance sank to his haunches and *made* Henry meet his eyes. "Henry, are you okay?"

"No," Henry whispered, powerless. Shouldn't you tell the truth to your friends?

Lance leaned forward and kissed his forehead. "We'll get clear of this," he promised, and Henry's eyes burned.

"Why? I mean, what possible reason do I have for staying out of jail? What am I doing on God's green earth that does anybody any fucking good?" The bitterness, erupting like that, should have been a surprise, and morbidly he thought of Martin Sampson's liver. Was this why it was called venting your spleen?

But Lance was apparently a healer, through and through. He cupped Henry's cheek, the touch making him suck in a breath. Oh, touch. Once upon a time, he'd been touched. Not a lot, not in public, but someone had wanted to touch him.

"You ride herd on a bunch of hormonally hyperactive models who need someone to remind them that the real world doesn't revolve around their dicks."

Henry smirked and used the end of his towel to wipe his eyes. "That's important," he said thickly.

"I can't do it myself," Lance said. He rubbed under Henry's eye with his thumb, not saying anything when it came away wet. "Now I'm going to leave you to get dressed, and the guys and I will make you something good for dinner, okay? No cleanup duty for you. And someone else can get the trash tomorrow!"

"That's awesome." He grimaced. "But, uh, Lance?"

"Yeah?" Lance stood and started straightening his black bag.

"I, uh, didn't bring in any clothes. My duffel's in the corner of the living room."

Lance laughed softly and closed the bag. "Brush teeth, comb hair—I'll be back in a sec." Then he washed his hands and exited, leaving Henry to brush his teeth and comb his hair and try to get his act together.

Two minutes later Lance appeared with a pair of soft shorts, tighties, and a tank. He set them on the back of the toilet, using his hand on Henry's back to establish space, and then moved back. He paused for a moment, then caught Henry's eyes in the mirror, and planted a soft kiss on the back of his neck.

He straightened and winked, leaving Henry alone and yearning.

The tighties he'd brought were Henry's.

The shorts and the tank were Lance's.

Henry put them on and didn't say a word.

That night, after dinner and some television, the guys disappeared into the back. Zep and Fisher (who had not yet paid rent, as far as Henry could tell, but who did contribute to all the household chores) were going back to have really noisy sex. Curtis came out right before the "Oh God, yes!" started.

Lance was sitting behind Henry in the corner of the couch, Henry between his thighs.

One arm was wrapped around Henry's chest, and had been since they'd sat down.

None of the guys had noticed—none of them had so much as looked at them funny—but as Curtis emerged from the hallway, rolling his eyes, the intimacy suddenly occurred to Henry, and he moved to get up.

Lance kept him where he sat.

"'Ssup?"

"Lance, can I, you know, use your bed? Randy's in the, uh, threesome bed, Billy's sleeping in my bed because he can sleep through fuckin' anything. Cotton's in Randy's bed, and, you know, you and Henry have the couch and the air mattress. Is that okay?"

"Yeah, sure," Lance said casually. His arm never moved from Henry's chest, and Henry fell into it, bought into the pretend, that togetherness, comfort, was that easy.

"Thanks, man. I've got a summer-session class at 8:00 a.m. I appreciate the chance to sleep."

"No worries," Lance said. "What class?"

"Physics 5-C. It helps with kinesiology, and it really helps with the study of prosthetics."

"Yikes!" Henry said. "Keep at it. It's good to have a goal."

"Yeah, well, I won't always be this hot and DTF. Gotta find something I'll want to do afterwards."

"Yeah," Lance said. "When you're super fuckin' old like me."

Curtis cackled and then paused. "Uh, Lance—you're still on the schedule six weeks from now. You, uh, still want that shit?"

"I'm not sure." Henry didn't have to look at his face to know Lance had assumed that carefully neutral look he used when he was trying not to talk about himself.

"Bobby still films scenes sometimes," Curtis said quickly. "Just, you know, I could use the cash."

He disappeared quickly, leaving a sort of numb silence in his wake.

"Bobby still films scenes?" Henry asked, scrambling to fill the silence.

"Sometimes." Lance kept that arm around his chest, and Henry finally acknowledged it, rubbing the back of Lance's hand fitfully. "He… he grew up in a hick town. I think it's his way of being seen. Reg sort of gets off on it, so it fits them."

"Mm." Henry tried to disapprove, tried to argue, find another way for them. After all, he liked Reg. One of the things in Jackson Rivers's favor was how gentle he'd been—how nonjudgmental, actually. Fuck. "I wish I understood," he said finally, melting against Lance and giving in. "My brain is such a muddle right now. I… I just know I'm scared and a little sad and I'm too tired to be an asshole about you guys filming porn. It was such a line in the sand, so black-and-white when I got here. Sex for money, bad. Sex for love, good, as long as it's a boy and a girl. But… but *I* don't even fit that idea." He thought of Martin Sampson with his head bashed in, and the way he'd run out of that hotel room, without taking the money Henry was going to give him. Why? Had he recognized Henry's name?

Henry couldn't put it all together.

"Just sleep," Lance murmured. "Fall asleep. I'll lie down on the mattress after the movie. I won't leave you."

"You feel so good," Henry confessed. "So safe. Maybe I'll figure it out tomorrow."

His eyes closed, Lance's arm locked over his chest like one of those bars on a roller coaster, and he dreamed of up and down, up and down, Lance's arms wrapped around him, the two of them inseparable, even in the chaos.

And in the way of dreams, their clothes disappeared, and he was kissing his way down Lance's bare chest, but he could never get past his navel.

"But how will I know you?" he whispered in the dream.

"You knew me before you kissed me," Lance whispered back.

Henry woke up sometime in the dark of night, shivering, craving the feel of Lance's mouth on his. He sat up on the couch, and Lance murmured, "I'm still here," from the inflatable mattress.

Henry grunted and stumbled to the bathroom, the shivers not easing as he relieved himself and stumbled back.

He couldn't make himself lie down on the couch alone again.

"Henry?" Lance said, sitting up gingerly.

"Can I…?" Oh God. He was an adult. He was a *soldier*.

"Yeah, sure." Lance lifted the blanket and patted the spot next to him. "You didn't even have to ask."

Henry climbed in and burrowed against him. "Thanks," he said, feeling naked.

"It's okay. Everything is okay."

He fell asleep believing that and slept soundly.

When he woke up again, the cops were pounding down the door.

ALLIES AND ALLY CATS

LANCE PACED around the apartment restlessly, his stomach churning. He'd thrown up once already, on purpose, and the purging seemed to have steadied his nerves a little—and made the giant breakfast he'd eaten feel a little less burdensome—but it wasn't enough.

He checked his phone for the thousandth time, drawing up short when it actually buzzed.

Released from questioning. Home in fifteen.

Lance took a deep breath and tried to still the shaking in his stomach.

Henry had looked so alone when he'd walked out that morning. The cops had barely given him time to put on a pair of cargo shorts and some loafers, and he'd been grumpy and unshaven and....

And dear.

Goddammit, Henry, why did you have to be so dear, so accessible, when you have a murder rap hanging over your head?

Lance thought that maybe he should have gone to work out, which he did on his half-days as often as possible, and then his brain quit. Just quit, and he sank down onto one of the kitchen chairs and tried to put his relief in perspective.

He was still sitting there twenty minutes later, staring at his phone message, when Henry burst into the apartment, looking irritated and hot.

"Henry!"

Henry gave him a scattered smile and then really took him in. "Are you okay?"

Lance stood up and scowled. "No! You were taken out of here this morning, and you looked terrified and—"

Henry's arms around his shoulders were a surprise. When had Henry become the comforter? "Hey, hey. It's okay. I mean, I'm not off the hook yet, but Cramer and Rivers, they really do seem to have my back!"

Lance wanted to pull away and demand what happened, but having Henry's arms around his shoulders, it felt just amazing.

"We texted John," he mumbled. "John contacted your guy, I guess, and then told us that Reg and Bobby had been... I don't know. Attacked? Someone broke into their house and was supposed to make Reg change his story but…." Lance had to pull away now. "I'm a little fuzzy on what happened next."

"Wait! I know this one! Bobby sat on the guy," Henry chortled. "Like, you know he's built like a fuckin' tank, right?"

"I'm surprised he fits through doors," Lance said honestly. Between the muscles and the height, Bobby was the giant country boy of your wet dreams—or nightmares.

"So the guy breaks into Reg and Bobby's place and starts yelling at Reg to change his story about what happened that day at the dumpster, and Bobby sits on the guy, and Reg called Jackson."

Lance frowned. "Like, the PI who beat the shit out of you, Jackson?"

Henry scrubbed at his face. "Yeah. I told you he was nice to Reg. I guess something about him said, 'This man will protect us from housebreakers.' Anyway, Jackson and Ellery show up and the guy kept talking about a tape. I guess yesterday they tracked down a tape of the dumpster—you know, to show I wasn't the one who dumped the body?"

Lance squeezed his eyes shut. "I should have thought of that. Apparently that's why they get paid the big bucks."

"Yeah. Hey, is there coffee?" Henry looked at him hopefully.

"Isn't it broiling outside?" Lance asked, moving for the coffee maker. "Never mind. I know you. Keep going!" Maybe it was the Montana farm-boy thing, but Henry could live on coffee on the hottest day.

Henry continued. "Well, apparently there were two different tapes—one the cops got and one Jackson and Ellery got hold of. But both of them were fake. It's sort of driving us nuts," he admitted. His voice dropped. "Jackson's downstairs right now, actually. He figured the tapes came from the super's office, so he's going to check Sternberg's security to see 'film school' as he keeps calling it. I thought…." He shrugged, and Lance saw a flush steal across his pale face.

Lance hadn't realized how much he needed that, had loved it, until right now, staring at Henry hungrily, gratitude and want vibrating in his stomach in a way that made lawyers and PIs superfluous.

"So I get to meet the great man himself?" He couldn't disguise the irritation in his voice. He was, he realized, reluctant to share Henry now that Henry was… well, *his*.

"He's my best chance," Henry said, like he believed it. "Seriously, Lance—Ellery and I got out of the courthouse today, and he was there with information and a plan and… I told him." He paused and glanced at Lance, as if looking for forgiveness. "I told him almost everything. Martin Sampson,

Malachi. I thought… you know. I thought you forgave me because you were my friend, and Davy forgave me because he's my brother. Like… like you were obligated. And you… you're kind. You're kind to everyone. My God, Lance, you didn't even laugh when Randy told you he really *did* have scabs from wanking off."

Lance grimaced. They'd guessed, of course, but when Randy had confided in Lance because he'd been too embarrassed to tell the rest of the house, Lance had needed to tell Henry so he could keep a straight face. "What *is* it with that kid?" he asked now.

"I've got nothing—it's like a medical condition or something. But see? I thought… if Jackson could hear the whole story and not hate me…." Henry's voice wobbled, and Lance hated himself a little. Henry was on the line for *murder*. He'd been brought in for questioning because he'd seen his one-night trick dead in a dumpster. He didn't need Lance's sudden weird bullshit jealousy.

"What?" Lance asked, voice neutral.

"Then maybe it's not just because you're kind," Henry admitted.

"Wait, what's because I'm kind?" Lance asked, some of the irritation fading.

"The…." Henry fidgeted, and Lance realized he was looking younger, more insecure by the second. "The… the thing. The thing between us. I… I—"

Lance's expression softened, but at that moment Curtis burst in, looking thunderous.

"Dude," Lance said, distracted. "Where'd you come from? I thought you were in school!"

"Ugh! You know what? That rent raise we got was bogus. Did you know that?"

Lance and Henry cocked their heads. "What rent raise?"

Curtis blinked. "The uh… never mind." He wiped his mouth hard and chewed the gum in his teeth harder. "He didn't tell you. It was me and Zep and—"

Henry and Lance met eyes. "And who?" Henry asked. "Where were you?"

"The super's office," Curtis snapped back.

"Did you see Jackson? He was heading that way."

Curtis's lower lip wobbled. "He… I was giving Sternberg a blowie to get two hundred off rent, okay? And this guy busts in there, and Sternberg gets all 'It just happens,' and the guy makes him confess that it was a scam. There *was* no rent raise. That was something he told some of us to get free blowjobs. So not only am I a whore, I'm a *dumb* whore, because I didn't even ask, I took his word for it when Zep and I went down with the cashier's check." He gave another vicious chew of the gum. "Fisher was giving some too. We wanted to spread it around because that fucker is *foul*."

"I'll kill him," Henry said. "I'm going to go find Jackson, and we're going to kill him."

"He wouldn't let me beat the shit out of him," Curtis muttered. "The guy—Jackson, I guess—told me that the cops would put *me* in jail but let him off. He's right. But God, *augh!*" Curtis stomped off to his bedroom, and Lance met Henry's furious gaze.

"I'll take Curtis," Lance said.

"And I'll go see what's up." He was all the way out the door before Lance even thought to ask him what they were doing after this.

When Henry came back—not more than ten minutes later, Lance would swear by it—it was to drag Lance to a crime scene—and to doctor the guy who was supposedly going to save Henry's ass.

"You need me to what?" Lance asked as Henry hauled him down the stairs.

"He hates hospitals and he's bleeding. I told him you were a med student—"

"Doctor," Lance corrected, although he'd been letting everybody else say med student for years. He'd been a student when he started at Johnnies—explanations were the suck.

"A resident's a doctor?" Henry asked, wrinkling his nose.

"A sergeant is a soldier?" Lance shot back. Henry was leading him to the super's office, and there were cops there already.

"Fine, you win, I'm stupid—"

"Wait! Is that the *super*!" They pulled short as paramedics passed by with a man on a stretcher who looked a lot like the asshole who took their money every month, only this guy was sheet white and covered in blood.

Henry made a sound. "Yeah, but he's being treated. Rivers isn't. Look—there he is."

The man wearing worn cargo shorts and a tissue-thin T-shirt didn't *look* imposing until Lance realized he was dripping blood from a wound on his shoulder and talking to the detective in front of him like it was an ordinary day.

Lance shook his head. "Yeah, he's going to need that treated."

"Rivers!" Henry called, and Jackson Rivers turned his head and nodded.

His green eyes had a burning intensity to them, and his gaunt, square-jawed face was still pretty in a faded way. And God, he looked so tired.

Lance realized that maybe it wasn't just porn kids who needed a nonjudgmental medical presence in their lives. "We can do this here or we can do this upstairs," he said, and was relieved when Rivers stopped arguing and picked the apartment instead of the crime scene.

LANCE GRIMACED as he stared at the network of scars on Jackson Rivers's back and plucked at the edge of his wound with the needle. The super had been carted away in an ambulance, because apparently the guy who'd sliced Rivers open had come back to silence the guy who knew why he'd been in the security booth erasing all of the video footage in the first place.

Ugh! The whole thing made Lance itchy. He hadn't even liked the superintendent—even less when he found out the guy had been blackmailing his kids for blowjobs. But going downstairs and seeing him hauled away in the ambulance had brought home just how close to danger they all were until whoever murdered Martin Sampson was found.

And seeing Henry's brand-new hero, standing at the crime scene, giving a detective shit while he dripped blood through his shirt, had made Lance even more worried for Henry. Henry seemed *invigorated* somehow. He'd been almost ecstatic when he'd come upstairs, more worried about Lance, about the thing blossoming between them, than he had been about proving his own innocence.

The fact was, Lance didn't give a good goddamn who killed Martin Sampson—as long as the guy and all his associates with knives and heavy blunt objects stayed away from the people he cared about. Lance wasn't a mystery kind of guy. The only puzzles that interested him were the human ones who presented themselves in the hospital or who interacted with him in his daily life.

Henry was his kind of puzzle.

And reluctantly, looking at the puzzle of scar tissue on Rivers's back, he had to admit that Jackson Rivers was his kind of puzzle too.

Taller than Lance or Henry, with dark blond hair and glass-green eyes, thin in a way that said he was coming back from an injury or an illness, there was still a swagger to Jackson Rivers that suggested he'd spent a long time trying to be self-sufficient.

The fact that he'd stood by a crime scene, bleeding, while he'd talked to the investigating officer and had needed to be cajoled into the bathroom of the apartment to get treated told Lance a lot about this man, other than that he hated hospitals.

Jackson Rivers's absolutely last priority was Jackson Rivers.

Lance wasn't excited about what that could mean for Henry. Under Lance's hands, Jackson twitched and held up his hand, then grabbed his phone and motioned for Lance to continue.

Lance concentrated on the stitching while listening to Jackson lie, bald-faced, to Ellery Cramer—who sounded like a boyfriend and not someone he was "boning"—about what he was doing. Jackson finished the call, and Lance went back to working on him. Lance played doctor like the pro he was—finished stitching the hurt, tried to give Jackson advice about maybe telling his boyfriend about the wound, but in the end, Jackson was distracted by the case.

And his color didn't look good. It was hot outside, and Rivers had bled a lot, and he looked pretty shocky, in fact. It pissed Lance off that Rivers wouldn't sit still long enough after being treated for Lance to get a bead on him.

Jackson ran to ask Curtis some questions, and Lance turned to Henry, frowning. "This guy? You're trusting yourself to this guy? Did you just hear him lie to his boyfriend—"

"Because Cramer would lock him in a cage to keep him safe," Henry said staunchly. "Look, I know it seems dysfunctional—"

"Not seems, Henry. That wasn't normal. I'm stitching the guy up and he's like, 'No, it's fine, everything is fine, see you tonight!'"

Henry sighed and rubbed the back of his neck. "But did you also see him freak out about the super? Take care of Curtis? And those were guys he didn't know. I mean, me, he sort of, I dunno, feels responsible for. He fought a guy with a knife who had the drop on him, Lance, and after he got stabbed, he still ran the guy down. I mean, I know you've got high standards, but even that has got to be tough enough!"

"You're pissed at him too!" Lance snapped, because Henry had been glaring disapprovingly as well when Jackson had done his tap dance with the truth.

"Well, yeah. But he thinks I'm an asshole, so I can yell at him. I want him to *like* you."

Lance raised his eyebrows. "Why?"

"I don't know. Because…." Henry bit his lip and smiled gamely and then scowled. "Whatever. Can we just not piss off the guy? We're going to go check out Sampson's father's practice. Rivers has some ideas about why his old man might have been the one to bump Martin off."

Lance recoiled. "That's *horrible!*"

Henry nodded. "Totally. But if it keeps me out of jail, it's worth knowing."

And then Lance had a terrible, terrible realization. "You *like* this!" he said in horror.

"Well…." Henry shrugged, obviously uncomfortable. "It's exciting."

"*I just put ten stitches into that man's back!*" Lance protested, a feeling of panic taking him over. "What if that was you?"

Henry's crooked smile almost blinded him, and he pointed to the butterfly bandage over his eyebrow and his battered knuckles. "It was me. I'm okay. You helped."

Lance's eyes grew huge, but at that moment, Jackson Rivers called them both into Curtis's room and made them promise to say Curtis had been in his room the whole time, to keep him out of the investigation.

Lance got it right away. Curtis's skin color had the potential of making the cops go rougher on him than they might have for, say, Cotton. Lance hadn't had to deal with too much crap because of his Filipino coloring or the shape of his eyes, but he knew what Rivers was saying.

After watching Henry with Rivers, Lance had a sudden realization.

Henry had arrived on his doorstep thinking his life, his career, everything about him was over, because his biggest mistake had become the sum of his existence.

But something about the last two days—the last two months, really—had been teaching him that he could make mistakes and learn from them. That his life wasn't over, that he was, in fact, a work in progress.

Oh. That was a little bit promising. Works in progress were… were growing, were learning new things.

Could fall in love.

Lance watched as Henry grabbed the scrubs he'd been wearing the night before—now freshly cleaned—and followed Rivers out the door.

"Text me!" Lance said weakly as the door was closing, and Henry turned to him seriously and nodded.

"Swear." He smiled then, and Lance could see the joy, the purpose. Yeah. This whole situation was fucked-up, but it apparently was teaching Henry something awesome about life, and maybe Lance needed him to see that before they moved forward any further.

As the door closed and Lance tried to contain his worry, he *really* hoped they'd move forward further.

HENRY CAME back that night exhausted and exhilarated. He took his turn cooking dinner, and then told the guys all about his adventures—the being questioned, the two different forged tapes, the fact that the super was in the hospital and by the way they should never, ever, *ever*, blow someone for rent without checking with the rest of the guys in the house first.

"But what did you do this afternoon?" Zeppelin asked, wide-eyed. "'Cause we got home and Lance said you'd come and gone!"

Henry grinned, looking at Lance with glee. "Well, me and the PI—"

"That Rivers guy who got stabbed," Fisher said, sitting practically on Zeppelin's lap. "That guy?"

"Yeah. Together we went to Scott's dad's practice, wearing scrubs. We pretended to be transport orderlies and went snooping around his office to see if there was something to indicate he was a douchenozzle."

"Was he?" Curtis had spent most of the afternoon seething in his bedroom, but hearing Henry back and working in the kitchen had drawn him out for dinner.

"Oh my God," Henry said. "Such a douchenozzle. Like big-time. He's been double-dealing drugs out of the hospital, and it's ugly. I don't know what we're going to do tomorrow, but I'll bet it's going to be looking around the hospital to see if we can find a distribution center."

"Did Rivers say that?" Lance asked.

Henry looked sheepish. "No. It's just… I mean, it's what I would do if I was in charge."

"Which you're not," Lance reminded him.

Henry shrugged. "Nope. Barely in charge of going to the bathroom. But I gotta admit it's fun to run around and play detective."

"Oh, hey," Curtis said, nose wrinkled. "Has someone been yakking in the bathroom? The pipes are starting to act funny, and it smells in there."

They were eating egg casserole—one of Henry's specialties—and the whole table groaned. "God, Curtis!" "Curtis, could you not?" "Seriously, at dinner?"

Henry stared at Billy. "Yakking?"

Billy's ears went red, and very carefully he avoided looking at Lance. God, it was a year ago—was that how long, a year and a half ago?—when Bobby had realized Lance and Billy were both bulimic as hell?

He'd been so disappointed—and so hurt. Bobby had grown up knowing what it was like not having enough to eat. The idea that they would voluntarily purge their bodies of calories, because they *felt* ugly—it had blown his mind.

For a few months, Billy and Lance had filled out calorie diaries, talked each other down from purging, stayed away from the laxative aisle in the store. Then Lance's residency had started and Billy had broken up with his girlfriend *again*, and Lance had gotten that really stupid online reviewer who liked to poke at his baby fat, and Billy had sprained his ankle and had been unable to run for a couple of weeks, and....

And suddenly they were avoiding each other's eyes when they were coming out of the bathroom again.

But in that time, they'd lost a whack of roommates and replaced them again with the current crop, and they were the only ones who knew.

Unless Henry tried to fix the damned plumbing.

"I can call Bobby," Billy said casually. "You've got enough on your plate this week."

Henry rolled his eyes. "I can check it out tomorrow night, after dinner with my brother." He looked hopefully at Lance. "Were you going to come with me?"

Oh crap. "I'm sorry. I took an early half-day today. I promised my buddy I'd make it up tomorrow. I'm sorry, Henry."

Henry shrugged, and he looked disappointed but not hurt. "I was really glad you were here today," he said. Then he looked back at Billy. "No, seriously, I can do it. Just make sure you guys have cleared out of the bathroom by the time I get back from Davy's."

There was a general consensus, and Lance could only thank God he'd be gone. It was easier to not look guilty when you weren't there.

"So tell us how your buddy chased the bad guy with the knife," Randy begged, and Lance wanted to groan. No. No hero worship of Jackson Rivers. Lance had met the guy—he was lost and damaged—and he hated that Henry and the others thought he was some sort of god.

Chasing someone into a rat's nest of apartment buildings after he'd just stabbed you sounded like pure suicide to Lance. The fact that it sounded like fun to Henry sent Lance into random sweats periodically, and that wasn't hyperbole, and it didn't get any better as Henry recounted the story. Lance would have thought he was exaggerating much of Jackson Rivers's stoic "I got this," but Lance had *been* there as he'd blown off his boyfriend while getting his back stitched up, and he knew it was true.

Dammit. He did *not* need to worry any more about Henry Worrall.

But that night, Lance nodded at Cotton this time, letting him know he could use Lance's bed, and crawled onto the air mattress while Henry— showered and wearing his boxers and a T-shirt again—turned off the lights and then went toward the couch in the dark.

"Henry?" Lance said tentatively.

"Yeah?" He sounded uncertain too.

"I mean, I don't mind."

Henry let out a soft laugh, but he got up and moved over to the mattress, slid under Lance's blanket, and set his own pillow down next to Lance's.

"Rivers and I talked about you today," Henry said, and Lance fought the temptation to kick him off the bed.

"Wonderful."

"Don't be jealous."

Augh! "I hate that you know what this is," Lance muttered. *He* hadn't figured out what it was until Henry had used that exact word.

"It's… it's what I feel in my stomach, thinking about you filming porn," Henry said baldly. "I… I tried to tell Jackson that. That's why we couldn't be together."

Lance's heart started pounding hard in his throat. God. This. This was terrifying. "What did he say?"

"He said there was sex for sex's sake and sex that meant something. And I said I'd just found my second lover dead in a dumpster."

Lance sucked in a tight breath. "Henry…."

Henry shook his head. "And he asked me which one hurt most. Malachi betraying me or finding Martin Sampson."

Oh God. Lance breathed through broken glass. "Which one?" It was a stupid question, but he needed to hear the answer.

"The betrayal hurt the most," Henry said, and they were so close in the dark, Lance could see the glint of his blue eyes, almost colorless, and feel Henry's breath on his face as he told secrets. "And I've been thinking all day about that. You'd never force me. And you'd never betray me. But I don't know if you could care enough about *me* to help me deal with all that other stuff. I'm… I'm not going to be okay with the porn right away. Can you deal with it when I'm an asshole about that? Can you help me not hurt you too much?"

"I can try," Lance vowed, suddenly needing to say the words. "Can you… can you deal with finding yourself? You're… you're so in flux right now. Do you really want to start something with—"

Henry's touch of lips on his own silenced him. Rough. A little gritty. Henry's lips weren't soft, just like Henry wasn't sweet, not on the outside.

Lance closed his eyes, suddenly so desperate for this, for this kiss, for this touch. He wasn't sure of anything—wasn't sure if Henry could even get out from under the cloud of suspicion he was fighting. The police hadn't seemed to take anything Lance or the roommates said seriously, particularly when they asserted Henry hadn't had the *time* to go out and kill someone and then hide the murder weapon.

But Lance, so pragmatic in every other aspect of his life, suddenly didn't care. Gruff, grumpy, practically a social throwback to the days when men like his father had ruled, Henry Worrall was rock-solid and responsible. He'd shown kindness to guys some people might assume were grown, corrupt, or stupid—and he'd taken a loosely knit bunch of assholes and bound them more tightly into the family unit Lance had craved.

And he'd been alone, and lost, and vulnerable for longer than even Henry knew, and not once had he asserted it wasn't his fault.

Henry would take ownership of a relationship, just like he'd taken ownership for trying to end his last toxic binding to a man who would rather force him than claim him.

Lance opened his mouth and let Henry in.

Henry tasted him, tentatively, sweeping his tongue along the seam of Lance's lips, venturing inside. Lance's low moan welcomed him, and he deepened the kiss and went a little further, exploring.

Lance rolled onto his back, giving Henry more room to maneuver, more control, and was surprised when Henry pulled back a little.

There was embarrassment in his expression. "I… I'm not a good kisser," he said, resting his forehead against Lance's temple.

"Wha—we were doing good so far!" He was pretty sure he'd been waiting for that kiss since March. "No disappointments yet!"

Henry let out a broken sound. "Mal and I didn't really kiss," he confessed. "I… it wasn't supposed to be a relationship."

"Then let's keep doing it," Lance murmured, brushing his lips along Henry's jaw. "Maybe that's all we need to do tonight. Just—"

Henry caught his mouth again, a little more confidently, and Lance almost cried. His body was aching already, feverish, needy, and Henry wasn't sure he knew how to kiss. He arched his hips unhappily, knowing they weren't at an angle where he could even grind, and Henry pulled back with an evil grin.

"I'm not great at kissing," he said, "but I'm hell at the blowjob. Wanna find out?"

And Lance almost said, "Yes! Just blow me and I'll be great!" But was that what he really wanted? He hesitated, and Henry pulled back, hurt.

"You don't want—"

"Keep kissing," Lance whispered. "Keep kissing me. I'm not going anywhere. You don't have anything to prove to me." He lunged up and pulled Henry back to kiss him again, and with some rolling—loud on the mattress—Henry ended up on top, between Lance's spread thighs, the kiss gaining momentum.

Lance's breath grew labored, and Henry's kisses grew more urgent, and their frotting quickened in pace.

Henry sat up, shucking his shirt, and Lance followed suit. They paused for a moment, staring at each other in the moonlight coming in from the front room window.

"Tighty-whities too," Lance directed. "I want to feel you."

Henry *hmm*d, and there was some more wrestling with clothes until he was back on top, and they were skin to skin. Lance sighed happily, luxuriating in their closeness in spite of the heat and the overworked air-conditioning of the upstairs apartment.

But suddenly Henry was shaking.

"Henry?"

Henry kissed him as a reply, mouth hot, body aggressive against Lance's own, and for a moment Lance responded in kind.

But he remembered that hesitation, that shyness, and lifted up, smoothing Henry's hair from his temples with both hands.

"Sh…," he murmured. "There's just us in this bed. We have all the time in the world, okay?"

Henry shook his head. "But we don't," he said brokenly. "What if…?"

"No what-ifs," Lance told him, keeping his voice firm. "Just you and me, and skin on skin, and nobody outside of us is gonna hurt us now."

Henry nodded. "You're… you're really brave with all that hope."

"You're really brave with all that chasing down the bad guys stuff," Lance told him. "It terrifies me. Your new friend terrifies me, but he's not here." Lance lunged up again, and the kiss went on, some of Henry's frenetic urgency easing, until they were moving against each other, their cocks bare on each other's skin, their arousal amping up.

More, and more, and more, their mouths moving deliriously, their rhythm growing slow and short and hard.

"Lance?" Henry begged, and Lance slipped his hand between them, wrapping his fist around Henry's cock in a basic hand job. Henry followed suit. Lance kept it slow, feeling Henry's sturdy thick base, squeezing the solid shaft until his hand caught on the ridge, rubbing his thumb along the slit. Henry gasped and did the same to him, but the kiss—that was the thing, and it didn't stop until Lance's entire body ached with need, and Henry whimpered inside his mouth and bucked once, twice….

He ripped his mouth away from Lance's so he could bury his face against Lance's neck as he came.

His cry of climax was one of the loneliest sounds Lance had ever heard, and before Lance could comfort him, his own orgasm rolled slowly out, until he was gasping, shaking, clinging to Henry with his free hand as Henry's hot spend cooled on the one below their waists.

Henry's ragged breathing stuttered against his throat.

"You okay?" Lance whispered.

"I'll go get a—"

Lance pulled his hand away and wiped it on the sheets. "We do plenty of laundry," he murmured, pulling Henry's hand and using the sheet to clean it too.

"I'm sorry," Henry said, not looking at him. "That was probably… stupid. Kid's stuff—"

"Hey." Lance kissed him. "There's nothing stupid about sex. It doesn't have to be anal or oral or penetrative to mean something. Yeah, with some guys a hand job is a handshake, and with other guys a kiss is a wedding proposal. This was something in between."

Henry laughed softly and moved so he could rest his head on Lance's chest. "You're really good at that, you know?"

"Good at what?" God, he felt wonderful. The pleasant buzz of sex pulsed along Lance's nerve endings, but more than that, having Henry, bare and vulnerable, draped over his body was filling all his empty places.

"Making me feel not stupid. Making my fuckups seem human."

Lance grunted. "You should see people in the hospital," he said. "Maybe they banged their thumb with a hammer or put on too much weight. And they won't ask for help. They don't go to a doctor until their thumb is six times its normal size and practically falling off. They don't ask for diet help until they can't get out of bed in the morning. Shame is a horrible thing, you know?"

Henry lifted his chin. "Oh," he said, his lips quirking in the moonlight.

"Oh what?" God, he was so handsome. The stark lines of his face were perfect, even his flat-eyed gaze.

"Porn," he said, a smile ghosting over his kiss-swollen mouth. "I get it now."

Lance would have sat up right then, but their adventures had left the mattress a little… soggy. "Get what?"

"No shame. I kept wondering—why porn? Why not waiting tables or folding jeans or something. But… but all the people in your life, they tried to make you ashamed, all at the same time. And you...." Henry bit his lip and rubbed his knuckles along Lance's cheek. "You don't play that fucking game. You took this thing that people wanted you to be ashamed of and told the whole entire world that you were proud of it. You did it naked and you did it in style. You're beautiful and you showed everybody that you were meant to be seen. That's amazing. That's... that's what makes you so fucking brave."

Lance's eyes burned. "That's really perceptive, soldier. I'm pretty impressed."

"Not nearly as impressed as I am," Henry said, and then he kissed Lance. It was a different kind of kiss, not exploratory, not building. Just... just a happy kiss, exulting in their bodies, still come-sticky, still soaring happily on sex-endorphin airways, but happy.

Lance returned it, until they were both a little sweatier, a little more breathless.

And then Henry broke off the kiss to yawn.

Lance laughed and rolled Henry off him and to the side. "Sleep," he proclaimed. "We will do this some more." The air mattress creaked. "*In my bed. And we will do it in an empty house, and we will be alone, and I will think of all sorts of ways to make noise, do you understand?"

God, please let this not be the only time. Please.

"Yeah," Henry said. "It's ours. We're not going to have sex with all the guys around, like soldiers whacking off in a barracks. I get it."

Lance's relief was palpable. "I've had easy sex," he told Henry. "And I've had it for pay. In case you were wondering, this thing you and I just did, it's a whole lot more important."

"I wasn't wondering," Henry said gruffly. "I'm stupid. I mean, God. My first relationship was a clusterfuck of entrapment—you know that. But I'm not so stupid I don't know this is special." He wrestled a little to sit up and then fell back against the fucking mattress again. "Should we put on our underwear?"

"No." Lance wasn't arguing about this either. "This way all the guys will know what we've been doing, and they'll all know it's you and me."

"Will they know it's important?" Henry asked, eyes searching Lance's in the darkness.

"They'd better." Lance swallowed. "I'm not sharing you."

"Me neither." Henry grimaced. "But that may make life a little harder when you're up on the schedule again."

Shit. "One thing at a time," Lance told him. "Once we know you're not going to jail, I can figure out if I'm out of porn."

Henry nodded, so sober Lance wanted to kiss him again, but that was just going to end up with them staying up way too late. "That's a deal," he whispered. "Anything. I surely would like to do this some more."

"My bed's not bad," Lance told him practically. "Maybe we can make Randy sleep on the couch for once."

Henry chuckled softly. "No. No no no no. There's not enough Febreze in the world."

They fell asleep giggling, naked under the sheets.

That thing they'd just done? It was for real.

DARK PROMISES

Henry sat in the dark kitchen, drinking dark coffee at ten o'clock on an eighty-five degree dark night, and tried not to think about his day.

As a result, every moment of his day flashed in front of his eyes like a giant strobe light, from morning to night, until his brain jittered more from memory overload than caffeine.

FLASH! Jackson Rivers, looking exhausted but composed, sitting down for once in his partner's office. Henry wasn't sure exactly what had happened the night before—whether Jackson had gotten away with coming home wounded or if there'd been a helluva consequence for pulling that shit on Cramer, but Jackson was looking both better and worse. Better because there was a sort of peace on his movie-star rugged features that Henry hadn't seen before, and worse because he was pale, like whatever illness had made him so thin in the first place was on its way back. Either way, their day of looking into Henry's case had begun, and surprisingly, so had Jackson's day of giving Henry some advice on how to get his PI's license. As they both figured—dryly—if Henry didn't get put in jail for murder, he was at least having fun tracking down who actually had done it.

FLASH! Skulking around the white-tiled corridors of UCD Med Center, looking for Martin Sampson's father's office. The scrubs they'd gotten that first day to view the autopsy had come in handy yet again as they'd sifted through Sampson Senior's office, looking for proof of the drug distribution ring they'd come to believe was the motive for Martin's murder. Henry had needed to get rid of some of his coffee right when Rivers had gotten trapped in the office's small supply closet. While Henry had been killing time on the john, he'd gotten Rivers's pithy texts:

Fucking Jesus, this guy's banging this nurse like he's ringing in the new goddamned year. Anal and no lube—what'd she do to him?

He'd been worried about getting caught, sure, but he'd also been exhilarated and sort of excited. The last three days he'd been part of an investigation, and sure, it had consequences for *him* because he'd be really excited about not getting arrested, going to trial, maybe going to prison, but it also had bigger consequences than that.

Martin Sampson was dead. And yeah, he'd been all about the street hustle until he'd figured out Henry was Davy's little brother. But he'd been a person—someone real to all the people Henry knew, and he'd been murdered. And Henry was going to get a chance to set that right by figuring out who really did it.

Did that benefit Henry? Well, yes. But finding who the killer was also benefited the memory of a guy who had maybe been sabotaged from the start. His father was a crooked drug dealer, and an all-around nasty piece of work. Henry had never thought he'd be grateful his own old man was a short-sighted homophobic redneck, but damn if Robert Sampson didn't make Paul Worrall look like a prize.

That gave him something he hadn't had since Malachi had bent him over and forced him to break the law.

It gave him purpose.

FLASH! The curve of Lance's throat when he'd thrown his head back while in the throes of climax.

It was the first time in his life that Henry could even say "making love" in his head.

FLASH! The sublimely uncomfortable look on everybody's faces when Henry asked who had been purging bile in the sink and toilet.

Cotton's game little wave. Billy's grim eye-roll. Fisher's embarrassed shrug. Zeppelin's sheepish grin. Even Randy's bashful look away.

Zeppelin had looked at Fisher and said, "Dude! Why? You're fuckin' perfect!"

And Billy had snapped, "So's Lance, but he's the one who takes the sink when the rest of us are going in the pot!"

Henry's face went cold, as well as his fingertips and his toes.

"All of you?" he rasped, looking at them helplessly.

"Not me," Curtis muttered. "I thought they were whacking off in the bathroom."

"Dude," Randy said, "I don't need to whack off in the bathroom. I pretty much bump a table and that's a candlelit dinner right there."

Henry looked at Curtis helplessly. "You're excused?" he said, because he was seriously at a loss.

But Curtis surprised him. "No," he said, looking away. "I'm not. I knew what they were doing. I… I should have said something, at least to all of them." He swallowed. "I was mostly just sort of jealous because I couldn't make myself do it."

But Lance! Henry wanted to flail his arms. *How could Lance do that to himself?*

But Henry knew the answer. All he had to do was ask himself what *he* had to be ashamed of, and he'd see the entire slideshow—every time Mal talked him into giving in, every time he closed his eyes and begged his family for forgiveness.

Lance had so much less to be ashamed of, but his body was on camera for everyone to see. The one place he could prove he had no shame was the one place he couldn't hide any flaws.

But Henry had felt him in the dark, had tasted his kisses, willingly and freely given, and knew Lance was flawless.

FLASH! The worry in Lance's eyes as he'd kissed Henry goodbye, while Henry was still in bed, drowsing, and Lance was off to work a twelve-hour shift.

FLASH! Jackson Rivers eating at Davy's table, looking exhausted still, cutting Kane's niece little shapes out of her sandwich while Ellery Cramer looked at him with that same worry.

FLASH! The worry in Kane's eyes as Jackson and Davy had spoken quietly about Martin Sampson, because Jackson couldn't investigate the guy's death without investigating his life.

FLASH! FLASH! FLASH!

All of it, *all of it*, swirled around Henry's brain in the big frightening amalgam of the things Henry was trying to right in the present, so overwhelming he didn't even see the scary things that had been trying to get him in the past.

And still it was all secondary to his worry about Lance, and the feel of Lance under his hands, under his body, the night before.

Click. The door opened, and Lance walked in, blinking.

"Everybody asleep?" he asked, puzzled.

Well, sort of. They'd all fled as Henry had stood there, gobsmacked, almost betrayed in a way. He'd put the sink back together, minus a heinous-smelling clog and a desperately needed uncorroded U-joint. He'd come back from the hardware store, and they'd stayed in their rooms, leaving the illusion he was alone.

"Sort of," Henry said, standing up. It wasn't the coffee propelling him. He just needed… needed….

He cupped the back of Lance's head and pulled him into a kiss, needy, thirsty, because he'd wanted to do it all day.

The images in his head receded, coalesced, until there was only this moment in time, Lance's mouth under his, minty with gum, but Henry didn't care.

"Wow," Lance breathed, beaming up at him. "That was…."

Henry kissed him again, and again, until Lance moaned and dropped his backpack and pushed gently at Henry's stomach.

"I need to shower," he confessed, grimacing. "I smell like the hospital and BO."

"Sure," Henry said reluctantly. He wanted to hold him. That was all. "Have you eaten?"

"Not yet." Lance batted his eyelashes at Henry, and even though Henry knew it was a lie, he laughed anyway.

"I'll make you something," he said. "You go shower, and then I'll tell you about my day."

Lance's smile went shy. "And then…?" he asked hopefully.

What had Henry thought? That he'd want this man any less when he found out Lance was imperfect? That he'd turn down a chance to be in his bed, to hold him, in favor of lording some sort of "Thou shalt not…." over him?

"And then," Henry told him, heart in his throat. "And then." He smiled and rubbed noses playfully, reveling in the affection, in the kisses, in the way Lance expected banter and fun and not just a blowjob and some ass.

"Awesome!" Lance kissed him quickly on the mouth and bent to grab his backpack. "I'll go shower and be out in a few."

Henry watched him go with what even he knew was worry in his eyes. By the time Lance came back, Henry had managed to put together a meal of riced veggies and cubed chicken, with a little bit of teriyaki sauce. Not original, but not heavy either. He plated it up right when Lance came out from the bathroom, looking a little uncertain.

"Here you go," Henry said, avoiding eye contact. "I hope it's not too heavy."

Lance nodded and sat down. "I, uh, saw the little filters on the drain."

"To keep the stuff that clogs it from going down," Henry said. "The sink was backing up and the pipes were corroded—the U-joint behind the toilet too. I went out and got stuff after I took everything apart. I'd just finished up when you got home."

"Oh." Lance pushed the food on his plate around a little, and Henry scooted close to him and grabbed the fork.

He took a bite and closed one eye. "It doesn't suck," he pronounced. "You don't have to look at it like it's poison."

"I'm not as hungry as I thought," Lance mumbled, and Henry sighed. Obviously, Lance was expecting the other shoe to drop.

"I wasn't going to say anything," Henry told him, not moving back. "I was going to let it go."

Lance put the fork down as if he was tired of the pretense.

"What would you say?"

Henry raised his eyebrows. "How about the fact that the only one who *doesn't* have an eating disorder is Curtis. Did you know *that*?"

It felt a little bit like vindication when Lance's mouth fell open.

"You did *not*," Henry supplied. "Well, they all know that *you* do. And now you know."

Lance pushed his food away and buried his head in his arms. "You never want to touch me again, do you?"

Henry draped his arm over Lance's back and told the truth. "I want to wrap you up and protect you from anything that hurts you and never let you hurt yourself again."

Lance shook his head. "This is my own—"

"Do you think I don't know that?" Henry's mouth twisted bitterly. "I have no place, no right, to interfere in whatever you're doing, however you live your life. But if you're waiting for me not to worry, it's not going to happen. You're a doctor. You have *got* to know all the bad things—"

"Heart murmurs, permanent acid reflux, rotting teeth?" Lance let out a bitter laugh. "I am aware."

"Yeah." Henry dropped a kiss on his temple. "So when I'm off the hook, and you and me are still sleeping together, and we manage to find a bed of our own, I think we should have a long talk about how we can help you not hurt yourself anymore."

Lance squeezed his eyes shut really tight, like he was trying to hold something back. "You think so?"

"Yeah," Henry whispered, feeling Lance's tremble against him. "I think so."

"Can we talk about the ra—"

Henry made a harsh sound, because he still couldn't say the word. Fucking Malachi—leaving him with this thing that had been done to him against his consent. "Then," he croaked. "Then we can."

"But not now." Lance sighed.

Henry held him a little tighter. "We can't do anything about mine," he said helplessly. "We can do something about yours."

"Oh, Henry—" Lance turned toward him, and Henry silenced him with a kiss. He pulled back tasting salt.

"Did the thing…." He swallowed. "The thing with Malachi make you not want to be with me?"

"No." Lance leaned his forehead against Henry's, and Henry got the feeling they were propping each other up.

"Bulimia doesn't make me not want to be with you." Henry closed his eyes. "It makes me want to shake you until you know you're perfect, but I still want to be with you."

Lance brought his hand up to wipe his face off. Henry grabbed a napkin from the table and started to mop up. He was so beautiful, even with his eyes puffing up.

"Can you try to eat a little for me?" he practically begged. "Stop if you think you'll have to hurl. Just a little. So you know I made you something good."

Lance nodded. "It was sweet of you to cook." His voice came out rusty, and Henry moved away a smidge to give him some room. "Talk to me. Tell me about your day."

"It wasn't bad," Henry said, swallowing past the lump in his throat. For once, he had good news and good stories to tell. "Rivers looks… well, I want to say sick, but mostly pale. Like his lips are a shade away from blue. He said something about heart failure back in November. I guess he was really sick and he fell into a swimming pool—"

Lance sat up and frowned. "Wait. *Wait.* Oh my God. His name. I never got a chance to look him up. I kept thinking Jackson Rivers and Ellery Cramer sounded really familiar. But *that's* ringing some bells."

"The swimming pool?"

"He ended up in the cardiac ward. He wasn't my patient, or my attending's patient, but word gets around. His doctor wrote a *paper* about him."

Henry blinked. "So you actually met the guy, and nothing. But his heart condition you remember?"

Henry had turned the light on over the table, and it made it easier to track the flush across Lance's cheeks. "Look, it doesn't happen often. He was sick, like, if he hadn't fallen into the pool and gotten stabbed, he would have needed to be brought in anyway. His temperature had to be around 104, 105 before the cold water hit him. Do you know *why* his temperature was so high?"

"Hit me." After three days in the guy's company, Henry could buy anything.

"He was chasing *a serial killer* around an empty apartment complex. The Dirty/Pretty Killer—"

"Oh my God," Henry said. "We heard about that *overseas.*"

"*Right*? So this PI guy, the guy trying to prove you innocent, he's the guy who caught the Dirty/Pretty Killer?"

Henry let out a gasp of laughter. "Wow. So, that figures."

"How?" Lance's shame, his sadness had evaporated, and Henry would do anything to keep that going.

"Well, like… just him. Like he wouldn't mention it—wouldn't brag. Wouldn't say, 'Look, Junior, I'm pretty good at this, maybe back off.' Instead he…." Henry bit his lip, sort of excited about this, in spite of the worry. "He showed me how to get my PI license, the classes to take, the test. Gave me links. So you know, I applied to junior college. Now I have some classes to add in the fall. I've got like… like—assuming I'm not in jail or anything…."

"A thing," Lance said, looking surprised. "You have a thing you want to do." Then his expression darkened. "A *dangerous* thing. You have a *dangerous* thing to—"

Henry stopped him right there. "Lance, what exactly was I doing before I showed up here—you remember that?"

Lance closed his eyes. "But—"

"And you may not have seen me naked last night but—"

"Scars," Lance said. "I've seen them—along your hip, your shoulder. Looks like road rash?"

"I got thrown by a blast. A ground missile hit the building behind me, left me concussed and skinned like a fish. But I wasn't the worst case there. I got up, dusted myself off, and pulled people to safety." He shrugged, uncomfortable. Just doing his fucking job, right? "I mean… in a perfect world, we would have met when I was, I don't know, retired military. All comfortable with myself and shit. And you'd have your own practice. And we would have been all mature and whatever. But we didn't meet then. You met me when I should have been doing something active and promising and yeah, a little bit dangerous."

Lance rolled his eyes. "You were in a *war zone*, Henry."

Henry met his eyes. "And now I'm in an apartment with porn models, repairing corroded plumbing. We all make adjustments, Galahad."

Lance shifted his hips. "We… we really can't use that name a lot. You understand that, right? I… I even went by Lance in grad school."

Henry stared at him. "Didn't that… didn't that sort of… I dunno. Negate the use of the name as a porn name?"

Lance stared back. "Well, uh…."

"I mean, wasn't that a thing with Reg? He didn't decide to go by a porn name until it was too late, and then he couldn't answer to it, so he went back to Reg? You want a name people can't look up on the internet, right?"

Lance turned away and looked studiously at his meal, shoving a huge bite into his mouth. "Tathe gway, 'rrnry!"

"You big coward. Aren't you a *doctor*, and you *literally* made your porn name your real name?"

Lance swallowed with a gulp and hid his eyes with his hand. "Did we not just cover that not everybody has their shit together in this business?"

Henry chuckled. "All done eating the big scary food?"

"Fuck you."

"Good. Now look at me. We're getting back to the hard thing." He waited until Lance had dropped his hand so Henry could take it in his own. "Can you deal with the PI thing? It's looking a lot less dangerous than the 'deployed in a war zone' thing, but not nearly as sexy."

Lance's mouth quirked up at the sides and he nodded. "I—you look really happy for a guy about to be arrested. I would like to see you be happy when, you know, there's nothing hanging over your head."

Henry kissed Lance's knuckles a little. "Wow. I'm a novice here. Is this what a relationship is like?"

"Sure," Lance said, obviously surprised. "This…." He frowned. "This is actually better than my last relationship was."

"Well, you don't need to sound so shocked," Henry muttered. "I mean, it wasn't functional or public, but Mal and I managed to keep a major secret for eleven years. We had to have *some* skills."

Lance was suddenly sober, and he searched Henry's eyes with his own. "Do you think about it like that?" he asked. "Like a relationship?"

Henry stood up suddenly, moving to put the leftover veggie simmer into a reusable Ziploc bag. He'd originally looked for butter-ware or leftover sour cream containers, but it turned out, nobody in this house ate anything with that much fat in it.

Ever.

He made himself busy in the kitchen in silence, knowing Lance was watching him through troubled eyes.

"No," he said at last. "I… I thought it was. I… I mean, we were together, right? There was this one time—right after we got through basic training, hand-to-hand and weapons combat—where we went on leave and Mal dragged me to this cheap hotel that…. God. I went and bought sheets for it, because we were going to be there a week but we couldn't afford anything better." He felt a grimace pass over his features. "Mal and Debbie were saving up for off-base housing."

Lance made a… well, not a sound, exactly. More like a breath. A long, slow breath out from his nose.

"Anyway," Henry continued, not sure what to do with that… breath, "we'd gotten the hard bang out of our system, and I said, 'Hey, why don't we go out to the bar and get some drinks or something,' and he said we weren't leaving the hotel room. And I sort of laughed him off. I showered and got dressed and was about to leave when he…." Henry's hands started to shake. He wasn't sure where this memory had come from or why it had chosen tonight to slip out. It was a long time ago, right? It's not like Malachi had meant it.

Right?

"What'd he do?" Lance asked, and Henry glanced up to see his eyes tracking Henry's movements as he played Captain Domesticity in a way that would have made his father sneer. Well, his father never had to care for a bunch of broke students/porn models who needed to save everything from half sandwiches to grilled chicken breasts if they wanted to have enough food to eat all month. And then, apparently, to throw it up.

"As I was heading for the door, he grabbed me around the throat and sliced my dress shirt off, from the back of the neck down. I'd put on a nice one—one of two I had, actually—and he caught some skin. I probably still have the scar. He let me go, and I was standing there, blood trickling down my neck, shirt in pieces and falling down my arms, and he put the blade away and threw himself back on the bed. I just… stared at him. He said—I'll never forget this—'You ain't going out there to find no one else, Henry. Just give that up right there.'"

"Henry—"

Henry shook him off. "Anyway, we worked really hard to keep the relationship a secret. That's where our… our partner skills were, you know? How to get laid without anybody knowing we were getting laid." Lance took another deep breath, and Henry couldn't look at him. "Man, you've got to eat some of that. I feel like I put you off your food—"

"That's not your fault," Lance whispered.

"Yeah, I know. But I'm the one who had to dredge up the weird shit right when I was trying to focus on you. So, another bite? Please? So I don't feel like—"

"I'll eat tomorrow," Lance said. "Right now, I'll throw it up, and not voluntarily. *Henry*. Are you even listening to yourself?"

"Yeah." Henry set the saucepan in the sink. "I am. I…." Damn. This had been such a good day too. In all of those pictures, that amazing slideshow behind his eyes, he hadn't seen Malachi's face once.

Not once.

Lance, the guys, Davy and his family, Galen and John—even Jackson Rivers and Ellery Cramer—all of them figured so much larger in his life now.

He'd forgotten he came from this.

"I hadn't realized how psychotic that was," he said weakly, leaning against the sink. "I thought, 'Oh. That's how guys have relationships.' But… but it's not Davy and Carlos. It's not John and Galen or Rivers and Cramer. It's not…." He swallowed. "It's not you and me."

Lance stood and leaned over his back. "It hasn't been yet," Lance murmured in his ear. "And it won't be, ever."

Henry nodded and let Lance hold him. "This night was supposed to go different," he said, disconsolately. "I was supposed to tell you about taking criminal justice classes, tell you about my day, and you were supposed to tell me about what it's like to work in a hospital when you're *not* hiding in the bathroom waiting for your suspects to stop banging, and you were supposed to eat and then we were going to… to… to…."

"Make love," Lance whispered in his ear.

"Yes." Henry took the two arms wrapped around his shoulders and clung to them. "I… eleven years of thinking I knew what fucking men was all about, and I didn't know men even *could* make love."

Lance emitted a cracked laugh. "Do you think you're the only one? I'm supposed to be a *professional* here. I had it so locked down. Why did I need a real boyfriend? I could miss all the chances I wanted, have all the hookups I needed, because I fucked on camera and it's all physical anyway."

Henry squeezed his eyes closed tight. "It's not."

"No. Not you. Never has been."

Just enough weight lifted off Henry's chest that he could breathe again. "Good. What do we do now?"

Lance nuzzled his ear. "I take you to bed, and we make love. And maybe we talk some more, and maybe we fall asleep. And when we wake up tomorrow, we do it all over again, and try to work on ourselves so we're better humans going to sleep each night than we were when we woke up. It's the only choice we've got."

"Jackson says this should end tomorrow." Henry turned in his arms. "He says either the cops will arrest me or we'll find the key piece of evidence that will turn the tide. So tomorrow night, I come home—"

Lance grimaced. "And I'm working and probably catching a nap in the crib."

Henry rolled his eyes. "Okay. So you come home the day after tomorrow, and you're exhausted and I'm here because it's the weekend and I've got nothing to do. What happens?"

Again, that searching glance. "We talk some more?"

Henry nodded. "It's your turn to do the talking," he said. "Because I feel naked in front of you already."

Lance let out a sigh. "Fair enough." His mouth crumpled. "Can we start the lovemaking, though? Please?"

Henry couldn't think anymore. Couldn't talk. He closed his eyes and lifted his face for a kiss, expecting it to be sad and shy after their conversation that night.

But Lance's mouth was hot and eager, and desire roared through Henry's body, burning away his inhibitions, his reservations—and seemingly his clothes, because one minute he was fully dressed in the kitchen, then in a flurry of having Lance's hot mouth on his and his impatient, grabby hands all over him, the two of them were naked and Lance had steered him toward the couch.

"There's lube under the cushions," Lance murmured in his ear. "And condoms."

Henry turned and fell to his knees on the floor, scrambling under the cushions. "I should get tested," he muttered. "I'm on PrEP, but I haven't been since... since...."

Lance's bare body over his own stilled his fumbling tongue. His fingers, however, were still active, and he produced the condoms and lubricant with an air of exasperated triumph.

"Who's been having sex on the couch?" he asked as Lance ran his lips down the back of his neck. "Besides us, I mean."

Lance chuckled softly, his breath hot and gentle on the curve of Henry's ear. "We're the only ones we need to worry about tonight," he murmured. "Me on top, you on bottom?"

Henry made a "Mm..." sound. "Only way I know how to do it," he admitted, in case Lance had "Henry the caveman" fantasies.

"We can fix that," Lance murmured. "I *love* to bottom."

Henry turned and caught his mouth, getting lost in the kiss again. "No new skills tonight," he mumbled. "Everybody plays to their strengths."

"Trust me," Lance told him, a wicked grin stealing across his features. "I... God, Henry. I want you so bad."

Henry shuddered and allowed himself to be helped onto the couch on his back, one foot on the ground and one knee propped up. He turned to Lance with wide, skeptical eyes. "You gonna feed me grapes?" he asked, but then he saw what Lance was doing.

Lance's head was resting on the side of the couch near Henry's hip, and his hand was behind his back and he was... he was....

He moaned slightly and then pulled his hand forward, wiping it off on the T-shirt one of them had left on the floor. The eyes he turned toward Henry were wide and glazed, and Henry realized Lance had been stretching his own asshole with lubricated fingers, and gasped.

His cock throbbed against his stomach, and he closed his eyes, only to open them again when Lance's mouth—God, so fucking hot—closed over him.

"Ahhhh…."

Lance's mouth engulfed him again, and Henry turned and bit his upper arm to keep from crying out. "I'm… oh wow. Buddy, I'm gonna come if you do that much longer."

Lance pulled back and gazed at his face through passion-blown pupils. "Someday. Someday, it's going to be my mouth on your cock, all day long. Nothing but dick. But not tonight."

Henry let out a stuttered breath. "You do talk sweet."

Lance gave a strained chuckle and snagged the condom from next to Henry, then ripped through the foil before slipping it over Henry's cock with practiced ease. Henry swallowed and stroked himself through the thin polyisoprene. "That's different," he murmured. "I don't usually wear one of these." Because usually it was him, hoping Mal had brought the lubricated ones this time.

"Yeah?" Lance stood and swung his leg around, straddling Henry. "Wait until you see this!" For just a moment there was the heady knowledge of his nakedness up against Henry's groin, bare skin to bare skin, and Henry stared at him, wondering exactly how this was going to work.

And then Lance positioned Henry's cock right at his own entrance, and the lightbulb that had been waiting to go off in Henry's head exploded.

"Oh! My God!"

Lance's smile was dreamy, pure sex. "Omigod. Omigod omigod omigod…." He gasped as Henry's cockhead stretched through his opening, and then suddenly Henry was inside him, and… oh Christ. Henry had to close his eyes against the orgasm that battered at his balls.

"I'm fucking you?" he asked in surprise, arching his hips up slowly and finishing the last few inches himself.

"That would be great, thank you," Lance said in a strained voice.

Henry grabbed Lance's hips, the flesh smooth and thick under his fingers and palms, and held him. He knew how this was supposed to work— just because he'd spent most of his sex time bent over something or on all fours didn't mean he didn't get the mechanics.

And Lance wasn't bent over, his ass out in supplication. He was facing Henry, his hands kneading Henry's chest, his beautiful face tipped up so Henry could see pleasure washing over it. Henry clenched his stomach and released, thrusting up and pulling back gently, easily, giving pleasure instead of only taking it.

Oh wow. Wow. Was this what sex was? Was it supposed to be this gorgeous?

Lance's cock, erect and straining, splatted against Henry's stomach and he got a good look at it for the first time.

"Oh, man!" Henry released Lance's hip to stroke it, to revel in the feel of it in his palm again, to pull back the foreskin and yearn to taste. He was good at the blowjob—he'd had to be because Mal didn't do patience—but he'd never really wanted to savor giving one. His memories of blowjobs were more "Mal's too tired to put a condom on, so Henry, c'mere and suck this thing, 'kay?" It was how he'd gotten so good at them—he'd been tired too.

But not now. Now he wanted this thing, this lovely column of flesh, in his mouth. He squeezed, and Lance's asshole tightened on his cock. Henry moaned and stroked some more, trying to find a rhythm between his hips and his hand. Lance gave a strained chuckle and wrapped his fingers around Henry's.

"Let me help," he whispered. "This sort of thing takes practice."

Henry closed his eyes against the burning behind them. "It's so good. So much better...." *Than I ever knew it could be.*

Lance let go of his hand and leaned over, and Henry did his best crunchie to meet him halfway. Their mouths met while their bodies were merged, and Henry moaned throatily. God, this was different. It was sex, but with all the beauty, the mystery that he'd always imagined it could have, and none of the dismissive shame of "just fooling around."

There was no "fooling around" about having his body inside his lover's. Unconsciously he quickened his pace, letting go of Lance's cock and grabbing his hips again.

He needed, needed so bad, so hard, he'd die if he didn't... oh God.... "Lance?" He wasn't sure he could do this.

"Don't stop!" Lance commanded, and Henry watched Lance stroking himself in a blur. Suddenly Lance's hand slowed, tightened, even as Henry's hips continued their relentless pace, and whiteness of semen exploded from the tip of his dick.

The visual threw Henry over, and he closed his eyes and lost himself, his orgasm sweeping from his toes upward. He clenched and cried out, coming into the condom, surrounded by heat, by pressure, by....

Love?

He made a sound low in his throat, not wanting to confront the scary word, not yet. Lance slumped over his chest, and Henry wrapped his arms around his shoulders, holding him, just holding him, while he all but purred.

"Damn, soldier."

"Yeah?" he asked. "We do okay?" His voice was more broken than he wanted to admit, and he cursed himself when Lance pulled back and caught his eyes.

"We did great," Lance whispered, rubbing his thumb along Henry's cheek. It came back wet.

Henry closed his eyes and said, "I don't usually do that. I swear, I'm not some sort of pansy-assed—"

Lance's finger, salty with brine, touched his mouth, and he stilled. "You've done a lot of growing, soldier boy. Growing pains hurt. Nothing wrong with that."

Henry nodded, eyes still closed. "That was really wonderful," he said. "I don't want to ruin it."

"Good." Lance moved off him, and Henry missed his warmth already. Fumbling, he reached down to take care of the condom, only to find Lance's fingers there first. Lance pulled it off and walked, shamelessly naked, to the bathroom, then came back with a washcloth. He was, Henry saw, smiling, wiping lube out of his ass as he walked.

It was the only awkward thing Henry had ever seen him do.

Lance gave a sheepish little smile as he neared the couch, and then bent down and started to wipe Henry off. "I'd clean you off with my mouth," he apologized, "but I *really* hate the taste the condom leaves."

Henry stroked his hair back. "I'll get tested," he said. "I...." He frowned. "I don't know why Mal always wore rubbers, but he didn't that last time. I mean, me and, well, his wife...." He cringed. God, he was a scumbag. "But he usually did and—"

Lance was doing that searching thing with his eyes again, and Henry wondered what he'd missed.

And then it hit him. "Oh."

Lance twisted his lips. "I'm sorry, Henry."

Henry took a deep breath and was... surprised... when it didn't hurt like he thought it would. Apparently being "guys just fooling around" meant Mal hadn't been faithful to Henry either. Well, that figured, right?

"It's not like he ever loved me anyway," Henry said, cupping Lance's cheek. "It's not like it was real." Eleven years of his life, wasted on a man he'd assumed had at least cared.

"This is," Lance told him, capturing his hand. "This is very real, to me at least. You will hurt me if you don't care for me."

Henry nodded, his throat tight, eyes still leaking annoyingly. "I don't ever want to hurt you," he said. "I... don't ever want you to feel like I didn't care."

"Oh, baby...." Lance bit his lip, and Henry had to say it, had to finish the thought, because that way he'd be clean, purged of the last bit of hurt, of hope, of misery that the last eleven years had given him.

"He never cared for me, did he?"

Lance shook his head. "No. I'm so sorry."

"But you do. And you're so much more than he ever was."

But that didn't stop them, the sobs that had been blocked up for too long—maybe since he'd stood as Mal's best man, watching as his lover married his sister—tore out of his throat, and he fell apart against Lance's chest.

And trusted that Lance would catch the pieces, so he could put himself back together again.

NEW HORIZONS

LANCE HAD been running all day. A six-car pileup on I-5 had all hands on deck in the ER, and with the impact of airbags on fragile chest cavities, a cardiac specialist was in high demand. He got another call about a possible heart attack during a shoot-out and hit the ambulance bay just in time to see Henry's new hero wheeled out on a stretcher, a tall, dark-haired man with a sharp nose and angular chin getting out behind him.

"Rivers?" Lance said in surprise, and found himself pushed aside by two ICU nurses who were chastising the patient.

"Really, Jackson?" said Dave, the tall nurse with dark freckles on pale brown skin. "Really? You invite us to a party next week and now you're gonna die on us?"

"As. If." Jackson was talking through an oxygen mask, but his irritation was quite clear. "See my shark in a suit? He's gonna bitch me back to health."

"Yeah," said Alex, Dave's boyfriend and thirty-five-year-old twinkie. "But he's getting tired. Jesus, Rivers, give the poor guy a break!"

"You're not—" Jackson took a gulp of air. "—going to leave anything for Dr. Keller to bitch at." They wheeled him through the corridor. "C'mon, guys, I called him first."

At that moment, a tiny African American woman with snow-white hair strode past Lance with a courtesy pat on his arm. "Excuse me, Dr. Luna," Dr. Keller said. "This is my patient. His husband called me from the ambulance. I'll take over if you don't mind."

She did just that, asking Jackson questions, running by his stretcher on their way to ICU. Lance looked behind him in bemusement to see Henry's lawyer sagging shakily against a wall.

"Mr. Cramer?"

Ellery looked up, wiping his mouth with his hand. "Dr.…?"

"Hi, I'm sorry. I'm Dr. Luna. I stitched up Mr. Rivers's back the other day. I'm Henry Worrall's, uh, roommate?"

Ellery straightened up and swallowed, his backbone going perpendicular to the ground and his shoulders squaring. "Oh, yes," he said, his eyes shifting back to the corridor down which Jackson had disappeared. "Jackson said you were very good."

"That's kind." Lance forced himself to take a deep breath. "I... uh, I heard there were shots fired? Is Henry, uh...." His voice wobbled. "Is Henry okay?"

Ellery heard the break at the end, though, and a pair of large dark-brown eyes snapped into focus.

"Lance?" he said, a slight smile on his face. "That's your name, right? You and Henry are in love?"

Lance practically swallowed his tongue. "Uh, I'm not sure how Mr. Rivers got *that*, but—"

Ellery shook his head. "It's true," he said, his eyes growing bright. "Jackson's usually right about those things. Henry's fine, Dr. Luna. All of us are fine except Jackson." A crack appeared in Ellery's façade then, and he wiped his face with the back of his hand. "Jackson's never fine, but, you know, he does his best. But Henry's okay. He won't be arrested, and he's no longer under suspicion."

"Thank God," Lance whispered, wanting to hold on to the wall. "That's... that's really great to hear. Here, let's get you to the waiting room, okay? You should hear something shortly."

"Thank you," Ellery said, his voice stronger than the paleness in his cheeks suggested. "That's nice of you."

Lance smiled crookedly. "I'm just so relieved to hear Henry's okay. I thought I'd return the favor. So, all the bad guys are in jail?"

Ellery grimaced. "Well, one of them is dead, one is heading to jail, and there are a few extraneous bad guys I probably have to brief the police about. But...." He waved his hand.

"Priorities," Lance said, understanding. "Henry's all about solving the puzzle and getting the bad guys. I'm more about saving the patient. It's a different way of thinking."

Ellery's social smile grew a little stronger. "Lance, my friend, I have the feeling we're going to enjoy being the only two sane people in a crazy world."

"Yessir. Your, uh, friend, Jackson Rivers—"

Ellery looked at him sharply. "Dr. Keller believes he's my husband. Perhaps we should let that, uh, stand?"

Lance couldn't protest. He'd been worried about Henry all week, and he wasn't sure he could ever eat again. He couldn't imagine how worried this man might be for Jackson Rivers, and how long he'd worried as well.

"He was giving Henry pointers on how to get his PI's license," Lance said. "I... uh... I'm a little afraid."

Ellery met his eyes. "I don't think Henry's going to end up in the hospital nearly as much as Jackson does," he said, and Lance couldn't figure out if he was speaking with bitterness or humor. "But...." He bit his lip, and a wave of weariness passed over his features. "You just have to decide if it's worth it. Do that right now. Before your relationship goes any further. Is the worry worth it?"

"Yes," Lance responded automatically. He heard his own voice in his ears and felt shock, but he wouldn't take it back for the world. "It's worth it."

"Then good luck."

They reached the waiting room and Lance gestured him in. "I'm afraid I need to get back to the ER. Usually I'm in the cardiac ward, but there are lots of hurt people today."

"I appreciate the guided tour," Ellery said. Then as though remembering who he was, he continued, "I hope to see you soon. Perhaps Henry could bring you by. He seems to fit right in."

"Thank you, sir." Lance nodded and backed away, trying to ignore the pounding of his own heart. He was halfway back to the madness of the ER when his pocket buzzed.

I'm fine. Case is over. Jackson's in the hospital. Will fill you in tonight. Don't worry, okay?

Lance stared at the text, his chest gradually warming as he caught his breath. *I'll always worry—but I'm glad you're okay. Met Cramer in the ambulance bay. Cool customer. Good guy.*

How's Jackson?

Talking when he got here. That's all I know.

Good. He won't die if he's talking. Keep me posted.

You too.

Lance was about to put his phone back in his pocket when it buzzed one more time.

Last night changed my life. See you tomorrow.

He smiled, touching the face of the phone foolishly before texting, *Me too. If Randy isn't banging someone in his bed, you can sleep in my bed tonight. Later.*

Will think of you. Later.

Okay, then. He could deal with this. Henry was safe, and he had an entire world to deal with. He sprinted toward the ER and another car wreck with renewed energy and purpose.

He had a boyfriend, and his boyfriend had a mission. He himself should know there were worse things in life.

LANCE STAGGERED home at nine o'clock the next night, after catching a few hours in the crib between shifts. Henry was reading quietly on the couch while Curtis sat in the stuffed chair with his laptop, and sounds of sex drifted out from Zep and Fisher's half of the bedroom.

"Randy and Billy?" Lance yawned.

"Went to see a movie," Henry said, getting up. "Here—hit the shower. Have you eaten?"

Lance shook his head. "I could eat," he said, because he knew he should, and because Henry would worry.

"Liar," Henry said with a grimace. "Go shower. I made something tonight you might not hate."

Lance emerged a dreamy half hour later and managed to find the kitchen table. Henry had plated chicken and veggies sautéed in a balsamic vinegar reduction that actually didn't make him overfull. "This is perfect," he breathed, trying to slow down between bites. "Where'd you get the recipe?"

"I asked the guys," Henry told him. "Apparently my mother's stew and spaghetti were part of the problem. You kids and your fuckin' carbs. Anyway, eat. Your bed's all made, clean sheets and everything. We can talk when you can see straight, 'kay?"

Lance managed to nod. "Morning?" he said hopefully. "I was gonna work out before my next shift."

Henry grimaced. "I actually got a thing I gotta do tomorrow."

Lance waited for a moment. "Go on…."

"Rivers sort of runs this… I guess halfway house for junior ex-cons. He and Cramer have a friend who's dating one of them. Anyway, I told him I'd go visit and see how they're doing. He's getting the feeling they're ready to move somewhere else, and Cramer sent me some info to help them out. Then I get to sort of vet more ex-cons to see who I think would benefit most from the house after they leave."

"Wow," Lance said, waking up a little just so he could marvel. "Rivers put you in charge of that?"

"He's sort of down for a bit. I guess he's got to go in for surgery in a couple of weeks, and he's under strict orders to eat well and sleep a lot and not go running all over the fuckin' world. I gotta tell you, I'm tired. I don't know how he does it."

"I hear you. Are you getting paid for this?" Because Henry felt like working for his brother made him a burden.

"Some," Henry said. "And he's got a friend who runs a housecleaning service too. Joey's not a bad guy. We figured I could go in on Fridays since, you know, you usually have Mondays and Tuesdays off. So, that'll bring in some extra income too, and I can still help my brother when he needs me, until school starts."

Lance had to smile a little. "Look at you, Henry. You have a life here. Friends, connections—not bad."

Henry shrugged. "Yeah, well, I'm doing some stuff Monday and Tuesday that'll not get me paid. I'll let you sleep in for the first thing, but the second might be up your alley, like, maybe you could help."

"What's the first thing?" Lance's brain hurt just parsing that sentence.

Henry looked away. "It's sort of... well, you're gonna think this is stupid."

And Lance wanted to scream. "Henry, do you have any idea how much I *don't* know about your last week? Any? At this point, I will take something stupid that will help me understand what happened here over something blind like 'Don't worry about it, Lance, it'll be fine.'"

Henry nodded, stood up, and wandered to the refrigerator and back. "I... look, there's ice cream that I buy and nobody's eating. Can I have some ice cream? Is that going to send someone over the fucking edge?"

"No," Curtis called from the couch, "but if you're getting those Drumstick things, get me one or I'm gonna think you're an asshole!"

Henry and Lance met eyes and smiled. "There's flavored ices in there too," Lance said. "Get me one of those, and we'll call it even."

"You want to come listen, legit?" Henry asked Curtis. "I mean, you could always pretend you're still working over there and get the whole story, but this way you can ask me to repeat the hard parts."

"Yeah, sure." Curtis closed his laptop and wandered over. "Wasn't finding anything good there anyway."

"Whatcha looking for?" Lance asked, finishing off his veggies and chicken.

"A job that'll pay as much as porn for as little hours." Curtis shrugged. "Not finding it. I mean, I get student loans and such, and I save money living here. Still, it looks like I'm in for another three years. No big deal."

"Joey's housecleaning service pays pretty good," Henry said. "But you might have to work there three days a week."

"I'll think about it," Curtis said dryly, which told them both that he really wouldn't. "Anyway, c'mon, Henry. You tell me and I promise to gossip, okay?"

"Okay." Henry dished out dessert and sat down.

Then he told them a story of violence and abuse and sex and drugs and murder, and how the drug-dealing porn star ended up dead in the dumpster, with Henry as the easiest guy to blame.

When he was done, Lance could do nothing but stare blankly at him, while Curtis served up the recap.

"So it was all about drug dealers and Daddy? Had nothing to do with you? Seriously?"

"Pretty much," Henry said, looking suddenly sad. "And don't get me wrong—Martin Sampson's father is a scumbag, pure and simple, but that other guy was a fucking psychopath. Man, I'm glad he's dead."

Lance and Curtis met eyes and then looked at Henry again. "And how did that happen again?" Because Henry's account had been sketchy.

Henry let out a breath. "So... do you want the scary version or the action adventure version?"

Lance closed his eyes and looked at Curtis, who shrugged.

"I'll take the 'Is this going to come back and haunt us again' version," Lance said.

Henry smiled faintly. "Probably not...." He bit his lip, looking embarrassed. "But that doesn't mean there's not wrap-up to it. See, Jackson called me this morning and asked... well, he asked if I wanted to come to a small memorial on Monday."

"For whom?" Who on earth would Henry be mourning?

"For Martin Sampson," Henry said softly. "Because he was an asshole, but he had help getting there, and it's just not right that nobody comes to his funeral. It's like... we want to say goodbye to the guy who might have been, you know?"

Lance and Curtis stared at him.

"That's... that's really...." Lance struggled for words.

"Stupid," Henry filled in with a roll of his eyes. "I get it."

"I was going to say wonderful," Lance said softly. "He could have been so very much more."

"Yeah," Henry agreed. "He could have. And I guess...." A flush washed over his pale features. "I guess I was his last scumbag straw. Like, that day I came to defend all the guys. He really loved my brother, and here I was, Davy's little brother, telling him he was a scumbag. And suddenly, he didn't want to be that guy anymore."

"And that's what got him killed," Curtis said in wonder.

Henry looked uncomfortable. "Exactly. So it only seemed right we sort of... honor that. Honor that there was a part of him who didn't want to be that guy. It's really important to Jackson that we not let that go."

Lance nodded and bumped Henry's knee with his own. "You sure you don't want me to come with you?"

"No." Henry shook his head for emphasis. "This is... it's my thing, I guess."

Lance raised his eyebrows, and Henry blinked, an entire conversation in that exchange.

You'll tell me later, right?

Yeah. But not in front of Curtis.

"So what's the thing you want my help with?" Lance asked, yawning.

"I'll tell you tomorrow before we split," Henry said gently. "You're so tired, you won't even remember."

"That's not fair." Lance yawned again. "I will too!"

Henry helped him up from the table and exchanged an amused look with Curtis that might have pissed Lance off if he could only stop yawning.

"C'mon, Dr. Feel Good—let's get some shuteye."

"This isn't fair." Lance pouted, stumbling along with Henry anyway. "You have this super exciting life, and I just—"

"Save people from heart attacks. Yeah, you're such a shut-in. C'mon, sweetheart, let's get you in bed—"

"Lie down with me?" Lance begged. "Just until I'm asleep. Or, you know. Bring your book. You can read it in bed next to me. Or your phone. Set your phone. Or—"

"Sh… sh, sh…." Henry kissed his temple. "Don't worry. You had me with 'bed.'"

They got to Lance's room, and Henry stripped out of his cargo shorts and his T-shirt before helping Lance into the twin-sized bed and sliding in next to him.

"Mm…." Lance burrowed up against him, snuggling his face against Henry's chest and stroking his stomach with an idle hand. "God, this is all I wanted. All, you understand. All I wanted. Two days and I wanted this. I saw Jackson's boyfriend, and he looked… looked like the world was caving in on him. It made me just… just really grateful you were okay."

Lance remembered to pull his head back and checked. "You *are* okay, aren't you? I mean, are you traumatized? Do we need a shrink or a counselor or something?"

Henry let out a strained chuckle. "I was a soldier, remember? Deployed? War zone?" He sighed. "It wasn't pretty, I can't lie. But I was less worried about the dead guy than I was about Rivers making it. Man, he scared me. All of Jackson's people were there, and he'd put himself in danger for me. And they were there and I was there, and it really was fucking terrifying."

"Fucking brave," Lance mumbled.

"Yeah." Henry dropped a kiss in Lance's hair. "Fucking brave."

"But… I still don't understand who killed the bad guy," Lance said, and Henry grunted.

"Have you ever… I don't know, walked into a staff meeting of people who were way above your pay grade?" he asked after a minute.

Lance tried to reason. "Once. Board members, trying to decide funding, I think. They were… well, sort of cavalier, I guess. I kept thinking that this funding decided if people lived or died."

Henry smoothed his hair back from his face. "Yeah. Well, Jackson and Cramer know people on that board. I figure at this juncture, they're my COs, so I just smiled and nodded."

"That's scary," Lance murmured, not sure he could wrap his head around it right now.

"It is. But in the end, I think it boiled down to Rivers and Cramer, taking care of their people. Me included. And you know what? I'm sort of okay with that."

"Really?" Lance asked, not sure he'd ever be.

"Look. When Jackson was looking like hell, I told him it would be okay if they arrested me—I knew he and Cramer and you and John and Galen and my brother would work to get me out. I'd be okay. And he said, 'Yeah, but you're my friend and I don't want you in jail.'"

"Wow," Lance mumbled, moved in spite of himself.

"Yeah. So he's got people that will do the same thing for him. That's why we're going to help him and Cramer put this case to bed."

Lance had to double-check to make sure his eyes were still open. "I'm sorry?"

"There was a loose end, a nurse named Frasier, who wasn't arrested. Rivers and I heard her having sex with Martin Sampson's father, and we're pretty sure she's been stealing drugs from patients and only giving them half doses—"

"Oh my God!" Lance went to sit up. "We have to tell the ethics board, and there's a whole department for that and—"

"And we have to get her arrested and provide cold, hard evidence first," Henry said, and Lance calmed down a little, because Henry was right. "Now lie back down."

Lance slid into bed again, his bones turning to jelly with that last burst of adrenaline. "Fine. Sure. Whatever."

"Well, do you want to help me find evidence or not?" Henry asked when he was settled again.

Lance was almost asleep, but he wasn't so far gone he missed what this was about.

"You want me to see why you like it," he said. "So I know why this is what you want to do."

Henry stroked his hair back again. "Yeah."

Well, couldn't argue with that. "Fine. Be reasonable. Sure."

"Good, now go to sleep."

"Night, Henry. Love you."

He fell asleep before he realized what he said.

APPRENTICE TO THE MASTER

HENRY LOOKED out over what was going to be another ball-burner of a day and fought a sense of letdown.

This was over. He wasn't under suspicion of murder anymore, and that was great, but now that Martin Sampson had been put to rest in a small vase of ashes currently being buried in a very small plot, he felt... adrift.

Purposeless.

He swallowed and tried to remember some of the thrill that had come from running around finding Martin Sampson's killer, and with that tickle in the belly, the excitement about jumping back into the fray, there also came the knowledge that Henry was entitled to ask questions.

And he was standing next to his brother, who could answer maybe the most pertinent question of all.

"So what made you fall in love with him?" Henry asked his brother as they lingered in the shade of a dusty pine tree at the cemetery. The question had been burning in his stomach probably since Lance had told him that "Scott" was Davy's ex.

Davy's smile was thoughtful, and for the first time, Henry realized his brother was over thirty, in a birthday that not even their mother had celebrated.

Henry knew the date—September 26th. This year, when Davy turned thirty-one, Henry would give him a card, maybe plan a birthday surprise with Kane. Kane might hate it, but it would be worth it to know Henry's brother had more than just his husband and their niece bringing him cake and a present.

"I was... floundering," Davy said. "And he told me it was okay—happy endings were for suckers. Only it turned out, I really wanted one and he... he really didn't think they were possible."

"There's more to it than that," Henry said, recognizing the adult censorship in Davy's voice. His own wobbled. "Please, Davy? I showed up on your doorstep full of lose. I just... just need to hear there's some hope that's not all I am."

David grimaced and rubbed the back of his neck. The little group that had gathered for Martin Sampson—aka Scott's—funeral had mostly dispersed, including a sad and scarred ex-boyfriend. Jackson and Ellery had been the first to go because Jackson had a doctor's appointment, and while he was still looking exhausted, his lips weren't blue, and that was an improvement.

"Want some ice cream?" Davy said. "I don't have to be at the shop for another hour. Let's get some fro-yo or something."

It was so close to something their mother would have said—and so close to what Henry had said to Lance the night after he'd gotten back from that double shift—that Henry had to laugh. "Sure."

They'd driven together—Davy was going to drop Henry off at the apartment on his way back to the shop—so in short order, they found themselves at one of those yoghurt by the pound places. Henry got the biggest size with all the chocolate, because he was in that kind of mood.

Davy got a tiny cup of sorbet with two gummy bears, because apparently once you were a model and the entire world saw your body up close and personal, that shit never faded.

"So you want to hear?" Davy asked as they settled in. "'Cause it's not pretty."

Henry rolled his eyes. "Jesus God, David. You've got porn models lined up the block who consider you, personally, as their wet dream. My entire household is like, 'Yeah, that guy, I'd hit that!' right down to my own—" He swallowed. "—boyfriend. Just... just can I see you not be perfect? Can I know... you know. There's recovery from being human?"

Davy gave him a sad smile. "Oh, Henry. I am so far from perfect. You have no idea the horrible things I've done. I hope you never learn about half the shit I let happen when I was trying to figure things out. But... but Scott. How about the breakup story? Let's do the breakup story, okay?"

"Sure."

"I broke up with him, and he... he sort of stalked me."

Henry swallowed. "Like how?"

"Well, I told him we were broken up, but he'd show up at my house and sort of... talk his way through the front door and into my bed. And I'd feel like shit, you know? Didn't I have any fucking spine?"

"But you see them," Henry said. "And you remember when they were your world. And suddenly, it's easier. It's easier to let them in."

"Yeah," David said, meeting Henry's eyes. "It was. But it wasn't good for me. And... and I was watching two guys, one of whom is still my best friend, self-destruct over... everything. Over modeling. Over each other. Over being in the closet. And I... I couldn't do it. If someone was going to be in my life, it had to be real. My friends were real. Scott was never going to be real. So...." He looked away. "This is so embarrassing. John did blow back then. And he'd just always have the mirror in the back bathroom. And maybe once a week when we were both up too late trying to edit shit and get it all uploaded and we were wiped out, he'd go back to the bathroom and come back sniffling and going 'And now I'm a fucking god!' And Scott was texting me, and I needed courage. So for my first and only time, I went back and took a snort too, then walked home."

"David!" Henry was flabbergasted. This was more unbelievable than the porn.

"You wanted ugly," Davy said, his blue eyes big and wounded. "You asked for this!"

"I'm sorry," Henry told him, and suddenly the weight of talking to his brother, human being to human being, sat on his shoulders. "I'm sorry. I'll shut up now. It was only the once? You swear?"

"Yeah." Davy shoveled a big mouthful of sorbet into his mouth, staring at his half-empty cup.

Feeling like shit, Henry dumped a bunch of his chocolate chips on top of his brother's tiny sorbet. "I'm sorry," he said again, humbly. "I... I guess it's scarier when you're not perfect. I thought it would be easier, but I'm dumb."

Davy looked up and winked, which must have been hard because his eyes were bright and shiny. "I've never been perfect, Henry. But I was sort of at my worst that night. Anyway, I got home, and Scott was waiting on my porch. John was right about that first time, by the way. I really *did* feel like a god, so I went inside, slammed the door in his face, and then came back with all his CDs, which I proceeded to throw at his head."

Henry couldn't help it. He giggled. "Bad to the bone, huh?"

"A hardened criminal," David said dryly. He gave Henry a shy look and took a couple of chocolate chips on his spoon, then closed his eyes as he chewed. "God. You and Carlos—you're gonna make me fat. Anyway, whipping the CDs at him felt damned good. But they might not have done it."

"What did do it?"

A fond smile passed over David's features—one that made him truly look like an angel, and not simply a really attractive young parent. "Carlos. He saw the whole thing. Scott was gearing up to get rough, and suddenly he had a broken nose. Next thing I know, Kane had moved himself into my house, along with all the scaly things. The original idea was that he'd sleep on the guest bed, but with all the terrariums, there wasn't any room. He just crawled in next to me." David shrugged, looking as sublimely happy as one person could be. "Stayed."

"That's… that's really sweet," Henry said, biting his lip. "That's…. God. That's…." He closed his eyes, his throat swelling. "I wish… I wish Mom and Dad could hear that story and know that it's… it's beautiful."

David blinked rapidly and shook his head. Then he took a bigger spoonful of the chocolate chips. "That is not ever going to happen," he said thickly. "I wish it was. I…. Trav emails me about once a month. You want me to forward that? You can write him back. He wants to know you're okay."

Henry's own throat felt swollen. "Yeah. What have you told him so far? Did you tell him about the investigation?"

David shook his head. "No. I figured if things went south, there'd be plenty of time, and if you got cleared, it wasn't something anyone back there needed to know."

Henry managed a smile. "Having my back like always. Thanks, Davy."

He smiled faintly. "Yeah, well, now that you've joined the gay side, I sort of want to keep you in my evil lair, you know?" His mouth went crooked. "It's good having family."

"Yeah." Oh Lord. He really was going to say this. "If you have the right kind. Thanks, Davy. For being here for me."

"What else was I going to do?" And he shrugged again, like it was no big deal, but Henry knew it was the world.

And because his brother was such a good guy, Henry needed to pose the hard question, because he needed help with this.

"I… I've been thinking, and it's not a great thing."

David looked at him, suddenly all alert. He straightened from what had become a slouch over his sorbet and cocked his head in a classic listening pose, and Henry wondered if this was the Dex that all the guys at Johnnies seemed to need so badly.

"What? What's going on?"

Henry let out a breath. "I…. Malachi. He… the further away I get from him, the more I realize the things he did… they weren't good things."

"Was there more?" this new David asked soberly. "Besides when you left—because that's bad enough."

Henry became suddenly invested in the chocolate cream in the bottom of his fro-yo cup. After that moment with Lance, telling him about the sliced shirt, the scar on the back of his neck, he'd had odd flashes of the last eleven years. Mal splitting his lip with a casual backhand after Henry had said, in all innocence, "Too bad we can't do this after you're married." Waking up in the middle of sex in their barracks. Henry had drawn a line about that, but Mal wanted him to know lines weren't for the two of them. The times Henry had just given in because the fight wouldn't be worth the implicit threat in Mal's smile.

"It wasn't every day or even every month," he said softly. "And I'm not saying I shouldn't have put an end to it long before. But it was always there. If I left, Mal would find a way to make me sorry." Deep breath. "In the end, I was sorry enough to leave anyway."

David's hand over his on the table helped still the shaking. "It's hard," he said. "To walk away from something like that. Especially when you're so convinced any relationship at all is wrong."

"You are really fucking generous," Henry said after a moment. "But believe it or not, this isn't about me—not really. It's that… that Scott went off the rails after you broke up with him, right?"

"Yeah?" David saw this was leading somewhere.

Henry hoped he was ready for where Henry saw it going. "And if Scott went off the rails after you ended a relationship like that, I'm wondering…." He swallowed. This was hard. "Davy, is our sister safe?"

He watched as the color drained from his brother's face. "Oh hell. Jesus. I… I wish I'd thought of that."

"It's not your fault," Henry said. God, his throat felt shredded, because every word was like glass. "I… I didn't exactly scream 'My brother-in-law is an abusive rapist!' when I got out of the Army." He stopped, sucking in a breath that tasted like blood.

"What?" David asked softly.

"It's the first time I said that word." He closed his eyes hard. He wanted to take it back.

"Which one?"

But Henry shook his head. "I can't. Not and function." And for the first time, he got why Jackson Rivers would risk heart failure and having his boyfriend break up with him over stitches in his shoulder so he could keep on keeping on.

God, sometimes you had to swallow the pain so you didn't fall apart.

"Henry, you're going to have to say it sometime. You know that, right?"

Henry nodded. "Yeah," he said. "But today, you and me have to talk to our brother so we can make sure our sister is okay." Debbie might never talk to them again—particularly if she found out about Malachi and Henry, but even if she didn't, they were gay. Her parents had written them off, and they were both aware of the fact that she had too. But she was still their little sister, whether she recognized them or not. They had to warn her if they could. Because they had to. It was only right. "I…," Henry said, trying to direct the conversation toward helping Debbie. "I… you know. My fuckups are my own."

"You were coerced," David said, brows drawing inward. "And yeah, there was a lot of gray there. But Malachi is a spineless weasel, and I knew that when you were in the eighth grade. But I left, and I didn't get a say in who Debbie married. And you and Mal…." He shook his head. "I didn't even know how to talk to you about that."

"I wouldn't have listened," Henry said honestly. "I would have made fun of you for being a…." He couldn't even say the word now. "But in a million years, I never would have admitted I was one too." He shook his head. "Nobody could have helped me there but me. And I did finally, but… but I didn't know how bad it had gotten until suddenly it wasn't there anymore."

"No," David said, searching his face. "You don't." He grimaced and pulled out his phone. "C'mon. I'm going to shoot Travis an email right now, and you can help me word it so I don't give away anything you don't want me to. You ready?"

Henry nodded. Better now than when it was too late, right?

He could only hope.

Davy dropped him off just as the heat was getting way too intense for the jeans and sport coat he'd worn to the service. He pounded up the stairs, hoping to have a cool shower and change his clothes before Lance got home from his workout.

What greeted him on the landing was a cross between a horror movie and a teen comedy.

"Uh…."

"Don't say anything," Randy said miserably.

"I've got to say *something*!" Henry protested, gaping at him. "What in the hell!"

"This wasn't my idea," Curtis told him matter-of-factly, but Henry looked at Curtis's hands and saw the black goopy seaweedy evidence all over them.

"You're still complicit," Henry snapped. "Zeppelin, Fisher, you too!"

"I tried to talk him out of it!" Fisher complained, holding up his pristine hands.

Zeppelin guffawed and tried to pick the stuff, which was apparently some sort of body—face?—mask off his hands. "Oh, ouch! Randy, this shit rips out your hair, did you know that?"

"Oh God." Randy's horror was absolute—as it should have been. His entire body, from his ankles to his face, was covered with whatever had been in the five or six big tubes of grooming goop swinging from the plastic bag on the doorknob. "God. Is it going to take out my hair?"

"I don't know! Does it wash off?"

Billy opened the door, sending the trash bag swinging. "Here," he said, holding out a soapy washcloth. "Hi, Henry. How was your funeral?"

"Uneventful," Henry said, still horrified. "Unlike my home life. Give me that." He snatched the washcloth from Billy and started to scrub the back of Randy's covered hand, only to find the stuff had dried with the consistency of polyurethane.

"Oh dear God." The horror wasn't going away. "Randy, can you even breathe?"

"Yeah, Henry," Randy said, sounding disconsolate. "It's supposed to be a face mask. I guess it's a hair remover too."

"What's it doing covering everything from your toes to your balls, man?" Henry gave up on the washcloth, noting that as the stuff dried it was peeling up in places, like it was supposed to. Great. Ripping it off would be easy for all of *them*, but hell on Randy.

"I was breaking out from the heat," Randy said tearfully. "I thought if maybe I put this all over myself, I could stop getting zits on my ass!"

"Oh, honey." Henry felt for the kid, he really did. Randy's complexion was that delicate ginger-and-cream kind that reacted badly to sun, soap, and a stiff wind. The thickest skin on his body seemed to be on his cock, and even that was exquisitely sensitive. "Did you think maybe you should test it on your face first? So you'd know if your ass and your abs could take it?"

"Whoa!" Zeppelin looked at him like he had solved climate change in one easy step. "Dude, that's brilliant! Where were you?"

"*At a funeral!*"

"You don't need to yell!" Now Fisher was almost in tears, so Henry held up his hands placatingly.

"Look," he said, racking his brains. "We need to give him at least four ibuprofen before we start to peel this shit off, because this is gonna smart, okay?"

"I'll be right back," Billy said. "And for the record, he was halfway covered when I got home from working out. This isn't my fault."

Henry just looked at him, and Billy held up his hands and backed out gracefully. Then he looked at Fisher, who was the most obviously distraught. "You run down to the drugstore. There's this stuff down there with lidocaine and aloe. We're going to rub it on his skin after we rip this shit off. We need it stat, so don't dawdle, okay?"

"Got it, Henry!" Fisher took off, his flip-flops sounding loudly on the stairs, the keys to his car jangling in his pocket as he went. That kid still did not pay rent. Henry didn't even know where he was *supposed* to live.

Without his shadow, Zeppelin was left standing helplessly with his goop-covered mitts in front of him.

"You," Henry ordered sternly, "go wash that shit off. And try to listen to your boyfriend now and then. He's obviously the brains of your particular operation."

Zep stared at him. "My boyfriend?" he said blankly.

Henry stared back. "You didn't know?"

"We're only fooling around!" Zep laughed, but not very convincingly. "You know, guys fooling around?"

Henry tried to wash the red out of his gaze. Zep was *not* Malachi, and no amount of Henry's past damage could make him that way. But still. "It's not fooling around when he's here six nights a week, Zep. It's not fooling around when 90 percent of the time, it's just the two of you. I don't even know where that kid lives anymore. Do you? Hell, I don't even know what clothes are his and which ones are yours!"

Zep opened his mouth and closed it, his goofy surfer grin deserting him for once. "But why would he want to be my boyfriend? The dude's rich and only has two years to go before he graduates!"

"Then what's he doing working at Johnnies?" Curtis asked.

"I dunno. One day we were on the schedule together, and we just never split up after that," Zep said, like that made perfect sense. His face fell. "I... you know. Assumed that's why we were only fooling around. He's got better dudes to do than me."

"Not according to him!" Henry would have shaken him, but God, that black crap was all over his body. "Maybe he's here because you're the only dude he wants to do!"

"Oh God!" Now Zep was almost in tears. "What am I gonna do? I don't want him to go off and do other dudes!"

"Well, *first* you wash that shit off your hands," Henry told him. "Then go change. When he gets back, you ask him if he wants to move in and pay rent, and maybe you two can be exclusive so you can stop talking Curtis into your bed, where he feels like the third wheel."

"Sorry, my man," Zep said automatically.

"It was cutting into my studying," Curtis said, a note of apology in his voice.

"Bummer." Zep sighed. "Sorry about the waxing you're about to receive, Randy. I should have maybe tested it out first."

Zeppelin went back inside, and Henry looked at Curtis. "Could you go get me a trash bag and rip it down the side? We need something for him to stand on so all this shit can get thrown away. It looks like it'll choke pigeons or kill fish or something. We need to contain it."

"Yessir." Curtis turned toward the door, and Henry had a sudden thought.

"Where's Cotton?" Because that would have made matters fucking perfect in chaos—if Cotton had been there to cry in sympathy as they hard-waxed poor Randy.

"He's on the schedule today," Curtis said. He frowned. "You know, he hasn't had a date in a month. That's pretty awesome. That shit was killing him."

Well, good. They had one guy who wasn't falling apart, bully for apartment 126C.

"Fantastic," Henry muttered, and Curtis took the hint and left. For a moment, it was just Henry and the perpetually horny kid who seemed to have one goal in life.

And now it was two.

"Randy?" Henry said into the quiet left to them. "What were you thinking?"

"Breaking out—"

Henry shook his head. "Sweetheart, the last couple of months you've been running around like a headless chicken. You're like, 'I want to bang all the things and then wank all the things and now, it's why not try all the things?' What's wrong? What's going to happen if you stand still?"

Randy gaped at him. "I… uh." He swallowed and two big tears rolled down the glossy stuff across his cheeks. "Do I have to talk about it like this?"

Henry looked around them. Everyone else was busy. "You have about five minutes to center yourself and take a deep breath," he said softly. "Five minutes to figure out what all this activity is about, so you can find a quiet place to go when we start ripping your hair out by the roots. Use your time wisely."

Randy swallowed. "I can't ever go home," he said hoarsely. "I… I just don't want to think about that."

Okay, then. "I can't ever go home, either," Henry told him. "Not to my parents' house. Not to the military, which was my home for nine years. Not to my abusive ex-boyfriend who happens to be married to my sister. I can't go back."

Randy sucked in a big breath of air. "Oh my God! Really?"

"Really, really. But you know what?"

Randy shook his head. "No." More tears rolled over the mask, dropping off his chin as clear as if they'd been coming from his reddened eyes. God, this shit was gonna suck to peel off.

"This is my home now. And I'm going to work really hard not to shit the bed while I'm here. You understand what I'm saying?"

Randy nodded, more tears following the first batch. "I'll remember that," he said gruffly.

"And another thing." Henry hated to bring this up, but, well, there were things Randy needed to know. "Use the pool at the gym from now on and not the one here. They use baking soda and not chlorine. I think that's why your skin's been so angry. Buddy, you're surrounded by guys who have made skincare their priority. One of us has got to have the answer."

"Doh!" Randy squeezed his eyes shut. "Oh my God, you know, you're totally right, Henry. That's probably the answer."

"Glad to help."

At that moment the door burst open and Billy came out with the ibuprofen and water, Curtis followed with the trash bag, and Henry figured Fisher would be back with the green aloe goop before they were even halfway done.

For Randy's sake, it was time to get a move on.

Lance got there when they'd just got to his legs and ass, which was the worst part.

His face had a little ginger scruff, and his chest hair was barely there. But his ass had a full complement of red fur, which might have added to the breakouts, considering the heat. Right as Lance walked up, Henry had grabbed a big strip of the black mask and yanked hard, wincing at the holler and whimper that emerged from Randy's already shredded throat.

"What the holy hell?" Lance asked, taking the stairs two at a time. Randy had buried his face against Billy's neck, and Billy was stroking his hair back and soothing him like he would a child, while the others tried to clean the discarded black seaweed wrap and the painful amounts of ginger hair from the cement.

"We tried using hair clippers on it," Henry said unhappily, "but that didn't work either. Nail polish remover, baby oil—nada. There was no choice. We had to rip the whole thing off."

"Oh, honey," Lance murmured. Fisher was already squeezing an almost emptied bottle of green goop over Randy's exposed skin. About the time they'd finished with his back, Henry had sent Curtis out for three more bottles.

They were down to two.

Randy whimpered some more, and Henry went after the next strip. He'd taken off his sport coat and jeans before he'd started ripping, and was wearing his board shorts and an old T-shirt—covered in ginger hair.

"Okay, Randy, we've only got a little longer here. I need you to be strong."

"O-o-okkkayyy, Henry!" Randy wailed, and Henry shored himself up and went for it.

Schwack, more hair. And there went Zeppelin with the washcloth, then Fisher with the green goop, and Curtis and Cotton finished up with a broom and dustpan.

Cotton had arrived about a half an hour after they'd started, which had been odd because he should have been busy for another couple of hours. He hadn't said anything, though—he'd just jumped in to help.

Bless the kid, he'd been the only one able to calm Randy down when they'd had to wax his balls.

And again. And again. Lance took over the green-goop duty and shooed Fisher into the shower, and together they soldiered on.

Finally—*finally*—it was over. Henry finished with the last of the washcloth, and Lance finished up with the lidocaine-aloe mixture, and Randy sobbed on Billy's shoulders.

"I suggest a cool bath with some oatmeal," Lance said. "Maybe wait until the rest of us shower. Then have somebody put the lidocaine on you again." He grimaced. "Then take two more ibuprofen and go watch some mind-numbing shit on television, okay? You're king of the remote control today—nobody's gonna fight you for it. You can even lie on the couch naked. We'll all find places to sit."

Randy nodded sadly, and Cotton said, "I'll go put an old sheet on the couch so he can sit down until it's bath time. How's that, Randy?"

Randy nodded again, and Billy and Cotton escorted him inside while Lance and Henry gave the porch a thorough once-over for all the hair they'd missed.

"God, that sucked," Henry muttered, tying the garbage bag in a knot. "I can't even believe how much that sucked."

"It would have been worse if you hadn't been here," Lance said. "Nice thinking on the aloe lidocaine, by the way."

Henry shrugged. "My mom put it on everything from mosquito bites to sunburns. I figured it couldn't hurt."

They both let out a breath. "So," Lance said, "about that errand we were going to run…?"

Henry shook his head. "Tomorrow. Man, they need us today." He looked out from under the landing, where the sun had barely started to lower. It was afternoon already. "Do we have enough ices for everybody? Fizzy water? Is there enough comfort in the fucking apartment for all those fucked-up kids?"

Lance gave him a lopsided smile. "Yeah," he said. "And you know what? We're part of that."

Henry grimaced. "You know, I was so excited about getting some better paying jobs and finding a way to move out of here, but…."

Lance nodded, and it was like they both shared the same thought. "How are we going to have our own sex in an apartment with five other guys?"

"Nooooo…. Doesn't one of us have to have a uterus before we squirt out sextuplets?"

Lance raised his hand so he could laugh behind it and then dropped it because like everything else on the landing, it was covered with ginger fuzz. He bent over double, laughing harder, until Henry wrapped an arm around his shoulders to bear him up. And while they were losing their shit, semi-hysterical with laughter, the door across from them opened up.

Henry could swear his freshman English teacher stuck her head out. A tiny, wizened, disapproving woman in her seventies glared at the both of them until they fell abruptly silent.

"Is that young man done screaming?" she asked.

"Uh… yes?" Henry said. "Yes, ma'am. He's going to be okay now."

"Ask me if I care if he's going to be all right," she snapped. "I dare you. Ask me."

Lance sucked air in through his teeth. "I give, Auntie. Do you care that our friend is going to be fine?"

"No! Now, ask me if I care about half your junior college having sex in your apartment at all hours of the day!"

It was Henry's turn. "Uhm, do you mind that our roommates seem to be having sex at all hours of the day?"

"Yes!" she shouted. "Yes, I very much *do* mind. And I don't care that you're all young men. I don't give a *damn* who you're screwing in there! Ask me what I care about!"

Well, they were in it now. "Uhm, ma'am?" Henry ventured. "What *do* you care about?"

"You assholes are *loud* as *fuck*! Now I tried to tell the super about it, but he got his head chopped off—"

"Throat slit," Henry corrected before he could stop himself.

"Henry!" Lance growled.

"I was there—I saw it! He got his throat slit!"

"I don't care if he got his spleen pulled out through his penis," the tiny harridan snarled. "He didn't do anything to stop the noise! Now we have a new super, and I tried to complain about the noise to *him*, but all he said was he needed to get his books in order before he does anything about it. So I'm stuck with you people, screaming 'Do me, do me!' all night long, and now, apparently, you're just screaming!"

Henry actually heard himself swallow. "We're, uh, sorry about that, ma'am—"

"And what is this fuzzy stuff!"

"That's our friend's body hair," Henry answered tersely, angry on Randy's behalf. "And a very expensive seaweed exfoliant depilatory."

"Go fuck in someone else's building!" And with that, she slammed the door in their faces and left them on the echoing landing.

"Good answer, Henry," Lance said.

"Shut up."

"You can tell she was really impressed."

"I don't want to talk about it."

"Are you going to want to talk about it to the super?" Lance asked, and they both winced.

"Sure," Henry said, trying not to scratch all over his body. "I'll just tell him that I've got no idea what she's talking about. I mean, who's actually on the lease?"

Lance blinked. "Uh… I have no idea. We go down and pay rent. I mean, it gets renewed every year, so it's got to be someone…."

They squinted at each other, and Henry got a niggle of curiosity and a really great idea.

"Let's go shower," he said. "And calm the guys down. And then I may need to call my brother or maybe Galen."

That seemed like a really awesome plan, but their day wasn't over yet, and he didn't get to that phone call for another week.

AFTER THEY'D showered—and of course by then, the water was freezing cold, but it was still hot outside so neither of them cared—Lance checked on Randy, who was lying on the inflatable bed because he said he felt bad about taking the whole couch. The aloe and lidocaine seemed to be working, as did the codeine Curtis had pulled out of his sock drawer that he'd saved when he'd gotten his wisdom teeth pulled the year before, and Randy was mostly comfortable and a little out of it, watching Pixar movies.

Curtis, Billy, and Cotton were all draped on one another on the couch, and Zeppelin and Fisher were having a quiet, intense conversation in their room.

Lance got out of the shower first, and as Henry scanned the room, he remembered that Cotton had come home early.

"Cotton?" he asked softly. "Is there anything wrong?"

Cotton's eyes grew bright and shiny and vulnerable, and Henry wanted to cry himself. Wow. This day had started with a funeral and had just gotten worse.

"Want to go talk about it?" Henry asked, and Lance looked at him in surprise.

Cotton nodded and followed Henry meekly to Lance's bed. Henry thought he should maybe put a sign up overhead that said, "Advice $.05"— but he didn't think anyone would get it but him.

"What happened?" Henry asked, sitting on the bed and bouncing experimentally. Yup—newish mattress, good box springs. He and Lance could have some fun on this bed, if only they could ever be alone.

"I… I was getting ready for my scene," Cotton whispered. "I was fluffing in a corner while John checked the light, and my scene partner was fluffing, and… and the guy was new. Young—maybe twenty—and he looked… I mean, he wasn't the same guy, but he looked just like… like there was this guy, before I started working for John. He used to… I mean, I did what he said, and that's how I knew I could charge for it, but he never paid me and I had to and… anyway, I started to cry. I started to cry and I couldn't stop."

Oh.

Henry held out his arm, and there was nothing sexual about Cotton's cuddle this time. "What'd John do?"

"He took me aside and said it was okay," Cotton told him, his voice broken. "Said nobody should have to do something that made them cry. I told him I didn't know what else to do with my life, and he said we'd think of something. When I'd calmed down, he gave me this… this card. Said there was a shrink there I could talk to—that it was on the health plan and everything. He told me not to worry about rent, but I said I had to pull my weight. He told me he'd find something else around the set for me to do. Anything, he said, except something that hurt me the way this seemed to right now."

"He's a good guy," Henry said, remembering all the shit he'd given John and Galen at first.

"But what am I going to do now?" Cotton wailed.

And Henry held him, just like Billy had held Randy, and told him it was going to be okay. "John's right," he murmured, when Cotton had calmed down. "Don't worry about rent. This group of assclowns has your back, okay? And it's not like anybody eats that much, right?"

Cotton sputtered tears against his clean shirt, but Henry didn't care.

"No, seriously. Call that shrink tomorrow. First thing. Lance and I will help. If you don't want to work for John, I've got a line on a guy who cleans houses. I know it sounds like… like a step down, but you know what? It's honest. It's honest, and there's skill involved, and this guy would be a fun boss like John. And nobody would expect you to take your clothes off, and nobody would hit on you—well, this guy hits on everybody, but he wouldn't if I told him not to—and you could work with your earbuds on, and it would be all okay. What do you think?"

Cotton wiped his face on Henry's shirt. "I think I've got options," he said with a little smile. "And I think… I think you and Lance and the guys would take care of me as long as I need. And I may need it for a little while. But not always. And some day, I'll get my shit together, and I'll take care of people too."

Henry hugged him again, tightly. "You'll be amazing at it," he said softly. "But first let's take care of you."

COTTON SLEPT in Lance's bed that night, and Randy—thank God—slept in his own. Zeppelin and Fisher took the queen-sized, which left Curtis on his bed, Billy on the couch, and Lance and Henry on the inflatable bed.

Billy was watching a movie quietly on his laptop, earbuds in, which finally—*finally*—gave them a chance to talk.

"How'd it go?" Lance asked quietly. They were lying on the mattress, under a sheet, while the fan whirred overhead. Henry suddenly wondered who he'd have to blow to get the air-conditioning to work properly and then laughed softly to himself.

No, no—that wouldn't work either.

"The service? It was fine," Henry said. "Rivers got hold of Martin's first boyfriend, and he said something nice about how we weren't mourning what Martin was, we were mourning what he could have been. How we'd have to work hard to try to keep the other Martin Sampsons of the world from falling through the cracks and becoming scumbags. It was really nice."

"Pretty idealistic," Lance murmured. "Hard to live up to."

SHADES OF HENRY 139

"It's good to have goals." Henry closed his eyes and smiled. That morning, when he and Davy had been standing under that tree, he'd felt that terrible sense of letdown. Now, talking about goals, about taking care of the porn kids—whoever lived under this roof—and thinking about the last bit of PI work he wanted to do on his own case, some of that letdown faded away, and that sense of purpose, the one that had sustained him when he'd been under suspicion, filled his belly. "I mean, that's what we're doing here, right? These guys?"

"Yeah." Lance blew out a breath. "What about afterwards? Did you and Dex talk?"

Henry's smile faded. "Yeah. I… I had this sort of awful thought, that if I wasn't around for Malachi to be a complete asshole to, he might turn on my sister."

Lance's eyes went wide. "Oh my God—abusers don't often just quit."

"We emailed my oldest brother. Travis still keeps in touch with Davy. He's going to keep us posted." Henry blew out a breath. "It's all we can do, really. 'Cause I keep thinking, what'll my folks do if Malachi suddenly starts whaling on my sister?"

"What do you think will happen?"

Henry snorted bitterly. "They'll tell her it's her fault."

Lance cupped his cheek. "It's not, you know."

Henry looked away. "I had some of that shit coming."

"No, you didn't. Not a damned bit of it," Lance growled. "You were like a frog in a pot of water. The water's fine at first. But then it keeps getting hotter and hotter, and you don't even notice until finally you're boiled alive. Only you were smart. You noticed. You got out."

"Don't try to make me heroic," Henry told him firmly. "Don't try to make me brave. If I was a fuckin' hero, I would have told him no the first time."

"Oh, Henry, you're a hero because you told him no at all."

Henry grunted. "Whatever." He yawned. "God. There was so much I wanted to do today. It all got completely derailed. We on for tomorrow?"

"Yeah, sure." Lance seemed put out that Henry wasn't going to whine anymore about Malachi, but Henry just couldn't. Who deserved to be subjected to that crap, right? "What are we doing tomorrow?"

Finally, something to smile about. "Well, you're going to get me into your work, and we're going to break some laws. You ready?"

Lance buried his face in his pillow. "Henry, you're killing me."

"Hey, maybe when we get back, the place will be empty. You ever think of that?"

"No."

"It could happen."

Lance glanced at him sideways. "Who says I want to?" he asked, clearly wanting to.

Henry actually chuckled and ran a gentle knuckle along the side of Lance's neck. "I do."

"God, you're cocky."

He wasn't, not really. "I just really, really, want it to be true."

Lance's shy smile peeped out from the pillow. "It is," he whispered.

Henry chuckled gently and lay back on the mattress. "I am so damned glad."

NOT MY JOB

"So HERE'S the thing," Henry explained as they were leaving the apartment. "You can't do anything that would put your job in danger."

Lance paused and looked at him in the much-laundered white scrubs he'd gotten that first day of the investigation. "You know, when we're done with this case, you can probably wear those as sweats or something. You seem to like them an awful lot." Truth was, he looked good in white, and Lance liked to imagine him in his tighties underneath the loose bottoms. He *really* liked to imagine Henry *naked* under the fabric, but it seemed best to curtail all sexual fantasies until they actually had some time alone.

"I'm serious, Lance. You need to watch yourself and your license to practice. Don't let me go over any lines, okay?"

"Like what?" Lance asked.

Henry rolled his eyes. "Look, you're the one who worked your ass off to be a medical professional. So, stop me before we do anything that would violate a rule or something, something you cannot do. I really want to wrap up this loose end, okay? Jackson's going into surgery in the next couple of weeks—"

"Hold up." They had gotten this phone call *that morning*. "Aren't we going to, like, some sort of party next weekend? At *his house*?"

Henry grinned. "Look, I'm just saying if the guy's gonna die, he's gonna do it in style. Besides, between you and me, I think that's Cramer. He seems to want to… I dunno, spoil Jackson. Like Jackson has a bank account and his own money and shit, but Cramer won't let him pay for anything. And they're always arguing about clothes—"

"Good!" The thing Jackson had been wearing when Lance had sewn him up had predated Lance's high school graduation.

"Yeah," Henry agreed, looking thoughtful. "It is."

"What do you mean?"

Henry shrugged. "He's let some stuff slip, not really complaining, though. I was like, 'My father's an asshole,' and he's like, 'My mother was a junkie—we've all got damage.' I get the feeling Cramer spoils him because he's going to need a lot of spoiling before he believes he deserves it."

"I know a guy like that," Lance told him, cursing for the thousandth time their living situation and the fact that he couldn't greet Henry with flowers and candlelight and a bottle of wine. Lance hadn't dated since Teddy, and Henry hadn't dated *ever*. What would it be like to have an entire evening alone with this man, and let him know he was cared for?

Lance would have to continue to wonder, because right now, they were busy fighting crime—and Henry was luminous with it.

"So I don't put my job in danger," Lance said, trying to focus. "That's easy, since I don't know what we're doing yet!" Henry had been sort of cagey about that, but then, they were supposed to have done this yesterday, only, well, seaweed exfoliant depilatories and a despondent Randy, who was probably going to spend the next week in either an oatmeal bath or the gym pool until his hair grew out, had kept them busy.

Henry sighed and waited for Lance to get in the car before pounding emphatically on his phone. "Okay, so here's what's going down. Goddammit, Rivers, I'm not a fucking kid!"

"What's going down is you're fighting with your new friend about who gets to play in the sandbox," Lance said dryly, starting the CR-V. "Anything else?"

He could practically hear Henry rolling his eyes.

"Wait… wait… oh! Hey! He called in reinforcements. Oh! Okay. That's cool. Very good."

Henry clicked some more and finally put his phone away as Lance made the turn onto Howe.

"Look, so I need you to get me into the hospital and past the patient areas. I need access to the offices of the board members—Sampson in particular. That's where Rivers and I went when we were looking for proof that he was selling drugs. Now, he confessed to the police—but Jackson's detective friend says they only gave a brief look at the office because of the confession. And one of the things Sampson *hasn't* done is mention Summer Frasier's name."

"And Summer Frasier is…?" Lance was still a little lost.

"The nurse who didn't give patients the full dose of drugs because she was saving them for her side business."

Lance frowned. "That still doesn't make any sense. She wouldn't get anywhere near enough to make a decent amount of money."

"We have proof she's doing it," Henry said. "We have pictures of her signature on two different electronic documents for the same patient. But we don't have the pills she's been stashing. We know where they are—but all Jackson got were shitty photos, no flash, because he was afraid of getting caught."

Lance's blood froze to a sluggish trickle. "Getting caught where?"

"Getting caught in Sampson's closet while they were having sex," Henry said, like, "Getting caught picking his nose" or "Getting caught eating cookies before dinner."

"This is going to be your life now, isn't it?" Lance asked in horror. "I mean, I keep thinking I get a handle on it, but you're going to be hiding under people's beds while they do the nasty, and I'm going to be texting you about a date and you'll be, 'Not right now, they're almost finished.'"

Henry appeared to think about it seriously. "I don't know, Lance. If you were naked and waiting for me and we had a house to ourselves, I might just stand up, take a picture, and say, 'I gotta go, my boyfriend is waiting.' I mean, I do want to make you my priority."

Lance ground his teeth. "You are being an asshole."

"And you knew this about me, and still, we have an inflatable mattress that is almost flat and might never recover. Now do you want to know how this needs to go down or what?"

Fucking *luminous*. It was infuriating and worrisome, but Lance couldn't even look at his face without wanting to bang him. *This* was who Henry Worrall was supposed to be. Not grim and angry, not hurt and lost. *This*. Cocky and excited and snarky and fun.

Lance might not understand it, but God, if this was what it took to make Henry happy, he had damned well better be on board.

"What do I need to do?"

"Just get me into the office. That's all you need to do. Now if you can't, if it's going to get you in trouble—"

"He's been arrested. There's no expectation of privacy there," Lance said. "Now if you were trying to hack his computer, that's doctor/patient privilege and that could be a thing, but if we're just, say, going into the closet to get some supplies, I can ask the office manager. No big deal."

"I like the way you think, Dr. Luna. This will be much more comfortable than hanging out in the dusty utility closet, listening to two criminals have sex."

"I thought you said you were in the bathroom when that happened!" Lance's stomach roiled.

"I was! But Jackson texted me a blow-by-blow. It was *so* not pretty. This will be much easier. Unless, you know, Frasier walks in."

"Why?"

"Because if she knows we're sniffing around, she'll have time to destroy evidence before we get the cops in there. I mean, Jackson's pictures showed a *lot* of prescription bottles that—"

"Those should have been locked up!" Lance's outrage over protocol felt silly, but medical staff was tested repeatedly on drug protocols. Things like what Martin Sampson's father had done weren't supposed to happen.

"Yes," Henry said patiently. "They *should* have been locked up. That's how we know they were illegal. But we also know the police just vacated Sampson's office—Jackson's buddy says they didn't find the evidence so they didn't search the closet. So this is important. We need to present this evidence to Jackson's department friend so we can get Frasier out of the medical profession, at the very least."

"Not in jail?" Lance asked, his outrage still fresh.

"Sampson committed murder—two and a half that we know about."

Lance was going to kill him. "Two and a half? What is that even—"

"His son, his old business partner, and his business partner's son, whom he accidentally overdosed on pills. The kid took them himself, but Sampson was in the room. Anyway, Sampson is up for murder, but there's no evidence Frasier was in on any of that. She may be arrested—that's not my problem. I would at least like to see her get her license revoked because she shouldn't—"

"She shouldn't get away with this," Lance said, coming out of his confusion to go with outrage again.

"No, she should not."

Lance narrowed his eyes and shook his head.

"Why does this make you so mad?" Henry asked patiently.

"Because it's dangerous," Lance said.

"It really isn't."

"You don't know that. Because it's dangerous and it's... it's unnecessary. You're not getting paid—" God, all of Henry's desire to be useful, and so much of it had seemed to be connected to his need to provide. This didn't do any of that, and Lance was confused.

"It's important, Galahad. Do you think I'm excited about you working thirty-six-hour shifts? Do you think I don't worry about you running into a tree or something on the way home? What about the fact that you're probably living on caffeine and anxiety, even though I tried to feed you fruit and egg white for breakfast? Do you think I don't worry? But this is important. It's a loose end I can tie up, and it's the start of a job I think I might really love. Jackson told me he's got contacts at the hospital who can get me in if it's dangerous for you, but—"

"No, no," Lance muttered. "No. You pulled out the real name and food, which means this is important to you. And I'm sorry I'm such a whiny baby. I...."

Henry gave him a fond smile. "You're a very by-the-book guy, Galahad. I get it."

Lance could hear his own eyeballs click this time. "Stop with the Galahad—"

"Nope. I'm the only one who gets to call you that. Galahad. Not Gally. Just Galahad. My own knight in shining armor." He squeezed Lance's knee. "I love that. You want to jump in and protect me. It's sort of awesome."

"Yeah, but apparently, I'm shitty at the job." Gah! Traffic on Folsom Boulevard—never Lance's favorite.

"Who says? Look at me. I'm a student. I'm a... a helper at a law firm. I'm a babysitter of adult children. I mean, a few months ago, I was just some helpless Army grunt—"

"Sergeant," Lance retorted.

"How did you know—"

"You told me, and I looked it up to see what it meant. You passed up promotions so you and your douchefucking ex could be lower ranking, but you should have been a sergeant for the last two years."

"Whatever. I'm over it—"

"You shouldn't be," Lance said. "I'm going to be bitter for you."

"Don't be," Henry said and his voice dropped, became low and intimate. "Because... because as corny and dumb as it sounds, maybe this was the path I was supposed to be on. You ever think of that?"

Lance's jaw eased up just a little. "Mm... maybe."

"Mm-hmm? And maybe this will be... well, different, but maybe life this way will be a little more fun."

"I'm fun?" Lance asked, not above fishing for a compliment.

"You're a whole amusement park." Henry's voice shifted again. "Or I assume you are. I'd really like some more time to find out."

Lance would *really* like some private time with him too. It was starting to drive Lance a bit mad. "I know! It's not fair!"

"How did you hook up before I arrived?" Henry asked, and Lance realized the answer was a little embarrassing.

"Same way everybody else did. Found a spare bed and went to town."

Henry made a happy little hum in the back of his throat.

"What?"

"I'm special," he said, the pride unmistakable.

"Don't ever doubt it." There was a thick, gooey silence in the car then, the kind that warmed Lance's chest before he turned his attention to the matter at hand. "So, since we're not breaking in or doing anything illegal, you're just going to ride my heel while I get permission from the office manager?"

"That's the plan," Henry said, looking out into the brutal sun with a sort of cheerful anticipation.

Lance tried to analyze the buzzing in his stomach.

To his surprise, he realized he was sort of looking forward to this too.

MARA, THE office manager, was a stout woman in her forties with cheerfully blond hair and cat-eye glasses. She had no problem letting Lance and Henry into Sampson's office now that the police were through with it, but she warned them that they weren't to touch anything, and they weren't to take anything out.

Henry held up his phone. "Just taking pictures, ma'am."

"That's what you're using?" Lance wrinkled his nose. "Somehow, I'm disappointed."

"I'm sure Jackson's got a long-range camera if he needs it," Henry said defensively. "He seems to work a little… I dunno, closer than that. Besides, he sent me his cop friend's number so I can text the evidence to him."

"That'll have to do," Lance mumbled. "So, Mara, let us in?"

"Sure!"

Sampson had an office in his own practice—his office in the hospital was opulent, but small. Plush rug, glossy oak furniture, a clear view over Stockton Boulevard.

"I wonder why he got one inside the hospital instead of in the office park next door?" Lance murmured. "Maybe he was here before the recent remodel."

"Maybe they wanted to shove him in a corner," Henry muttered. "Lots of awards and shit for show, but seriously, if he's practicing medicine somewhere else, what does he need an office in here for?"

Lance thought about it. "Ostentation," he said, looking at a couple of cases carefully crafted for some obscure humanitarian award. "He has it."

"He does indeed." Henry moved behind the desk to the small utility closet. "You're the one with the key."

"Are you sure the cops didn't check this?" Lance asked as he opened the door and stepped back. He was hoping to catch the interior with as much light as possible.

"I asked Cramer," Henry said. "Neither he nor Jackson had a chance to mention it to their detective friend. Jackson said he'd contact the guy today. The fact is, they wrapped up the main bad guys and all they really have on Summer Frasier is some paperwork and Jackson's story about sex in the office."

"But is this really your job?" Lance asked, hating the whine in his voice.

"Well, is it really not? I mean, *you* can have your version of internal affairs check her out—but by that time, she'll have cleared the evidence. This is...." Henry grimaced. "It's a loose end, and I don't like those. And it's driving Jackson nuts, and he needs to chill and get better. And... and I don't want to be the guy who's sloppy. So we're doing this."

Well, Lance couldn't really argue with that. Henry Improvement was apparently not done in half-measures.

"God, that's tiny," Henry observed as Lance opened the closet. "I don't know how Jackson took a breath in there. But look!"

"Holy wow," Lance murmured, getting a good look at the pill bottles arranged neatly in box flats—four shelves of them in the back of the closet. "This is not legal."

"And that," Henry said, pulling his phone out and starting to take pictures, "is why we're here."

At that moment, they heard Mara's voice raised in the hall. "But Ms. Frasier, don't you need a key to go in there?"

Oh seriously? Now? Henry and Lance met horrified glances—and did the obvious thing.

They dove into the closet.

"What are you doing?" Lance asked, mashed up between a shelf of polyisoprene gloves and Henry. For a moment his baser animal kicked in and he leaned a little closer to Henry, smelling baby shampoo and Old Spice and danger.

And there went his libido, right along with the pounding of his heart.

"Not that," Henry whispered back, his nose bumping up against Lance's jaw. He showed Lance his phone screen, and Lance saw that he'd sent the brightly lit pictures of the pill bottles to a Det. Sean K, as well as to Jackson Rivers.

A text appeared from Rivers: *Great. Where are you now?*

Henry's honest reply surprised him. *Stuck in the closet with Lance. She showed up.*

Texting K-ski. STAY PUT.

Will do.

Henry kept the phone out, but he cast Lance a meaningful look over his shoulder, and Lance rolled his eyes. Then the outer door to the office slammed shut, and they could hear Summer Frasier tearing through the room, muttering to herself. The pounding on the computer was easy enough to discern, as well as her cry of frustration when it was locked.

She went through the drawers in the desk, cursing. "Dammit, Robbie—where would you put that shit?" and then they could hear cabinets opening and shutting with force.

They both knew where this was going. Lance bumped Henry and gave him a worried glare, and Henry nodded, holding out his palm. "Stay. Put," he mouthed and then, oh God, he opened the door and slid out of the closet.

Lance gaped in the sudden darkness, his mouth opening and closing in surprise.

What. The. Hell.

And outside, Summer Frasier apparently had the same thought.

"Who the fuck are you?"

"Oh! Hey, see the hands up here?" Henry's voice had a note of surprise, nothing more. "You were pretty quick with that thing, there, Summer. I think maybe you should put it away."

Put it away? Lance closed his mouth completely, breathed through his nose, and tried not to panic. Put what away?

"Who in the fuck are you!"

"Oh, honey, I'll tell you who I am if you stop waving that thing around. I mean, it's not very big, but you're a medical professional. You've seen what even a small one can do, right? How'd you get that thing through the gates, by the way? I mean, I had to go through metal detectors—just me and my cell phone here."

And he knew. He totally knew what "that thing" was that she should put away.

Oh dear God. This "loose end," this "nurse with some extra evidence" was waving a gun around in Henry's face.

Lance's stomach dropped, and he had to work to stay standing.

Henry had just told him to stay put and had walked out there to face a desperate woman with a gun? Oh God... Lance was seriously going to be sick.

He swallowed down his nausea and held his breath so he could hear.

"I came up through the executive entrance," she sniffed. "Robbie gave me a pass, so I could...." Her voice dropped. "So I could visit when he needed me."

And oh, she didn't sound happy about that.

"Ah," Henry said softly. "I wondered about that. I mean, he wasn't very nice to you. I wasn't sure if it was an affair or something else."

"It's none of your goddamned business!" Summer shrieked. "What are you doing here, anyway?"

"I'm here for the same reason you are," Henry said. "To find the evidence against you. Except I've already found it and sent a picture to the police. Don't get upset, but they're on their way over."

Lance blinked hard and thought seriously about killing his brand-new boyfriend. He'd said *what*?

"Don't get upset?" Summer's voice hit an octave Lance wasn't even sure dogs could hear. "What in the hell—"

"Look, Summer," Henry said, his voice low and soothing. "I need you to answer a question for me. Be honest. How did you think this was going to turn out?"

"Wha—what?"

"That's right. Think about it. When did this have a happy ending?"

"I...." She caught her breath. "I wasn't supposed to even be with him. I... I was just out of school and I was hired in their practice, you see? And one of the other doctors wasn't there, and Robbie said, 'Deal with the guy!' so I did! Only I was *wrong*, because I shouldn't have even been there and he almost died!"

"See?" Henry said softly. "You were in over your head from the start, right?"

"And Robbie...." She had to catch a sob. "He said if I went... went along... you know, just bend over, Summer, it'll feel good, I got an itch... and I did, because I'd worked so hard and I'd lose my license and he... he... made the bad part go away."

"And you were trapped," Henry said, his voice low and compassionate, like he knew how she felt.

Oh God. He knows how she feels. He really, really, does.

And he kept going. "You couldn't get out, because you'd screwed up. And you had to keep doing what he told you, because even if he was the one who fucked you in the first place, he was the only one who could keep you out of the fire, right?"

"Yeah," she said softly. "I thought… he was so desperate to keep me there, doing stuff for him. I thought he might care for me. I hated myself so badly by then, he could be the only one."

"He didn't give you up," Henry said. "We caught you first. So if nothing else, you have that."

"I… it's not what you think," she said hoarsely. "I… the thing I did. Where I screwed up. I prescribed too big a dose. And the guy almost OD'd. And this doctor I work for now—he's terrible. He almost kills people every day. And I… I mean, I'm already so fucked anyway. I'm trying to keep his patients from getting addicted, because he doesn't seem to care. And Robbie caught me doing that and said I might as well give *him* the extra drugs." Lance heard a terrible weariness in her voice. "I'm so tired. I'm so damned tired. I was so proud, you know? I'd be a nurse. I'd help people."

"Sh… here, honey. Give me that. That's a girl. Thank you. Yeah. Yeah. I know. Our lives get screwed up sometimes and we just have to clean up the mess and go on."

"I'm gonna go to jail," she wailed. "And I deserve it!"

"A little bit yeah," Henry told her, and even in the closet, Lance stifled a laugh. Because that was Henry—dead honest, even while comforting a criminal. "But I've got some friends who might make that a little less painful, okay?"

"What's gonna happen to Robbie?" she asked pitifully.

"He's going to go to jail for a lot longer," Henry said, voice grim. "I hope that's okay."

"I don't know." And she was lost. So lost. Lance could pity her because he imagined that's exactly how Henry had sounded when he'd shown up on his brother's doorstep. With a little more asshole thrown in, of course.

"That's fine too."

"Worrall?" The voice was muffled, but the pounding on the outside door cut through two rooms.

"Come in, Kryzynski," Henry called. "She's unarmed, and she's given the gun to me. And by the way, nice timing!"

"We were literally across the street, questioning someone else in the hospital." The voice got louder as, presumably, the door to the office opened. "And I'll take that. Ms. Frasier?"

"Yessir?"

"Okay. Here. If you like, you can take your sweater off, and we can put the cuffs on in the front. You can cover them with your sweater that way."

There was another clatter as more officers entered the room. "Okay, guys. Go search the closet for the stash."

"But don't shoot my boyfriend!" Henry called immediately. "Lance, come out of there—nobody's weapon is drawn!"

Lance peeped out to discover a scene right out of Friday night television. A group of policemen surrounded Henry, who had his arms protectively around a woman in her midthirties with a bony jaw and bold knife-blade of a nose.

She wasn't conventionally pretty, no—especially not when her eyes were swollen with tears and she had too much mascara running down her cheeks. She'd sounded a little naïve, a little impressionable, easy prey for a handsome, smooth-talking doctor.

Henry was right. She was going to do jail time, and she'd certainly get her license revoked. But Summer Frasier's life wasn't over, not yet. There were second chances for people who got sucked in over their heads, who did the wrong things because they'd felt too trapped to even see the right ones.

Henry was living proof.

"Okay, Summer. I'm going to turn you over to Officer K-ski here, and he's going to read you your rights."

Kryzynski arched an eyebrow. "K-ski?"

Henry shrugged. "It's how Jackson has you on his phone. I think he forgets how to spell your name."

Lance had seen Kryzynski before, when Jackson had stood bleeding over the building super, the day Lance had stitched him up. He was a midsized man in his early thirties with sandy brown hair and ice-blue eyes. Lance had to admit he'd be a little tempted, at least to crush on him, if Henry hadn't been standing right next to the guy wearing purloined scrubs and an almost transcendent expression of triumph on his square-jawed face.

Kryzynski rolled his eyes. "And how is everybody's favorite pain in the ass?" he asked. "I haven't seen him since that night."

Henry gave an epic eye-roll. "Still planning a party next weekend. You're still invited. If he doesn't drop dead, I think it'll be fun."

"Oh my God. He's such an asshole. He'd better not fucking die."

Henry nodded. "That *is* the general consensus. See you there?"

And Henry got a brilliant smile and a hand extended in return. "Looking forward to it. Thanks for the assist, Mr. Worrall."

Henry took his hand and pumped firmly. "I'm looking forward to doing some more of that," he said happily, and Detective Kryzynski dropped his hand like a hot rock.

"What do you mean?"

"I'm taking criminal justice classes next semester," he said smugly. "I'm going to go after my PI license. You know, maybe help Jackson out when he needs it."

"Oh, dear God." The friendly look of camaraderie had changed to slowly dawning horror. "That is a very bad idea."

Henry grinned sunnily at him. "Well, between you and me, I think Jackson's going to teach me everything he knows."

"Oh God, I do not need this in my life!"

Lance could only look at the guy in sympathy. He'd met Jackson Rivers too—the idea that Henry might be training to be a PI in Mr. Rivers's image could hardly be a comfort.

Henry clapped him on the shoulder. "Just say thank you, Detective. It's really all I need."

Kryzynski's low growl of irritation was hardly reassuring.

IT TOOK an hour of paperwork and answering questions before Lance and Henry got to leave, and part of that was spent tracking down Summer Frasier's immediate supervisor. Lance hadn't missed the fact that Summer thought she'd been helping because Dr. Scheideman was too liberal with the opioids. And while the argument of a woman under arrest for all sorts of charges wasn't necessarily gold, Lance thought it was at least enough to have Mara put in an inquiry.

"Is it going to go anywhere?" Henry asked quietly after Mara had sent off the email, and Lance shrugged.

"It usually takes more than one complaint to start any sort of proceedings," he said, knowing the red tape got even worse than that. "It's not a perfect system."

Henry let out a deep breath. "Well, we do our best, right?"

"Yeah. It's going to take someone weeks on the computer with clearance to see if Summer Frasier was telling the truth. But we won't let it drop." In-house investigations could get ugly and heated—but Lance was pretty sure Dr. Schearer had his back.

Henry had winked at him then, and they'd resumed the paperwork part of their day.

Lance had to admit he was glad Henry had insisted on packing a change of clothes after that. It was his *day off*, for heaven's sake. He'd love to spend it *not* wearing scrubs and his ID lanyard. They changed before they left the hospital.

"Where to now?" Lance asked.

"Mm… how about the office." Henry was staring at his phone. "You can swing by and meet everyone. Jackson's sister works there as a paralegal, their friend AJ might be there, as well as Ellery. You can see I'm not being befriended by wolves."

"They could *actually* be wearing wool sweaters that make them look like *real* sheep, and I would not be convinced," Lance told him acerbically. "Oh my God, Henry, you scared the crap out of me." That moment when he'd realized Henry was facing an armed suspect was not going to leave him alone.

"She wouldn't have used the gun," Henry said, pausing as they neared Lance's car in the lot. "She wasn't even holding it right. It was fine."

"Have you ever seen a gunshot wound close up?" Lance asked, knowing the answer was probably yes and not caring. "I've seen what a gun can do, whether or not someone knows how to use it—it's all fucking bad!"

"Well, yeah," Henry said, and he had the same absurdly gentle tone in his voice that he'd used when talking Summer down from the ledge. And goddammit, it was working! "Yeah, guns are bad. But that's why we need to talk people into giving them up and not shooting them, right?" He turned toward Lance in the bright hot of what was still an early morning. "C'mere."

Lance tried to resist, but Henry tugged on his hand and pulled him close. "You think this makes it okay?" he asked, wanting to melt against Henry anyway.

"Yes." And there, in broad daylight under an unforgiving sun, Henry leaned in and kissed him. "I do," he whispered, smiling. "This makes everything okay."

Lance thought there needed to be more. He followed the kiss, harder, parting Henry's lips and taking his mouth unapologetically. His blood was rushing hard through his veins and a vortex of anxiety was opening up in his chest and Henry was the only thing—*the* only thing—keeping him from disintegrating into a puddle of fear.

And then Henry responded like wildfire, sweeping through Lance's body, consuming him, evaporating the fear and leaving a solar flare in its wake.

Lance moaned and collapsed limply against his chest. "This is so not fair," he said. It wasn't. "You're so good at what you just did. And you need to do it. And I'm going to be afraid every day for the rest of my life."

Henry regarded him with a faint smile, the lines in the corners of his eyes reminding Lance that he was an adult, and one who had chosen a hard life of service and loved it, and needed the same thing now.

"But will you also be happy?" Henry asked. "Because I'm happy right now. I... I didn't actually know that a relationship *could* make me happy. Is that enough?"

Lance closed his eyes and took his mouth again, pulling back only long enough to say, "Yes," before he all but devoured Henry against the side of his car.

They finally separated when the heat got too much, and Lance hyped up the AC as they drove through the heart of Sacramento to Ellery Cramer's office on F Street.

"Hope you're prepared for a hike," Henry said. "Ellery has clients right now, and the parking is for shit." He directed Lance to a spot by a meter on the side of a tree-lined street, and proceeded to be as good as his word by walking two more blocks without another parking place in sight.

"You weren't kidding about the hike," Lance muttered. "Yeesh. How far is it to get coffee?"

"Another block," Henry said. "Jackson has a skateboard that he keeps threatening to use. Ellery tried to pay me to get it out of the back of his car and throw it away, but I'm sort of on Jackson's side here. I'm thinking I'll buy one of those razors—"

"And a *helmet*!" Lance protested.

"No. No helmet. Anyway, it could come in very handy."

"You're going to make me old fast," Lance said seriously. "Fast. So fast. There's going to be no milestones. You're going to give me a heart attack. I'm going to wake up at thirty with gray hair and arthritis and a heart condition and I'm going to say, 'That's okay, kiss me again, and at least I'll die happy.'"

Henry's chortle as he turned into a parking lot next to a green Victorian that had been converted into office buildings was not reassuring. They took a left and then another left before Henry guided him up a flight of stairs that landed right by the elevator.

"Accessible," Lance said approving.

"Yup. They've worked hard to make it friendly." There was already pride in his voice.

There were three doors on the second floor, and Henry opened the one leading to the corner offices. Lance entered an obviously newly refurbished space, pleasant, done in muted blues and mauves, with a colorful area rug on a hardwood floor and comfortable fabric-covered couches.

There was a basket of toys in the corner by a sturdy, child-proofed end table, and Lance's heart did a little stutter. There would be children in this room, hoping their parents wouldn't be going to jail for most of their childhood. There would be mothers concerned about the adults they raised. There would be hope and despair in this room, just like there was in the ER or the ICU.

This was what Henry wanted to be a part of. Something important.

"Henry, how you doing? Still pissing people off?"

Henry turned diffidently to a stunning and curvy African American woman who sat behind a receptionist's counter that led to the back offices. She wore her hair in loose waves with bright magenta ends, and was dressed in one of those sleeveless shell/skirt combos that made every professional woman Lance had ever met as intimidating as hell.

"Hi, Jade. We, uh, were sort of tying up a loose end for Jackson. Lance, this is Jackson's sister and Ellery's paralegal. Jade, this is my friend, Lance."

"Friend?" Jade said, her face set into stoic lines. "That's what we're going with? I'm so disappointed in you, Henry."

Lance watched in fascination as Henry's color went from peach and tan to a magenta very close to Jade's hair.

"Boyfriend," Henry mumbled, looking at Lance sideways. "He's my boyfriend. It's new."

Jade's severe expression melted as she offered her hand to Lance. "So very nice to meet you," she said. "Are you here to keep Henry in line?"

"Absolutely," Lance said with his own sideways look at Henry. "He needs someone like that." His heart beat triple-time, he was so excited to actually hear the word.

"Mm-hmm." She glared at Henry again. "Tying up loose ends. You do know we can't pay you yet, right? I mean, not that I mind one less thing for Jackson to do, but—"

"I know," Henry said, with unexpected humility. "AJ first."

She sighed. "Well, we might have another path for AJ, so that would put you next on our roster. I've got to tell you, I'd rather feed you to the cannons than that kid, so I'm rooting hard for it."

Henry cocked his head. "Where is he going?"

"Well, we might have a line on a scholarship for him at an electronics school—so, surveillance, computers, technical stuff."

"That would be great," Henry said softly. He looked at Lance and smiled a little. "AJ's a great kid, but, you know, I'd be worried about him doing what we just did."

"And what did you just do?" Jade asked sweetly.

"Yeah, Junior," Jackson said, emerging from the hallway with all the swagger Lance had seen even when Jackson had been bleeding on his bathroom tile. "What exactly did you just do?"

Lance leaned casually against Jade's counter when Henry's cocky grin weakened his knees.

"Nothing you wouldn't do," Henry told Jackson, all teeth.

"Oh dear God," Jade said. "Did you learn nothing from our little adventure last week? Nothing?"

"Hey," Henry said, on the defense. "It was not my fault. Lance got me in all legal and shit, and I took those pictures and sent them to you and K-ski—"

"K-ski." Jackson gave a cat smile to Jade. "I like it. We're keeping it. Can do?"

Jade grinned back. "It's going in the contact files, so noted." Then she looked back to Henry. "Continue, Junior."

"And then Summer Frasier got there, and we dove into the closet," Lance said baldly, because he was not about making this into a storytelling moment.

"Oh!" Jade clapped her hand over her mouth, but that in no way hid her delight. "Caught? You got *caught*!"

Henry arched his eyebrows at Lance and turned back to her. "Well, once we shut the closet door, I texted the evidence to everybody, and then, when it was obvious she was heading back to the closet anyway, I stepped out and shut the door behind me."

"Classy," Jackson said, and he and Jade nodded together in agreement. "Very nice. Your stock is rising already."

"See?" Henry directed the comment at Lance, and then turned back to finishing the story with relish. When he finished up with telling Kryzynski that he planned to stick around a while, Jackson laughed softly, and for the first time Lance caught the breathy sound of someone who was not getting enough oxygen.

"Well done," he said soberly. "We need to find some way to pay you. I have the feeling—" He took a deep breath. "—we'll be asking you to help until I'm back to full strength."

"Or maybe beyond," Jade said pointedly, but Jackson just shook his head.

"When are you going in?" Lance asked, and Jackson's mouth twisted.

"A week from next Monday, if I can keep putting on weight. You guys are coming to Ellery's party, right?" He darted a look over his shoulder. "He's invited like a thousand people. It would be great if Jade and her boyfriend weren't the only ones to show—" Another inappropriately deep breath. "—up."

"Sit down," Jade said softly. "You got your nitro?"

"I hate this," he muttered. "I hate it so bad."

"Yeah, baby. It's a picnic for the rest of us. So much fun. Your lips are blue. There is a *couch* right there in the reception room. I'll go get Ellery."

Jackson started to move slowly to the couch, regulating his breaths with every step. Lance put a steadying hand out to take his elbow on instinct, only to be met with a withering glare.

"I. Dare. You."

Lance assumed his best bored expression and took his arm anyway. "When you're all recovered, you can come to the apartment and kick my ass. I'm fine with that."

"Henry, deck him," Jackson breathed as they sat him down on the couch.

"Yessir. I'll get right on that."

"I hate you. You're fired."

Henry winked at Lance. "I'm not even on the payroll yet. I'm not scared."

Jade came bustling back out from the offices with Ellery in tow. He looked a little more composed than Lance remembered, but the worry in his eyes hadn't changed.

"Here," he said, handing Jackson a tablet. "Was that so hard to ask?"

"It was sudden," Jackson told him, shoving the tablet under his tongue. He let it dissolve a moment before swallowing, his cheeks already getting ruddy again. "All better now. Go talk to your client."

"Go home and rest," Ellery said, no compromise in his voice. "You did a solid morning's work on the computer, now go sleep."

"We can take him home," Henry offered, but only because he opened his mouth before Lance did. "It's no problem."

Ellery gave him a grateful smile. "You guys can hang out—swim, raid the refrigerator, whatever. I would…." He bit his lip. "I would just really like to know he wasn't alone all day."

"I'm fine, Counselor," Jackson murmured but without heat.

"I'm not."

Jackson closed his eyes for a moment. "I can take myself."

Lance stood up and said, "Get used to losing that fight for a while. I'm going to go get the car."

He didn't meet Henry's eyes on his way out, because in that moment, watching the fiercely independent Jackson fight over comfort or help or self-care, he'd seen his life with Henry, as Henry did the same.

He hurried back the two blocks they'd come, wondering if he'd have to call in reserves if Henry got hurt, wondering if Henry would have as many people gathering around him as Jackson Rivers seemed to.

But then he remembered the day Henry had found Martin Sampson's body, and the way the apartment had rallied around him. He remembered the day before, when Henry had gotten home from a funeral and launched into papa bear mode, taking care of one of the kids.

Henry might not have learned good parenting from his own parents, but he'd definitely picked up on responsibility from the military and kindness from, where? Maybe his brother. But somewhere.

Yeah, Henry would be a handful if he got hurt, but Lance would have help taking care of him, just like Ellery Cramer had help taking care of Jackson.

Ellery had been right, that one day in the hospital. They had a lot in common. At least Lance would apparently be able to learn from a master.

OBVIOUS SOLUTIONS

HENRY HAD to admit that Jackson was an appreciative audience. They sat in Ellery Cramer's spacious American River home, a movie paused on the big-screen TV, while Henry regaled his new mentor with the story of the poor porn kid and the really effective exfoliant depilatory.

"Oh no!" Jackson sympathized. "Poor kid! I mean, that *sounds* hilarious, but... oh, man. Ouch. How's he doing?"

And that was Jackson. In the closet, listening to Summer Frasier come unglued, Henry had wondered what Jackson would do. He'd remembered the memorial service for Martin Sampson, and the way Jackson had found the one human kernel in a man who had hurt so very many, and he'd had his answer. Seeing the gun hadn't scared him—he'd recognized an amateur gun handler from the get-go—but the thought of Lance in the closet *had*. If Lance had jumped out in some misguided attempt to save Henry's life, his chances of getting shot would have gone up exponentially. It had been absolutely imperative that Henry control the situation.

And in order to do that, he had to see Summer Frasier as a human being.

It hadn't been hard. He'd apparently had a lot of experience being human himself.

"He's been taking a lot of oatmeal baths," Henry admitted. "And we asked John's permission and got him some edibles to chill him out while the hair is growing back. It's weird—he's always been sort of hyperactive anyway, but now, suddenly, he can sit still long enough to think things through."

"I wonder if he's got some other issue," Lance said thoughtfully. "You're right. Those edibles are really helping him think. Ugh. We've got a mental health caveat on our insurance. We should probably take him in."

Henry grunted. "I can do it tomorrow. He'll still be eating pot gummies and the idea won't freak him out quite so much."

"You guys are a good team," Jackson said drowsily. He'd played the charming host for the first hour, asking them if they wanted to swim, locking his psychotic cat in his bedroom. But after Henry had paused the movie to talk, he'd looked more and more exhausted. "You going to play mom and dad to all John's lost porn stars for a while?" Jackson asked Henry.

Henry grimaced. "Well, it's good when couples have things they can do together," he admitted. "But it would also be really awesome if we had time to do each other together."

"Oh God!" Jackson groaned, covering his eyes with his hand.

"Henry!" Lance complained in embarrassment.

"Sorry!" Henry nonapologized. "It's… God, I'd really like to sleep in a real bed that's actually meant for two grown men."

Jackson chuckled. "Yeah, I can see why that might be important. But it's not like that's the only apartment in the complex, right?"

Henry stared at him. "What?"

Jackson just rolled his eyes and then worked really hard to keep them from fluttering shut.

"Go to bed," Henry said softly. "We'll stay here until Ellery gets home."

"Fuck," Jackson muttered. "Fuck this shit. Fuck it to hell. I'm so done. And no, Junior, I don't need help getting to bed."

But Henry was already on one side, helping him up. "Sure you don't."

"Most days aren't like this," Jackson insisted. "This is the first bad day I've had since—"

"Since Friday when you almost died," Henry nagged. "Yeah, I get it. Now get your ass into bed and don't let your cat eviscerate me."

"Well, don't get too familiar with my cat and he won't get ideas," Jackson told him peevishly. Lance had gotten up and was on his other side, waiting in case Jackson suddenly needed him. He didn't, but he did sink gratefully down on his bed when he got there. Billy Bob, his tattered three-legged Siamese cat, was lying on the coverlet, looking affronted when Henry pulled it back so Jackson could lie down. "I'm fine," he grumbled, even as Henry tucked him in.

"You're a pain in the ass," Henry told him. As he turned away, he saw Billy Bob butting his head against Jackson's chin. Without a word, Jackson lifted his covers and the cat wiggled in, then curled up against his chest, licking his chin as Jackson fell asleep.

"Aw," Lance said as they emerged from the room. "What a sweet animal."

"That cat scratched up my face, you know. I tried to be nice to him, and he jumped on my head."

Lance raised an eyebrow in pure skepticism. "I remember the scratches. What did you do to the cat?"

"Nothing," Henry muttered. "I pet him. I swear to God."

"I don't believe you. But did you hear what he said?"

"Yeah, he said don't get too familiar with the cat." Which made Henry sound like some sort of pervert, and he was not pleased.

Lance snorted. "Come sit down. No, not on the other side of the couch—next to me. I know we're babysitting, but we're adults and even teenyboppers get to feel each other up in front of the TV."

Henry rolled his eyes. "Teenyboppers? Are we in our forties now, Lance? Is that what people our age call kids these days?"

Lance shut him up with a kiss. "I'm serious. Because your friend, who is feeling like complete crap, by the way, just dropped an amazing idea in our laps, and I would like to talk to you about it."

Henry snuggled closer. "Can't we make out first?"

Lance kissed him, hard enough to make Henry's head swim and his nipples point and his cock stand up and take notice. Then Lance pulled back and glared at him.

"What?" Henry mumbled. "Wha'd I do?"

"We're not having sex on a stranger's couch," Lance told him. "And we're not going into the guest bedroom either. Are you horny now?"

Henry leaned his forehead against Lance's. "Yes!"

"Well, we'll probably find a way when we get back to the apartment because I've already made it clear that I have no shame when it comes to you. None. I'm a big doormat."

Henry almost choked. "*That* is hilarious. Oh my God, if you were a doormat, I'd have spikes in my feet."

"*Henry*! Do you want to hear this idea or not?"

Oh please. Like Henry hadn't seen the idea too. "You want to rent an apartment in the same complex. I'm not stupid, Lance."

Lance seemed to deflate a little. "But… why aren't you excited about this idea? And by the way, I was *dying*, trying to figure out how to keep an eye on the guys while we got some privacy."

"I'm not stupid, but I *am* broke. Remember? I don't make half the rent. Even if Ellery can scrounge up some money for me, I'll be going to school. I'm stuck on that couch until I get a job that pays!"

Lance smacked him on the top of the head. "You're so stupid."

"Ouch! What?" Henry rubbed his head and tried to figure out what he'd missed.

"I don't need you to pay rent!" Lance snapped, absurdly enough keeping his voice down. "I just need you to move in with me!"

Henry blinked. "Lance, we've been sleeping with each other for a week."

"But we already live together! And seriously, if we get a separate apartment, and it doesn't work out, you know, move back into the flophouse!"

Henry laughed softly and sprawled across Lance's chest. "Galahad?" he said, trying to be reasonable.

"I don't trust that name."

"You should. It's amazing. Do me a favor and relax, okay? We've got some privacy, we've got a movie. We've got air-conditioning. I am, at this moment, a very happy guy. I may even get lucky tonight, and that makes me even happier." He kissed Lance's cheek, giddy all over again that this guy seemed to want him. "I haven't been this simply happy in a long time. Let's not fuck with the happy. Not now. Let's make out on the couch and pretend we're teenyboppers, okay?"

Lance grunted. "Fine, but I still think it's a perfectly good idea—"

"It's a great idea. But it's not going to happen this week, or even next week. This weekend, Ellery's having a party, and he's invited some of our friends and my brother, and you know what?"

"What?"

"I'm looking forward to that. Because last week, when Ellery was issuing invitations left and right, it was always followed up with, 'As long as Henry's not in jail.' So I'm not going to jail, and I have a boyfriend, and I did something sort of heroic this morning. There may be more shit to come." He sobered. "Malachi is still out there. I still need to pass my classes and get my license. There's always shit to sort, but...." He swallowed, suddenly unable to joke about this. "A few months ago, I was trying to get out of an abusive relationship I wouldn't even admit was happening. Can we just let... let a good reality sort of sit on our shoulders a little? Please?"

Lance let out a breath. "Sure," he rasped. "It's... this morning, you walked into a room and confronted a woman with a gun. And I get that you're still high from that, but it made *me* realize that you are... really special to me. And you're going to be doing shit like that a lot more than I'd like. So I don't want to waste any time."

Oh. Oh wow. Henry took his mouth, savoring the sweetness. "It's never wasted when we're together. We'll find a way."

Lance sighed and kissed him back, and Henry spent the next few hours on the couch, learning the joys of having a boyfriend you could kiss indiscriminately, and who was as much fun to talk to as he was to have sex with.

More, in fact, because there was respect, and kindness and humor in all that banter, and the sex was a promise, not a threat.

ELLERY GOT home about two hours later, right when Jackson got up. Jackson looked much better after his rest—his color was good, his eyes twinkled wickedly as he gave Ellery crap about saving the world while Jackson was down for a nap.

Henry and Lance made a quiet exit while Ellery was trying not to swoon all over his boyfriend, because it was obvious the two of them needed privacy and that every moment alone for them right now really was a sorely treasured miracle.

"Dinner?" Lance said on the way out to the car. "We could go somewhere."

"What would you want to eat?" Henry asked, keeping his voice neutral.

Lance let out a sigh. "It would be mostly for you," he admitted.

"Which is nuts because we skipped lunch." Then Henry remembered his own words about just letting them be happy, and let it go. "Anywhere you'd eat," he said. "I mean that."

"Okay. I've got a place. Bratwurst for you, grilled veggie kabobs for me. We can do this."

Of course they could. Lance made his way to one of those industrial-chic places with a polished concrete floor and sanded wood tables. Inside would have been unbearably loud, but outside on the patio, with the river breeze picking up through the tree-lined boulevard and the sunset sky overhead, it wasn't bad.

They chatted about movies and books—Henry had read anything and everything when he'd been on deployment, and Lance was insanely jealous, because the only things he'd had time to read were medical journals.

It was a fun moment, until their server, a happy, perky girl with blue ends to her curly brown hair and an infectious laugh, left their plates on the table with a happy wave. Lance looked at the veggies on his plate—absolutely lovely grilled mushrooms and pineapple and peppers—and then he met Henry's eyes across the table, his face sober.

"Want to see something?" he said, out of the blue.

"Here?" Henry raised an eyebrow and tried to make it dirty, just so he could see Lance's smile again.

"Yeah." Lance reached into his pocket and pulled out his wallet. He had to dig a moment, but eventually he pulled out a picture. With visible reluctance, he handed it over to Henry.

"Oh my God!" So cute. Round little cheeks, round little chin, and the same great, comforting ear-to-ear smile. "You make me want to have kids, and I gotta tell you, kids drive me nuts."

"I'm fat," Lance said shortly. "Can't you see it? I'm rolling in it. It's gross."

Henry looked back at the picture, thoroughly wounded for that happy little boy. "It's *adorable*. Who told you that little boy was gross? They should be shot!"

Lance looked away. "No one had to tell me—"

"Oh yes they did," Henry snapped. "Just like someone had to tell me that being gay was bad." He looked at the picture again, absurdly hurt for the kid in the little school uniform, his eyes sparkling with the same wicked humor Henry had seen in Lance's eyes every day for the past few months. "You're beautiful."

"Fat," Lance whispered. "I heard it every day from my parents. When I hit high school and started working out, they were singing my praises. Of course, I knew it was to deal with the stress of the big gay secret, but God, that was addicting. The better I made my body, the better son I was. And then... then when I started at Johnnies, you know, you start reading reviews. And suddenly I was that little fat boy again. And the more ripped I was on camera, the more praise I got on the websites and...." His voice wavered, and Henry swallowed hard.

"You're sitting on the other side of the table from me," he said randomly. "I've never had this, where I needed to touch someone to reassure them. Why are you sitting on the wrong side of the table from me?"

Lance tilted his head. "It's my fault that we're not next to each other?"

Henry shook his head. "No. It's your fault because you don't look at this little kid and see that smile. And those eyes. And... and the guy I've been falling in love with for months. It's your fault because you don't look at your body and see how beautiful you are, and how much I... I depend on you. How smart you are." His voice was wobbling off its axis, and he couldn't seem to get it to spin right.

"I... I don't know how to stop... stop hating food," Lance said miserably. "I... I look at your french fries and I think about that fat little kid—"

Henry got up and moved to Lance's side of the table, squeezing over on the bench. Deliberately he reached across the table and dragged his bratwurst and fries over. "I see fuel," he said, making sure he had Lance's complete attention.

"That's very healthy of you," Lance said dryly.

"I see a really beautiful guy letting his vegetables get cold." Henry took a deliberate bite of a crispy french fry.

Lance let out a breath. "I see carbs," he said. Henry could hear his swallow. "I love carbs."

"But can you live with yourself if you eat them?"

"No."

Henry pulled a mushroom off a kabob and dipped it in the balsamic glaze before popping it into his mouth. "That's pretty good," he said. "Here. Have one."

Lance smiled briefly. "Okay." He crunched the mushroom, and Henry could feel a part of him relax.

"I looked up bulimia, you know," Henry said conversationally. "I'm gonna be a PI. Figured I'd sharpen my skills."

"So what did WebMD tell you?" Lance asked, his voice as arid as Death Valley.

"It told me that it's a long-term condition. That even if you never throw up another meal, you're going to be playing Peter and Paul with your intake for the rest of your life. That stopping the purge cycle could lead to weight gain, but it's still better for your heart. That every day you need to wake up, look in the mirror, and love who you see, and remind yourself that this person you love needs to eat to survive."

Lance wiped at his face with his napkin. "WebMD didn't tell you that," he said, voice broken.

"Not all of it. I'm gonna be a *good* PI. I looked a few more places."

Lance breathed in hard through his nose, keeping his face averted, and Henry leaned his head on his shoulder. "Will it help if I tell you every morning that I love who I see?"

"Why wouldn't that help?" Lance's voice cracked.

"Will it help if I suggest you see a shrink when Randy goes? And that way, you can come back and tell everybody what it was like, so they won't be so afraid?"

Lance breathed in again. "Well played." Because Lance would go first so the guys in the apartment could break their own cycles, and Henry knew that about him.

"I'm glad you think so. Look at me, being all affectionate in public. Isn't that cool, how I changed? Isn't that proof that anybody can? Even practically perfect and healthy and well-adjusted people."

That got a strangled laugh from Lance. "Why would I—"

"Face it, Galahad. You won't be happy with yourself if you get all weird and emo about my job when I know you're hurting yourself every day."

Lance broke then, wrapping his arms around Henry and holding him so tightly Henry couldn't even dream of them being apart. Then he buried his face against Henry's cheek and wept softly, and Henry let him, not caring about stares, not caring that their food was getting cold. They were in the Lavender District for one thing—there were lots of same-sex couples, not just in the restaurant, but everywhere.

But for another, this, Lance trusting him with the pain, the uncertainty, the purging—this was the thing Henry had never been given with Mal. This was a part of Lance's heart that nobody else would get to see—or even, as far as Henry could tell—would appreciate. Henry would stand up on their table and shout, "I'm gay, motherfuckers!" if it would help Lance not hurt himself.

If it would help the two of them be okay.

Lance's breathing finally grew even, and he let go, grabbing some more napkins to clean up his face—and Henry's. After a quiet moment, he turned back to their food and snagged another mushroom.

"I'll make the appointments tonight online," he said. "One for me, one for Randy. See if we can start a trend."

Henry kissed his cheek. "Good."

They ate then, side by side, enjoying the quiet and the coolness of the falling evening.

Lance took a final bite of vegetable and breathed out. "I love you too," he said. "I love you a lot."

"Wasn't too soon?" Henry asked quietly.

"Apparently not." Lance closed his eyes as though just appreciating the evening. "Apparently it was exactly the right time."

"That's a first."

Lance laughed a little. "Maybe it's the start of something awesome. We can only wait and see."

They didn't have sex that night, which should have been a terrible disappointment. But what happened instead was quieter and more magical.

When everyone had gone to bed, they ended up on the couch, talking quietly.

They made plans.

An apartment, when Henry could help with the rent. Some furniture. A PI's license for Henry, a fellowship for Lance after this year of residency. A house in a couple of years. Did they want kids? Maybe. Lance liked them.

Would Lance want to meet David and Henry's oldest brother if he came to town? Of course. Would Lance introduce Henry to his sister the next time they had lunch? He was dying to. What would Henry do if he didn't like PI work? A law degree? Possibly—possibly not. So many things to do, so many places to go. Vacations neither of them had ever taken, but wanted to take together.

Henry sat back against the corner of the couch, his arms around Lance's shoulders, thinking about the future in a way he never had before.

That sense he'd had when he'd arrived in Sacramento, that his entire life was over? That feeling was a bad memory.

The letdown at the end of the case had faded, and what was left was a building thrill of what his life could become.

Somehow, in the past few months, the future had gone from a wasteland of loneliness to an exciting, living thing, something that he could change, something that he'd already changed. Yeah, he had a past—and Malachi still loomed large, a shadow Henry might never truly escape, only learn to live with. There was a reckoning there, and Henry knew it. But even that felt less awful, less full of shame, less covered in guilt and remorse.

Henry had so much more to do now.

The future was *exciting*.

He had control over his future in a way he never had before.

And it all started with the man in his arms.

HUNGRY

"So, Dr. Galahad Luna—"

"People call me Lance." Lance gave the psychiatrist—Dr. Stevenson—a brief, professional smile.

"It says here you're a resident at UC Davis. What are you doing here at Kaiser?"

Lance grimaced. "You're actually on my health insurance from my other job, and since I was taking a friend here from that job anyway…." He held out his hands so Stevenson could make the obvious connection.

"What's your other jo—oh."

Stevenson's balding head came up from the file he was scanning, and he looked at Lance again in mild surprise. "John Carey Industries. Wow. Okay, so, eating disorder. Is that *all* we've got going? Just making sure."

Lance fought the temptation to roll his eyes. "Why? You used to seeing a lot of train wrecks in porn?"

Stevenson's homely features, his sagging jowls and eyes surrounded by wrinkles, became sober almost immediately.

"Yes," he said. "Some fairly well-adjusted guys, one guy who told me, 'Hey, I'm so over therapy but you seem nice,' and a bunch of other guys who came to me with eating disorders and then quit porn and came back and said, 'You know, it's weird, I can eat a whole cheeseburger now. Go figure.' But yeah. Maybe it's because your boss has decent health insurance so I catch a lot of you before you go nuclear. But since I sort of got known for treating you guys, it's been…."

"Interesting?" Lance supplied, arching his eyebrows, as if he was talking to a colleague.

"Hard," Stevenson said instead. "Because you're all young, you're all bright, and you're all beautiful. And getting you to see that is so difficult." His eyes wandered someplace far away. "It's worth it," he said after a moment. "But not easy."

Lance grunted. "Tell me about it."

Stevenson cocked his head. "No, son, that's your job."

Lance swallowed. "Look, my eating disorder is… pretty standard. I was a roly-poly kid, and I got tired of hearing about it, so I leaned up. Then

I took this job where you can see a tic-tac against my stomach if I eat it close enough to a scene, and I got pretty good at tossing my cookies. I'm… I need a calorie diary and a nutritionist and, well, basically to quit porn and to settle down and make my life about not tossing my cookies. Am I right?"

"Wow. It's like you're a medical professional or something."

Lance rolled his eyes, and in response, the doctor pulled out a bag of… knitting?

"In this heat? Are you kidding me?" Lance could feel the stickiness from outside still oozing on his skin.

"It helps me not strangle cocky young assholes who think they know my job," Stevenson said irritably. "Now tell me some more about how you've got your eating disorder licked."

Lance let out a breath and closed his eyes. "You're right. I don't. I really don't. I just…." He laced his fingers behind his neck and decided to talk about what was really bothering him.

"My boyfriend got out of an eleven-year abusive relationship," Lance said, because *that* was the thing that had been chewing on his heart on the way over. Bulimia, yeah, yeah—Lance was functional, but Henry's denial scared him. "The guy had him over a barrel too. Either they keep fucking in the closet, or the asshole would wreck his military career and out him to his family."

Stevenson put his knitting down. "This is new."

"Yeah." That was aces. Lance loved it when he was a medical anomaly. "Well, my guy said stop, and the asshole said go—and he did exactly what he wanted and kept fucking going." Stevenson sucked in a breath, and Lance plowed on. "And my guy won't even say the fucking word. He took a dishonorable discharge to get away from his brother-in-law—yeah, you heard me—and he's been getting his shit together for the last couple of months. And he seems to be doing good. Great. Like… like he was just waiting to be free to see what an awesome human being he could be. Me and him, we watch over this group of porn kids—"

"My last patient?" Stevenson said, and Lance nodded. "He mentioned you both. Seems to think of you like parents."

"Right?" Lance said, standing up so he could pace. "Like, neither of us want to just leave them alone—they… they seem to need some steadying, you know?"

"I am stunned," Stevenson said.

"You're a real sarcastic asshole, anybody tell you that?"

"It only comes out in a safe place." Stevenson picked up his knitting again. "It's my reward for dealing with people who will jump out of their skin if I breathe in too hard."

Lance lifted a shoulder. "That's fair." He exhaled. "So yeah. When I leave here, I want the calorie diary, the newest treatment plan, all the mental games I have to play in my own head to get over my fucking self so I can eat a sandwich and not puke. I am *down* for that shit. But right now, before I even concentrate on that, before I can even *think* about that, I need to know two things."

"Shoot."

Lance looked over at him. He was knitting, but he was also gazing at Lance thoughtfully, so Lance thought he'd run with it.

"The first is, are we doing these kids a favor, hanging around, trying to find a way to not bail on them? Are we giving them false hope or screwing with their self-sufficiency? My heart says no—my *heart* says they need us. But we all have shit we carry from our upbringing. My parents were like, 'Hey, you are a truly self-sufficient being in your twenties, so if you want to continue contact, you need to stop being gay.'"

Stevenson let out a pained grunt. "Motherpusbucket."

Lance's eyes went wide. "Excuse me?"

"Sometimes the wrong people really *do* end up in therapy. I'm sorry. I've just… I hear that story a *lot*, and I am never ever happy about it, and I will never get over it, either."

A teeny corner of Lance's soul began to warm up a little. "So does that mean I don't have to?" he asked gruffly. "Me and my boyfriend—it's okay if that still hurts?"

"Yeah, Lance. You had a support system for much of your life, and it disappeared. It's okay if that hurts for a good long time."

It was difficult to swallow, but Lance managed. "Good," he said. "We'll get to that. So, is it wrong, me and Henry, trying to help these guys out?"

"No," Stevenson said, unequivocally. "Don't let them become codependent on you. Don't get in their way of growth. But if they need to know someone's there to care for them, and you two, you decide you're their people, that works. You brought Randy here when you realized he needed more than you, right?"

"Yeah," Lance said. "And there's at least one more guy we need to bring in, but he's closer to Henry, so I'll let him do it." Lance growled. "Which brings me to my second question. The one that's driving me batshit and I need it answered before I can concentrate on myself."

"Go for it. I'm going to need a couple of weeks to unpack this conversation anyway."

Lance gave him a one-sided smile, because he realized he wasn't being easy.

"So Henry's parting gift from this psycho who kept him in the closet was being forced."

"Raped?" Stevenson qualified delicately, and Lance looked at him, actually met his eyes, so the guy could see how serious he was being.

"Yeah," he whispered. "And sometimes, when he's talking, shit just slips out. Shit like 'Yeah, Malachi sliced my shirt right off my body once, to keep me from leaving the hotel room.' Or, 'Gee, I hope my sister's okay.' And when he showed up here—his brother works at Johnnies—he looked like hell. His dad had pretty much beat the crap out of him, and Henry's not a small guy. He let it happen. And I'm *worried*," Lance burst out, so relieved he almost cried. "He kisses me in public now. He smiles. He cracks jokes. He's still sort of a grumpy asshole, but that works for him. And I'm like, 'Okay, when's this going to come out?' I can control my eating, or if I can't, *now* I know that there is a headspace and some hard work that will let me do it. I have faith that will work. But I can't control when all of this is going to burst out of Henry, and I don't know how bad it's going to be."

"Oh. Well. Just when you think you've heard it all…."

"What?" Lance demanded.

"You are reasonably functional. I'd like to see you get the bulimia under control. I'd really like to see you gain ten pounds, even if it's muscle. But yeah, you're right to be worried. Your boyfriend sounds functional too, but that's some baggage he's carrying around." He shook his head, his fingers moving of their own volition in wool that was a military-green color. "Does he seem to be violent?"

Lance thought about Henry, being kind to Summer Frasier when she'd had the gun.

And then he saw him body slam Martin Sampson into a full dumpster.

"When he's protecting us," he said after a moment. "And not… not to extreme. He doesn't beat people to a pulp—he gets them out of the way. He doesn't yell at people. He talks them down from the ledge."

"So… so there may come a day when some of this gets out," Stevenson said softly. "And he's going to need someone to talk *him* down."

Lance nodded. "Yeah. That's what I was asking." He blew out a breath and flopped onto the very comfortable couch. "So I just need to be ready."

"Yeah. He's got a sense of freedom, from what you've said. Out of the military, out of this relationship—he's not going to see he's keeping himself in his own prison until something reminds him."

Lance shook his head. "He's a really good guy," he said. "I… we talked last night, and I could see our entire lives unfolding. Like this was the guy I'd been waiting to fall in love with since I was twelve years old."

"There's nothing wrong with falling for a guy with baggage," Stevenson said softly. "It sounds like you're ready to work with him to lighten the load."

"I am," Lance said, his eyes burning a little.

"Now what can we do to help lighten *your* load? Without sticking your fingers down your throat, of course."

God. Lance felt wrung out already. But he also knew he'd trespassed on the doctor's good will enough. "Okay, so, let me tell you the sad story of a fat little kid named Galahad, and how everyday his father said, 'What a little chunk! Are we skipping dessert tonight, Gally? I think that would be best.' And I'd leave the dinner table hungry so I could stop being fat little Gally."

"I'm riveted," Stevenson said, and Lance looked at him in surprise, because he seemed to have lost his sarcastic edge. "No, truly," the doctor told him, apparently in all sincerity. "Because that's a real story about you, and now we're getting somewhere."

Lance swallowed. "God," he muttered. "I knew this was going to suck."

"Had it all figured out, did you?"

"Yeah." He swallowed again and was about to wipe his eyes on his shirt, but then Stevenson used a knitting needle to point out the box of Kleenex right next to him. He grabbed a couple and wiped his eyes.

"Didn't count on the pain?"

"I'm a doctor," Lance lamented. "I should know better."

"Oh, sweet, sweet naïve little porn star. Nobody ever does."

And then they really got to work.

LANCE DROPPED Randy off at the apartment and then took off for work—a twelve-hour shift—getting back around two a.m. Henry was asleep on the couch, still in his cargo shorts, arms wrapped around his knees, his head leaning on the couch back. He looked like a child who'd just nodded off. Lance woke him up with a kiss on the temple.

"Hey," he said. "I'm going to shower. There's no one on the inflatable—I'll join you."

"Mm. D'you eat?"

Lance smiled. "Not yet. Want to make me something?"

Henry's return smile, sleepy and gratified, was one of the most beautiful things he'd ever seen.

He really *had* been reading up. Veggies and tofu this time, with a hint of coconut milk and some spice. "I was going to do curry," he said a while later, propping up his chin on his hand, "but that gives me gas sometimes."

Lance paused midmouthful. "And that would be bad?" he baited.

"Well, *awkward*, maybe. But, you know. You're dealing with a guy who has bent over in a Port-A-Jon—my definition of *bad* is really pretty loose."

"No!" Lance protested. "No! We are not going to talk about that, not right now."

"No?" And there was something in Henry's voice, something almost desperate.

"No," Lance said, tracing his firm, grouchy lower lip. "I hereby make that a rule. If you have waited up to feed me and talk to me and maybe sex me up after my shift, we're not going to talk about your ex. Because you need a place in your life where nothing's going to hurt you. His memories are going to be cropping up for a good long time, Henry. You may never be clear of them. But here, late at night, when I want nothing more than to touch your bare skin, nothing's gonna hurt you. Is that okay?"

"Yeah," Henry whispered. "Very gallant, Galahad." He looked at Lance's plate, which wasn't cleaned—but it wasn't full, either. "And nice job on the food. All done?"

"All done," Lance said softly. "But not with the food."

"With what?"

Lance shook his head. "You never ask me. Do you realize that? What a gift that is?"

Henry looked confused. "Never ask you what?"

"If I'm quitting porn."

Henry looked away. "It's not my place. I mean, I know that. I've been working really hard to not... not drag morality into all of this. And that means what you do professionally."

Oh, that hurt to say. Lance could tell it did. But he'd said it. And even though his face was red, and he was really uncomfortable, he'd been trying to give Lance his space about his job since he'd arrived in March.

"Well, I am," Lance told him, and the words were like a weight off his chest.

"Because of me?" Henry swallowed. "This was… this was your act of defiance, Galahad. It wasn't mine to regulate or to try to control."

"Not for you—for me." Lance took a bite of tofu and closed his eyes, savoring the taste. "Because I don't need the money, and because I don't need the fuck-yous, and because I'm not ashamed of anything I've done. But doing this thing to a point where it could hurt us, could keep hurting *me*, that would be something to be ashamed of." He looked at Henry carefully, trying to gauge his expression.

"I can't lie," Henry said, looking embarrassed. "I'm fucking *thrilled*. I just… I don't want you to regret quitting—"

"No," Lance said. God, look at him. Tough and grumbly and… sweet. Strong and protective and… empathetic. He was a throwback to a homophobic age who was trying gamely to throw his old identity away and embrace the one that fit him best. "I can't say I can always go back, but I can be perfectly comfortable leaving it in my rearview right now."

Henry was still searching for what he probably thought would be the appropriate response, so Lance gave him a moment by putting his plate in the sink and rinsing it off. He was entirely unready to find Henry's arms around his waist and his mouth on Lance's neck as he pulled him close.

"Can I be a caveman now?" he rasped. "Say dumb shit like, 'Mine! Lance mine!'"

Lance chuckled and thrust back against him. "Yeah. I'm good with that."

Henry licked the whorl of Lance's ear. "Mine," he said, but it came out as seduction. "All mine."

"Yes."

And then he shucked Lance's sleep-shorts to his knees, along with his briefs, and turned him by the hips until he was leaning, bare-assed naked, against the counter.

"Henry?"

Henry sank to a crouch in front of him and nuzzled his upper thigh. "Mm…." He stuck out a treacherous tongue, licking the crease between his thigh and his groin, and Lance spread his stance, bending his knees a little, giving him better access. Gently—so gently—Henry took Lance's testicles into his mouth, plying them with his tongue, rolling them like precious things, and Lance put his hands on the counter to support his weight.

"Henry, maybe a be-*ed*?"

Henry opened his mouth and took the balls in his palm, where he treated them like finest porcelain, while his hand moved up to Lance's cock.

"I have not tasted this yet," Henry said deliberately, sticking out that pink tongue again. He touched the end, swollen, getting bigger, and dabbed a little at the pee-slit, just enough that Lance knew he was there.

"You're not tasting it now!" he complained, and Henry's throaty chuckle almost sent him down to the kitchen floor.

"Give me some time to savor it," he stalled, licking Lance's head again.

Oh wow. Henry was right. He was amazing at giving blowjobs, and Lance had sworn not to invoke the evil ex's name ever again during the late night, but that asshole hadn't known a good thing when it had licked him on the penis. Henry licked around the bell, sucking the head lightly into his mouth, plying his tongue with teasing little flicks before releasing it again. Lance caught his breath and gripped the counter harder, because oh my God, he wasn't going to make it long if Henry kept doing that.

Right when he'd moved one hand to the back of Henry's head, to beg for pressure, for grip, Henry engulfed his prick in one long, smooth move, all the way to the root.

Lance used his hand to moan into, because wow. Just... wow. Henry dropped Lance's balls with enough "plop" to make them ache pleasantly and used his hand to grip Lance's cock, his stroke firm and sure while he kept using his mouth, his magical mouth, to titillate, to tease. Lance's eyes rolled back in his head and his knees shook—oh, man, this was amazing. This was *tremendous*. Lance, who had been getting professional-quality blowjobs for nearly three years could safely say this was the best blowjob he'd ever had.

It was too good. "Henry," he begged, massaging Henry's scalp with his fingertips. "God, please. I'm going to co—" Henry flicked Lance right behind his balls, right at his taint, and sucked and swirled all at the same time.

Lance's fingers tightened in Henry's hair, and he bit the palm of his hand as he climaxed, his entire body threatening to crumble from the one orgasm.

It almost wasn't fair.

"C'mere," he croaked. "Let me kiss you."

Henry swallowed on his way up and then went to wipe his mouth with his sleeve, and Lance could read the work of Henry's ex-monster all over that semi-ashamed gesture, but he refused to invoke him.

"Let me taste myself on you," Lance clarified, licking at his lips, at his chin, at the trickles down his neck. "Let me lick my come off your mouth."

He took Henry's lips in an all-out mauling, a possession that allowed him to suck, to swab, any last traces of come from Henry's mouth. He pulled back after the last touch of sweetness and kissed him almost chastely on the corner of his lips. "You have a filthy mouth, Henry Worrall. Let me clean it for you."

He kissed Henry again, sliding his hand down to the front of Henry's cargo shorts and finding his erection strong and hard, thrusting against his briefs. He kneaded, and ran his lips down the side of Henry's neck.

"Did you get your results yet?"

Henry had gone in Saturday for a blood test, and the results were supposed to be up on the website today.

"Negative," Henry said, thrusting against his hand.

"Good. Because I'm going to drink you all up."

Now it was Lance's turn to sink to a crouch before Henry, but Lance wasn't going to play coy. Hard and fast, without mercy, he stripped Henry's shorts until they fell to the floor, and took that amazing cock in his hand. Henry was porn length, and thick, with no foreskin, but an aggressively wide head.

Wrapping his lips around Henry's cock was almost decadent, and allowing his tongue to swirl around it, tasting him, was better than dessert.

Lance knew tricks too, knew about twisting his grip, about teasing Henry's taint, about digging into the pee-slit with his tongue. He'd used these tricks without shame in his videos, and now he used them without hesitation to bring Henry to an abrupt and startling edge.

"Lance?" Henry asked, his hands shaking in Lance's hair.

"You ready, Henry? Because I want your come down my throat."

Ah! The seductive power of words. Lance pulled Henry into his mouth again and was flooded, Henry's come overwhelming his senses, pumping mightily down his throat as he swallowed.

He kept just a tiny bit in his mouth, though, so when Henry tugged him up, pulled him into a kiss, he had some taste to share. He knew he'd done right when Henry sucked on his tongue and moaned, wanting more.

"We have all night," he whispered in Henry's ear.

"You have work tomorrow," Henry whispered back, and Lance whimpered softly.

"No!"

"And so do I," Henry sighed. "I'm driving Galen around tomorrow. Apparently he's got plans."

"Aw, man!"

Henry kissed him then, and backed them both toward the mattress, their shorts and underwear left where they'd stood.

"I'm getting hard again," he whispered in Lance's ear. "I'll never get to sleep like this. You?"

"God, no."

Henry's mouth still tasted like come. Lance had plans to taste that some more.

Ah! There was something so fulfilling about bare skin, about Henry's hands touching him *everywhere*. About their chests rubbing together, their thighs.

Their cocks.

Henry's hands, palming down Lance's backside made him almost delirious with want.

"Inside me," he whispered. "I want you."

Henry pulled back and frowned. "Are you sure?"

And if Lance had had the ex-monster there, he'd have killed him. "Yes, Henry, I'm totally sure." Deliberately he walked to the couch and grabbed the lube from between the cushions, noting clinically that there was a lot less of it. He handed it off to Henry, who wrinkled his nose.

"Seriously?

"Who do you think?" Lance asked because he had to. "Zep and Fisher?"

Henry grunted. "Billy and Curtis," he said, and Lance felt his jaw drop.

"No!"

"I'm saying—sometime in the last week, they both realized they were men who liked to have sex with other men, and they qualified."

"Are you sure?" Billy who was almost subversively quiet and Curtis who was unapologetic about liking porn and…. "Oh!" Lance suddenly got it. "They were on the schedule together last week."

"Hunh," Henry said, and Lance frowned.

"What is that word?"

"It's just a word. They seem to have a pretty powerful connection. Does that happen often?"

Lance shook his head. "Almost never. Johnnies is like the one place you can have really raunchy sex and not have to worry about strings."

Henry's eyes searched his face. "Unlike here, I guess."

Lance's breath caught. "This is home. This is having sex with someone in your home. That's…." Oh, how embarrassing to say. "That's magic."

And suddenly, they were the only two people in the apartment again. The only two people in the world.

"It is," Henry said. This kiss was untainted with memories of the ex-monster, unsullied with doubt. Lance wanted him. Therapy had left him cleaner than purging, an empty shell that yearned to be filled. Henry's warmth, his muscular arms and solid chest—he was shelter and sustenance in the same hard body.

Lance fumbled the lube bottle into Henry's hand and bent over the couch, tilting his head when Henry kissed behind his ear, down his neck, to the join of his shoulder. He made himself vulnerable, allowing for Henry's strength and his bulk to have control. His gratitude, when Henry breached him with two slick fingers, was acute. Stretching was good, was more than foreplay, was invasion. Lance's breathing quickened, and he bent over, giving himself to Henry who fingered him boldly, kissing along his spine, his shoulder blades, his triceps, as he thrust inside.

"More," Lance breathed, not caring if it was more fingers or Henry's formidable cock. Another finger breached him, and he hit the couch with his fist. "Good," he moaned softly. "So good." And while Henry thrust into him with his fingers, he continued the gentleness on the rest of his body. One hand made its way to Lance's nipples, plucking that wonderful string that led directly to his groin, and he hit the couch again. "God! God! More!"

He was expecting Henry's cock and got another finger instead. He buried his face in the couch cushion, gripping the sides of it with clenching fingers and let out a groan.

"You're killing me," he cried. "God, Henry, fuck me."

Henry spread his fingers instead, and his entire body shook.

"Please!"

"Is that what you want?" Henry whispered. "Is that what you *really* want?"

"Your cock," Lance begged. "God, you."

Henry's fingers disappeared, the emptiness enough to make him weak. Henry's cock was next, just a bit thicker, filling him completely, thrusting hard and fast down to the balls.

Lance screamed into the couch, pounding with both hands, until Henry's arms caught him around the waist and Henry whispered harshly in his ear.

"Stroke your cock. Hard. I want to taste your come."

Oh wow. Wow. People didn't say things like that on a porn set. Lance went boneless, moving one hand down to his cock as directed, and squeezed. He began to shake right as Henry began to fuck, brutally hard, but not fast.

Fast would have been merciful.

Lance was reduced to whimpering into the couch, orgasm sweat breaking out over his body as he stroked himself.

"So good," Henry murmured. "So tight. It's like you're trying to trap me inside."

Sweet talk—it seemed to be Lance's thing. He gave a cry and came, the heat spilling across his fist driving him higher even as he pumped more. Henry kept fucking through the climax and he moaned as Henry hit his sweet spot, even as he was coming. Again! Again! Again!

Henry bit the back of his neck and groaned, rutting harder as Lance squeezed him with every muscle in his ass. He came in a scalding rush that Lance could feel, thick and good, and collapsed against Lance's back. Lance managed a partial turn, holding his hand up defiantly, and Henry sucked on the webbing between his thumb and forefinger, licking shamelessly, tasting Lance's spend like his last meal.

The change of position forced him out of Lance's ass, and Lance felt the trickle of wetness down the back of his thighs, shivering with the decadence of it.

And then Henry pulled back and pushed him facedown into the couch again, and licked a trail down his spine. His mouth right above Lance's crease was a promise, and his tongue, lapping at his rim was….

Oh God.

It was everything. It made a lie that sex was ever dirty, that making love needed to be clean. Lance all but sobbed into the couch and allowed an aftershock to wash over him, wiping the memory of any other lover from his bones.

He was practically helpless in the aftermath, and Henry pulled at him gently until he found himself on the mattress, on his side.

"No washcloth," he murmured. "No underwear. Your body, sweaty and good under the sheets."

"Too late," Henry said a moment later. Lance felt the washcloth along his groin, and then Henry's bulk over his body as Henry wiped at his crease. "Spunk ripping out my body hair—not my favorite."

"I just want you all over."

"Wow," Henry said, touching his face with fingers damp from cleaning. "You sound out of it."

"Subspace," Lance said. "Doesn't happen a lot. So floaty."

"Mmm…." Henry burrowed his face against Lance's neck, and Lance welcomed him. "Think we'll sleep well?"

Lance managed a soft bark of laughter. "Yeah. Best dream I ever had."

And it was.

BABY STEPS AND BABY MODELS

"GOOD MORNING, young Henry. Good to see you in fine form today. I notice you dressed well."

"Morning, Galen." Henry wore one of three collared shirts he had. He did that when he drove for Galen, probably because he'd seen too many movies. "Where are we going today?" John had left the car parked in front of the house since he'd run an errand before taking his bicycle to work. Henry wasn't sure if he was trying to keep to one car or stay healthy, but either way, Henry was the chauffeur today.

"Hm… downtown. The courthouse, the headquarters for the Bar Association, and the mall."

"The, uh, mall?"

"I personally use a tailor, but we need you to have something… anything to wear."

Henry rolled his eyes, even as he was offering his arm to help Galen down the porch stairs. "I'm naked now?"

"No, but you aren't particularly presentable."

Henry grimaced. "Uhm, Galen, you know this thing I'm doing is… uh, temporary." And now, remembering the past two weeks during which Galen and John had literally thrown the full force of John's business into his defense, he felt bad about that. He'd thanked them, but there was no way to thank someone enough for saving your ass.

Galen laughed and patted Henry's shoulder. "Oh, I know you'd like to think so, and you have been very honest about apprising us of your class schedule and your hopes for a PI's license, and I think both goals are admirable. In fact, I am more than proud of you—if you could find a way to hide the razor burn on your neck, you'd be all that is a respectable picture of ambition."

Henry tripped and barely avoided falling to his knees. He recovered, but then he had to wait for Galen to stop chortling before he could help the guy into his car.

"Oh my God," Galen chuckled as Henry turned the ignition. "Your face! It was priceless. For God's sake, did you think we didn't know?"

"Goddamned Martin Sampson," Henry muttered, making his way under that lying Sacramento shade. Galen was fully dressed in a linen suit, but the heat was oppressive already.

"Oh no, Henry. We knew you were gay long before Martin Sampson. Your brother told John a long time ago. He was worried about you even then, because he knew what a horrible secret that was to keep. I didn't mean to mortify you—I promise. I'm just quite happy to see you this morning. And even happier to see you happy. Is that terrible?"

"No," Henry said, humbled. "That's kind. Thank you."

"May I ask who was the young man with the scruffy chin?"

Henry laughed, mostly because Lance was usually so clean-cut. "Lance. Roommate. You know, the flophouse—"

"Oh!" Galen sounded truly surprised. "Well, don't you have good taste. I take it you two will want to be moving out soon?"

Henry grunted. "Are you trying to marry us off?"

"Are you trying to throw a good thing away when it apparently likes you enough to rub itself all over your neck?"

And he couldn't help it. The *goofiest* smile crept out as he remembered Lance doing exactly that. "No," he mumbled. "But I'm living on my brother's charity right now and can't afford to share rent."

"Oh," Galen said softly. "Well, I think I have a solution for you, but I do need to make these stops first. You were hoping to work for Mr. Rivers and Mr. Cramer, were you not?"

"When they can afford me."

Galen's chuckle was quite subversive. "Well, we shall see that they afford you at the soonest possibility. Do you have any idea where you *want* to live?"

"Same complex, if possible," Henry said. He remembered coming up the stairs and finding Randy, on one of the most agonizing days of his young life. "Right next door if we can get it. I mean, I know some of the guys might move out, but I get the feeling anyone who ends up in that place is going to need a little bit of… I don't know… adult supervision. You get what I'm saying?"

"I do." Henry glanced in the mirror and saw that Galen was working on his tablet—but that didn't stop him from talking. "In fact, I think that's a great idea. You do know John took out the lease on that apartment like five years ago, don't you? So he didn't have his boys on the streets. He hasn't had to pay rent once—he won't say so, but he's pretty proud of that."

"Oh wow." And Henry's opinion of John, an addict in recovery and pornographer, rose exponentially. "That was when…." Henry didn't like to talk about this.

"That was when he was still using, yes. He was a drug abuser, but he tried not to be a scumbag. I think, if nothing else, you might have learned a little tolerance in the past couple of weeks."

And Henry must have learned something, because he finally recognized that tone in Galen's voice.

It was defense against hurt.

"I just think it was really great," Henry said, his voice thick. "I think those kids there, they were lucky to have John and my brother, trying to do right by them. I mean, Davy—he was the family's promise, right? Going away to school, getting his degree. We all thought porn was such a step down. But it's not that simple. You should hear the kids in that apartment talk about Davy and John. There's this… this reverence, you know? It's like they need to believe in someone. I get that now."

"Well," Galen said, sounding stunned. "I guess you *have* grown. And I think—if your stiff-necked pride won't get in the way—that I can get you and your young doctor a place not only in the same complex, but in the same building. And be patient. I have the feeling the perfect solution to the rest of the matter is coming your way."

Henry let out a sigh. "Always so cryptic. Do you enjoy that?"

He imagined Galen's lean, pretty face with a wicked tilt to his lips. "Oh my God, I really do. Just like I'm going to enjoy dressing you like a Ken doll and paying your salary for it. I've always wanted to be a sugar daddy."

"I am unimpressed with your attempt at lechery," Henry said, doing his best Galen impersonation. "If I have learned nothing else in the past few months, it's that you and John and my brother and his husband are really good people."

"That is disappointing," Galen murmured. "However shall we spend our time if we're not antagonizing each other?"

Henry smirked. "Nice suit, Galen. Do I need to bring you a mimosa when you're seated at your chaise?"

Galen made a sound that was almost a purr. "Oh my boy, only men in bow ties and Andrew Christian underwear can bring me *my* mimosas. We'll have to find something else for you to do."

Yeah. Henry suspected he and Galen would find a way to deal. He just didn't think it would be on the day of Ellery and Jackson's party.

"WOW," LANCE said, his feet dangling in the water. "That's a lot of people."

The house itself was pretty full. Ellery had done the job of a good host, introducing everybody to everybody, and Henry had gotten to say hello to

Jade as he'd made sure Galen got seated. He'd driven at John's request, and Henry had gotten the feeling John and Galen were up to something. There had been a lot of murmuring as Lance had remarked on the beauty of the homes by American River.

Once they'd arrived, John had kissed his boyfriend on the cheek, told him to play nice, and then had come outside with Lance and Henry.

Ellery's sizable pool wasn't full—but it was busy. Jade's twin brother had brought his wife and kids out there, and Davy and Kane had brought Frances. The older kids, River, Diamond, and an adopted son named Anthony, had made themselves Frances's personal playmates, and the competition to see who delighted the little girl more was fierce and awesome. Bobby, Reg, and John were taking advantage of the deep end, tossing a ball back and forth and talking idly, while Davy and Kane sat on steps in the shallow end, watching Frances like twin buff hawks.

"I remember when Kane was paying for Frances's cancer treatment," Lance said softly. "His sister wouldn't even let him in the house, and he was doing three scenes a month. Look at them—they're going to be miserable when she hits dating age."

"They'll be wonderful," Henry said with a faint smile. "They'll respect her decisions and tell her the truth as they know it and be kind when her heart's broken. It's really all she can ask for."

"Wow." Lance leaned on him a little. "My heart's all full now. Let's adopt tomorrow!"

Henry snorted. "Maybe we can wait until I can afford rent on half an apartment—"

"You're being stubborn." Lance sniffed. "I'm a doctor. Like *a doctor*. I know residents don't make much, but I've been saving for almost three years. I could furnish an apartment and pay rent and even buy a new car and have enough savings for a rainy day."

Henry rolled his eyes. "And I'd be what? Your kept man? Jesus, Lance, don't you want to respect me?"

"I *do* respect you!" Lance protested. "I'd just really like a chance to respect you more, in private!"

Kane turned toward the two of them and smirked. "He being stubborn?" he asked Lance.

"He's afraid of not being able to make rent." Lance's frustration was obvious, as was Kane's horror.

"Dexter, have I ever paid rent?" he asked.

"Not once," Davy replied dryly. "It wasn't a requirement. I had a place to stay—you needed one."

Kane stared at Henry in exasperation. "You're making things difficult on purpose," he announced. "Get over yourself." And then he turned back to Frances, who could now swim from kid to kid to kid all by herself.

"See?" Lance said pointedly.

"No," Henry muttered. He couldn't stop staring at the back of Carlos's head. Davy turned to him after a moment and gave a half smile.

"A real partnership means money is the least of your worries," he said.

Henry rolled his eyes. "You're smitten. I get it. He's cute, he came with a kid and a snake and some turtles. But I'm not going to agree that it's okay that I don't have a real job."

All three of them—Davy, Lance, Kane—groaned and covered their eyes with their hands. And that's where they were when Jackson emerged from the door to the patio. He looked better today than he had the last time they'd been there, but Henry could spot the telltale red crescents in his pale cheeks. He'd taken his medication like a good boy, but that surgery in a week was no less necessary than it had been when he'd collapsed in the middle of stopping a murderer. Nobody was talking about that now, though. He was being social and charming, and because he was Jackson, apparently, that was enough.

He visited his sister-in-law first and said hi to the kids, who seemed to adore him.

"Jump into the pool, Uncle Jackson!" the oldest, the girl named River, begged.

"Sweetheart, Ellery actually bought me an outfit to wear to this shindig." He held his hands to the lapels of his ocean-green dress shirt and gave a showy tug. Henry noticed his shorts—slick bajas in dark brown— were also not threadbare or tattered. Ellery had apparently gotten his way with this, as he did with so many other things, but probably because Jackson had trouble giving with the big stuff.

"Aw, man!" The two boys were disappointed as well, but Jackson told them to enjoy the pool and they could have hot dogs and cake when they got out.

"Cake?" Rhonda—his brother's wife—asked. She arched a shaped eyebrow at him, and he seemed to melt. Rhonda was gorgeous, model-quality stunning, with skin a rich earthy bronze and an elegant oval face, but it was more than that. Jackson's family, however they had come to be, seemed to be the one thing that could ground him.

"Ellery had a bakery just sort of go to town," Jackson admitted. "I mean, my idea of a barbecue and his are very different."

Rhonda's laugh was deep and layered. She knew this man, and she was as worried as the rest of the world. "You let him plan all this? Good boy. Make sure you eat some of that cake."

Jackson winked at her and then walked over to where Reg, Bobby, and John were treading water.

"Did Ellery and Galen talk to you?" John asked, flicking Henry an inscrutable glance before turning back to Jackson.

Jackson rolled his eyes. "Yes and yes. Are you kidding me? Seriously, you waited until now because you knew he'd be less stiff-necked about it, didn't you."

John gave him a toothy grin and neatly bopped the ball as it came his way from Reg, who hadn't picked up yet that he was talking. "You give us too much credit," John said. "We just wanted Henry to feel like he had a reason to stay in the area."

Henry frowned. "I wasn't planning on leaving!"

Jackson looked at him from across the pool and then moved closer. "That's the point, Junior. Staying."

Henry blinked at him. "I've got nothing."

Jackson laughed, the sound breathy but true. "Galen has just asked to be Ellery's first partner. Which means they are both paying rent in that office, which means we have some money freed up." He grimaced. "Ellery's mother has come up with some sort of scholarship scam for AJ—" He looked over his shoulder, because Henry had been sure he'd seen the quiet, almost timid gopher and friend hanging in a corner of Ellery's living room with his boyfriend. "It's a chance for him to go back to school, study electronics and surveillance and basically that end of the business."

"Something that'll keep him out of danger," Henry said baldly.

Jackson shrugged. "Some of us are more comfortable with it than others. How about you, kid? You want to join the firm? Be their information gatherer while I'm laid up? Help when I get back on my feet? You'll have flexible hours when school starts, and of course, you'll be Galen's driver because hey, he's part of the firm, but...." Jackson's eyes twinkled, reminding Henry of Jackson's perpetually horny friend who had offered him a job cleaning houses. "It beats working for Hurricane Joey—"

"And his nine-inch dick," Henry filled in wickedly.

"Right?" They shared a memory, Henry realized. A good one, of an exciting day. Jackson had almost died that day, but Henry had been cleared of murder.

And they had both lived to tell the tale.

"So, I can tell people I'm…?" Because he didn't have a license, not yet.

"A PI in training," Jackson said, winking. "Are you?"

Henry grinned. "Yep."

"Good," Kane said without even turning from watching Frances. "I'll be by next week to help you move."

"No need," Lance said. "I'm buying all new furniture and having it delivered. Are you kidding? Do you know how excited I'll be to *not* sleep on something that's been in that apartment?"

Kane actually turned and nodded at the both of them. "That is probably the better choice," he said sagely. "You guys come by afterwards. We'll make you dinner."

Jackson extended his hand and Henry took it. "See you Monday morning," he said. "Galen already confirmed. You and me—we're gonna have to work together without killing each other."

"That'll be a challenge," Henry said. "I can't wait."

TINY DEMONS

LANCE WAS never sure how John did it. Did he know the person who owned the complex? Did he have blackmail material on someone? Lance knew some of the guys rented out for spare change—had sexual favors been exchanged? Lance had no clue.

But whatever his evil powers, he really did get Lance and Henry an apartment to lease in the same building. Downstairs and to the right, apartment 126B.

Two bedrooms, one bath, new carpet, and it smelled like new paint and not old jizz.

The guys in the flophouse were ecstatic.

All four of them.

When Lance and Henry had told everybody they were moving, Zeppelin and Fisher had their own news.

"Yeah, dude," Zeppelin said, like this would surprise everybody, "I think we have to move too. And quit porn."

"Only if you want to," Fisher said, his voice clearly indicating that he wanted to.

"Dude, the only reason you started was for me. I can't even believe you did that. Most romantic fucking thing I've ever heard." Zep turned a besotted glance to his boyfriend—and his one and only, now that they had declared themselves apparently—and Fisher seemed to melt.

"My dad has property," Fisher said to everyone else, while still staring into Zeppelin's eyes. "He's got a little cottage out in the back, and we can live there rent-free while I go to school and Zep teaches yoga. It'll be good." He smiled at all of them with so much happiness, Lance couldn't even warn the two of them that they were too innocent to go out in the rain.

So that left Billy and Curtis, now unabashedly taking the queen-sized bed, and Cotton and Randy taking the two twin-sized beds in what had been Lance and Randy's room.

Lance had quietly asked Billy, Curtis, and Randy if he needed to pitch in Cotton's portion of the rent, and had gotten a resounding no. Cotton was never going to be homeless again—that was a pact they all made, and since

Henry still planned to cook them all dinner once a week, they'd never go hungry again either.

And Henry had been right. Once Randy had started going, and Lance had told everybody he was going to therapy to treat his eating disorder, Billy started going again, and so did Cotton.

Zep and Fisher were quitting porn—Lance suspected porn had been their only impetus behind the bulimia, so he was going to cross his fingers.

So the move, which consisted of getting furniture delivered and buying their own household items over the span of two weeks, was pretty seamless. So was Henry's new job. Since Jackson had gone through surgery with flying colors, he was issuing all the commands from mandatory bedrest at home. Henry said he slept a lot, but he also sounded better. He'd even had some conversations during which Jackson had been eating, which was encouraging. Ellery said they were going away in a week, sort of a vacation before Jackson came back to the office, and Henry was all for that.

And Lance was so looking forward to going to Henry's brother's house for a family meal.

He'd stayed with Johnnies for the family, and this was like proof that it didn't go away.

Dex and Kane's house was—like so many houses in midtown—small. It had a tiny front yard but a decent backyard with a big shady tree and a terrarium pit with running water for the four big turtles that Kane had accrued both before and after coming to live there.

The most interesting thing about the two-bedroom, one-bath home, was the giant glass wall that showed off the king snake and the iguana that lived in Frances's room. It caught shade from the backyard tree all day so the reptiles didn't cook, and people could look out and watch the critters while they were eating at the picnic table in the backyard.

This was a special occasion. They grilled turkeyburgers and hot dogs, and Henry and Lance brought a green salad in a brand-new container, as well as some sliced fruit.

"Bunny!" Henry cried, picking Frances up and swinging her around. "Look at you, all brown from the sun! You are beautiful!"

Frances giggled. "I've worn my swimsuit every day for a month! Uncle Kane says I have to get a new one!"

"Uncle Dex already got her a new one," Dex said, coming out from the house. "But it wasn't pink, and Uncle Dex is apparently a loser who doesn't know pink is the thing."

Frances giggled again. "I like rainbows too."

Dex squeezed his eyes shut. "Of course you do!"

"Put me down, Henry. I want to play in the sprinklers."

"Wait a second, bunny. Have you met my friend Lance?"

Frances's eyes narrowed. "Your friend or your boyfriend?"

Henry winked at him. "My boyfriend."

Frances smirked. "Your boyfriend or your *husband*?"

Henry's eyes got big. "Wow, bunny, that's moving pretty fast. We just moved in together."

She rolled her eyes. "But all good boyfriends end up husbands. Right, Uncle Dex?"

Lance saw the long-suffering look between brothers, and his heart did a big squishy roll in his chest.

"The best ones do, bunny," Dex said. "Henry and Lance will give it their best."

"And I'll get to be a flower girl and wear a dress, and you'll let me keep the little silk pillow, just like I did for *your* wedding, right, Uncle Dex?"

Dex squeezed his eyes shut again. "Yeah, bunny. They know the plan."

Lance snickered as Henry put her down. "Wow, Henry. Are you ready for all her plans?"

"No," Henry said blandly. "No, I am not. I suspect that is the case of all seven-year-old girls, and I'm glad she's Davy and Carlos's."

"Thanks, little brother. You're a peach."

Henry smirked. "Pink, Davy. Remember, pink. Also, rainbows. Whatever you bought was crap, and you'll pay for that forever."

"Aces. Go help Kane on the barbecue and make yourself useful."

Henry gave a salute, and Dex came to sit next to Lance on the picnic bench. He wore the air of a man who wanted to talk quietly.

"What's up?"

Dex gave him a brief smile. "You're very perceptive. Is that a doctor thing?"

"Yes. We get mind-reading capabilities in our first postgraduate year. It's in the curriculum."

Dex wrinkled his nose. "Sarcasm is so attractive. Welcome to the family."

Lance chortled and then sobered. "Seriously, what's going on?"

Dex swallowed and glanced at his brother. "So, Trav called today. Malachi transferred stateside about three months ago, and Debbie was waiting to join him in Georgia. She was getting a little upset because he wasn't relaying any orders or any travel plans. She'd let the lease expire on their house—she had to move in with our parents this week."

"Oh no," Lance said. He could tell where this was going.

"Mal went AWOL a week ago and cleaned out their savings."

Lance closed his eyes. "What. A. Scumbag."

"Yes. Well, he's a scumbag who knows where I live, which is not exciting. But he's also a scumbag who wants Henry back."

"You know this how?" Because Lance had held out hope. God, Malachi had been such a user. How important had Henry been to him, really? But apparently, Dex knew.

"I know this because he had no other reason to leave," Dex said. "I had Trav ask Debbie some questions about how Malachi had been doing. She admitted he'd been drinking a lot and talking about Henry a lot. She was the one who suggested he transfer to Georgia so she could see him and maybe get him back on track." Dex swallowed angrily. "Trav says she started crying. Malachi may not have been close enough to hit her, but he sure did say some shitty things to her from deployment."

"So he knows Henry's in Sacramento?" Lance had to make sure.

"He does. And he could show up here any minute."

Lance scrubbed at his eyes with his hand and tried to keep the fear at bay. Henry had been so happy, so optimistic. Was he ready to face his biggest demon? "You haven't told Henry?"

"I just got off the phone with Trav an hour ago. I've been trying to do the math to figure out how long it would take Mal to get here by bus, or if he could get a plane ticket as an AWOL serviceman or even if he stole a car and drove. When's this guy going to show up on my doorstep? And I've got nothing. But I wanted you to know so you could let the guys in the other apartment know, and—"

"And I'll call Rivers," Lance said, pulling out his cell phone. "He has a contact at the police department. I'll ask him for K-ski's number. Henry has friends."

Dex smiled faintly. "He does. That's good to know. Maybe tell his friends to have some MPs on standby, because they can take Malachi into custody. Make your call. Then, if you can play with Frances while Carlos deals with burning things at the grill, I'll tell Henry. I really don't want Frances to hear. Her… her father wasn't a good person. She's had enough of that in her life."

"Understood," Lance said, shuddering. God, he felt Henry's compulsion then. The one that said "protect my family"—the one that had led him into danger with Jackson Rivers, and had led him to face down Summer Frasier with a gun. Lance would do anything to protect Henry. He just hoped Henry had the healing in his heart to protect himself. "I…. Henry doesn't deserve this."

"No," Dex told him, clear-eyed. "No. He never deserved this."

Which was great that they both agreed on that. But would Henry agree if he had to see Malachi again?

THE NEWS was a cloud, but like most clouds, Henry shrugged and acted like he had an umbrella. But he did tell Lance to be careful and make sure there was someone with him at all times.

"I am not sure what Malachi would do if he knew about you," Henry said. "I… I would rather nothing bad happen to you, right?"

Lance heard the quiver in his voice and gripped Henry's hand tight.

"You know I bench press as much as you do, right?"

Henry rolled his eyes. "You know Mal and I were trained in combat. It didn't stop him from getting the better of me. Emotional warfare works because the bad guys play to win."

There was no arguing with that, so they ate dinner instead.

Turkeyburger, lettuce, tomato, pickles, some ketchup, no bun. Lance checked his calorie diary and saw that he was under, so he took a teeny bit of fruit salad and settled in. Henry watched him put his phone away and stroked his thigh. A team. They were doing this as a team. It made it easier.

"You got room on that phone for cake?" Dex asked hopefully. "We made little cupcakes with applesauce for you guys."

"I get white sugar and butter," Frances said smugly. "Because Uncle Dex says I'm so sweet."

"I get them because I eat whatever the hell I want," Kane said without compunction. "But you guys feel free to have applesauce without sugar, because I can see where that would be fun."

"Subtle, Carlos, real subtle," Dex teased, and the conversation devolved into good-natured kidding about all manner of subjects as they finished dinner.

Henry and Lance were cleaning up when Kane went into the house to get dessert. They all heard the hard, almost frantic knock at the front door, and Lance and Henry met eyes right as Kane hollered, "Dexter, keep Frances where you are, 'kay?"

Henry set down his dishes and ran out the side gate to the driveway, Lance hot on his heels.

Lance remembered to shut the gate, and he was pulling his cell phone out right as he witnessed poetry in violence.

A tall, lanky, brown-haired man came flying off the porch to land, flat on his back, on the small patch of lawn in front of the house. Kane leaped off the porch to stand over the guy when Henry got there, staring in confusion at the wild-eyed stranger on the ground.

"Malachi?" he asked, puzzled.

"Henry, get this motherfucker off—"

Kane bent down and grabbed the guy's ear, then, while Malachi's arms windmilled, he pulled him up very slowly, Malachi howling all the way. When he got him up, Kane locked Mal's arms behind him, hauling them up against his shoulders until his struggling stopped.

Dex's husband was nobody to mess with, and Lance would never forget that again.

"You will use good fuckin' language in my house," Kane said flatly. "And nobody's leaving you alone with Henry." He looked over to Henry and shook Malachi hard enough to make him whimper. "Right?"

Henry's mouth twisted up at the corners. "Right, Carlos," he said. "Lance, can you get K-ski's number?"

"Yup."

"Text him and tell him to get the MPs over here. We've got an AWOL soldier."

Lance's fingers flew, and the response came so fast, he was pretty sure Kryzynski had been sitting on his phone. *Three-minute arrival. They were going to case the place anyway.*

Thanks, sir.

Tell Henry to hang in there.

"Henry!" Malachi begged. "Man, I came all this way just to talk to you." He sent Kane a fulminating look. "Alone. Don't I deserve to talk to you alone? After all we been through?"

Henry's mouth parted, and his eyes grew shiny bright. "Kane, you can let go of him. It'll be fine."

Lance's heart crashed to his feet.

Malachi gave an arrogant grin, and Kane let his arms fall to his sides. Mal drew his elbow back quickly, like he was trying to get Kane in the kidneys with it, but Kane grabbed it between his forefinger and thumb. "I will crush your skull like a walnut," he said easily, and Malachi took a few hurried steps away, yanking his arm from Kane's apparently painful grip.

"Henry, come here," he said. "We need to talk."

Lance looked at Henry again, his heart aching. *Please, Henry, don't go with him. Don't. You're not his. You never were.*

He saw the indecision in Henry's face, the stoicism. Henry had been determined to do it all alone, from paying his share of the rent to keeping this man—and their terrible secrets—locked in his heart. But God, that wasn't him anymore. Couldn't he see that?

For just a moment, Lance could see Henry forgetting all the hard-learned lessons of the last couple of months, and his heart almost shattered.

Then Henry shook his head. "It was easy when we were alone," he said softly. "Wasn't it?"

Mal wouldn't meet his eyes. "You and me, we had a good time alone, right?"

Lance wasn't even aware he'd moved until Henry turned and put a gentle hand on his chest. "No, baby," he said softly. "Not over him."

"Me and you," Mal snapped, trying to intrude into their contact. "We're how it's supposed to be, right, Henry?"

"I thought so," Henry said. "But… but that's only because I didn't know what good was." He dropped the hand from Lance's chest and turned back to Mal. "You had me so fooled, I thought good was when you remembered lube or didn't knock me around. I thought good was when we got leave together and you didn't have to tell people I broke up a bar fight with my face. That's not a good time, Malachi. That's a bad time. That's eleven bad years of a *very* bad time. You think I'm going to go back to that now?"

"Henry, it wasn't like that!" Mal cajoled. "I only ever hit you when you got ideas about leaving, and look at us—"

"You destroyed my career, Malachi. I had a right to leave, and you took the Army away from me. You think that means you care?"

Mal shook that off. "It was a shitty job, anyway. C'mon, man. You can't just dump me. We've been tight since grade school!"

"And that's where it should have stayed," Henry snapped. "You're *married*, Mal. Did that escape your attention?"

Malachi grinned like a salamander, and Lance's gut churned. "Is that what's got you so turned around? You want me to leave your sister? I left your sister—"

"You left my sister pregnant and alone and broke. With my *parents*, where Dad can knock her around for not being good enough to stay married to you, because that's such a treat." Henry swallowed and shook his head. "I can't do anything about that. Debbie, my parents—they're not going to listen to me now, or Davy. But that's their world. This is mine. And in my world, I deserve a guy who cares about me."

"I didn't care about you?" Malachi demanded, his voice breaking. "We had each other's backs, Henry Matthew Worrall. We were in each other's back pockets since we were kids! I *loved* you, goddammit!" Mal reached out to grab his arm, and Lance started to hit the Call button, because he'd be damned if Mal laid a finger on Henry again.

"You *raped me*!" Henry roared, breaking the contact, and Lance almost dropped his phone.

Mal sneered. "I didn't do nothing that you weren't begging for—"

But Henry held up a hand and took a deep breath. "I said no. I took a promotion to make it illegal for me to say yes. And you did it anyway. It may never go to court, but you know what? I'll press charges anyway."

Mal gasped. "You'll what? You'll tell all those people that—"

"The people I need to care about me know," Henry said. "They still care. I work in a law office now. I've got some help with the charges. Hey, it *may* go to court. There's precedent. Because you and I both know you didn't have my consent. You say that word to yourself—say *consent*. Say *rape*. Tell yourself that's who you are. Say it until you believe you're a bad man, Malachi. Say it until you know you're the bad guy."

"You were fucking your sister's husband," Malachi sneered, advancing in on him. "That doesn't make you a fuckin' saint!"

"My big mistake was thinking we had a relationship," Henry said, taking his own step forward. "It was in thinking I had a choice. I was coerced, and you're the bad guy. And I've made some mistakes—God knows I have—but you are a mistake I'm not going to have to live with. Not again. Someday, I'm going to be married to a nice man who would rather chew off his own wrist than hurt me. He's a doctor, Malachi, smarter than me, but he still thinks I'm something. That's a relationship. That's how I know what you and I had was bullshit. That's how I know I don't ever have to go back to the military, or even back to Montana, to know I'm home."

Malachi grabbed both arms this time and shook him. "You're talking crazy!" he shouted. "You and me, we're what's real!"

Henry broke the grip again in a classic self-defense move, and when Malachi tried to grab him again, Henry broke it again. "Keep your fucking hands off me!" he snarled. "You don't ever get to fucking touch me again!"

Malachi hauled his hand back and slapped Henry in the face, hard enough to split his lip and bloody his nose, and Kane and Lance both moved in to stop that shit, but Henry was closer. He pulled his elbow back and took him down—two punches to the nose, the jaw—and Malachi's knees wobbled as he held his hands in front of his face.

"Henry?" he moaned, his voice broken. "Henry, you hit me.... I'll fucking kill you, man. You and your little pissy boyfriend. You fucking hit me!"

Henry wiped his split lip and bloody nose on his shoulder. "You're the bad guy," he said, and Lance heard the tears in his voice—but the strength too. "And I've got good guys ready to stand up for me now, but I don't need them to beat you."

Mal dropped his hands and snarled, feral as a wounded bear. With a howl, he rushed Henry, who had the presence of mind to step back and trip him, so he flew forward and ended up sprawled face-first on the concrete. And then Henry did a thing that terrified Lance to the bones.

He flipped Mal over and sat on his chest and started to beat him. "Stop it!" Henry screamed. "Stop it! Just fucking stop it! You don't have the fucking right! Just stop it!"

"Henry!" Lance cried, afraid to get in his way. "Henry—you will *kill* him!"

Malachi was still trying to fight, but he was getting solidly whaled on, right into the ground, and God, Lance remembered that fear, that the violence wouldn't end, that Henry wouldn't be able to stop.

"Henry!" Lance screamed. "*Stop it!*"

And Henry paused, looking at Malachi's bleeding face, and sucked in a breath like a sob. "Lance?" he said, looking up.

"Here," Kane said softly. "Go see Lance, Henry. I'll hold him down, okay?" And Kane hefted him bodily off Malachi, who groaned a little to prove he wasn't unconscious, but otherwise wasn't moving, not this time.

Henry stumbled up and into Lance's arms, and Lance held him tight. "I'm sorry," he sobbed, fighting for breath. "I'm sorry. I'm so sorry."

"You stopped," Lance told him, closing his eyes. "You stopped. You beat him, Henry, and you stopped. It's okay. You stopped."

"I'm sorry. I'm sorry. I'm so sorry."

Lance held him tight as they waited for the MPs, and hoped that someday, *someday*, Henry would realize he didn't have to apologize for defending himself. Didn't have to apologize for winning.

HENRY HELD up as he spoke to the MPs, neither of whom batted an eyelash as he talked frankly of the reason he'd left the military and of Malachi's going AWOL. Malachi could stand by that time, but he was too busy sputtering blood and venom against Henry for the MPs to so much as take his statement.

"We'll get him to the infirmary, but it looks like he got a pretty solid blow in. This is clearly a case of self-defense."

Henry nodded and held the ice pack that Dex had run out to him before going back into the house with Frances, and Lance watched helplessly as ugly black bruises bloomed on Henry's biceps, where Malachi had shaken him. Self-defense indeed.

"We can hold him on the AWOL charges," the first officer, a seasoned man in his thirties named Carlson continued. "But if you can press charges for the original assault, he can do some time. That way, you can get notified if he's released. Stalking laws are there for a reason, Mr. Worrall."

Henry grunted. "It's the best we can hope for, thank you. I'll have my lawyer file charges tomorrow."

Carlson tilted his head in response and then looked at his partner uncomfortably before saying, "Look, I know it's not my place here, but good for you. This happens way too often. Male or female, everybody deserves to be safe."

Henry just nodded again, and Lance could see his shoulders start to hunch.

"He's done," Lance said quietly. "Can we take this up tomorrow?"

"Yup." Carlson turned toward where Malachi was being helped inside the back of their vehicle. "He's not going anywhere for at least another twenty-four." He handed Henry his card. "Have your lawyer call this number."

"Thank you, sir."

The MPs left, and Lance wrapped his arm around Henry's shoulders and started to guide him into the backyard, where Dex was fussing over Kane to see if maybe he'd injured a hair on the back of his hand while handling a seasoned combat veteran on their front lawn.

They got to the gate and before Lance could open it again, Henry threw himself into Lance's arms and wept.

"You did so good," Lance whispered. He remembered his fears for Henry, the violence, the suppression. "God, you did so good."

But Henry didn't say anything, just shivered in his arms until he could function again. After a few long moments, he pulled back and wiped his face on his shirt, leaving a bloody streak against his shoulder. Lance yearned to take him home and tend to him.

"We need to reassure my brother," Henry said gruffly, "and save Carlos from all that whatever Davy is doing." He rolled his eyes in a patent attempt to make things normal. "You'd think the guy had to make an effort or something. Jesus, what a tank."

Once Lance might have fought him, but now he knew better. "Yeah," Lance said, keeping his own voice from quivering. "Try not to piss him off."

Henry gave a crooked smile. "You know me."

Lance just nodded and followed Henry into the backyard again. Henry Worrall's heart was good—so good. But sometimes he had to find a way on his own.

FORWARD HO!

OF COURSE, Jackson had to come into the office that morning. Wonderful. Fantastic. Henry was so pleased.

Henry could have asked him to leave. He was talking to Ellery as a client, not an employee, but asking him to leave felt wrong, somehow. His nose throbbed, as did his lower lip, and the bruises on his arms, and his split knuckles, and these were things Jackson knew about, and Jackson would know why they were important.

Jackson had been one of the first people to tell him he was okay. Without knowing about the rape or the abuse, Jackson had looked at Henry and told him that maybe his choices weren't awesome, but he wasn't a bad guy, and he had much of his life to live and live better. That had meant a lot to Henry.

It meant enough to let Jackson in on the whole truth.

He finished talking and looked at Ellery expectantly. Lance had offered to come in with him for this—and so had Davy, for that matter—but these two men were relationships Henry had forged on his own, and he needed them to see him for who he was without the people who made him look better.

He'd expected to feel something—anything—when he saw Malachi Daniels again. Helplessness, rage, grief.

He'd felt all of those things, but he'd also felt… let down. He knew such better men now. How could he not have known Malachi Daniels had never been worth his pain?

But that didn't mean he didn't worry about Jackson and Ellery, his new bosses, men he'd come to admire. Would they still look at him the same?

Well, Jackson's wrinkled nose and arched eyebrow looked familiar, although on most days he would have been pacing the floor instead of sitting in the adjoining stuffed chair in Ellery's opulent office.

"What?" Henry asked defensively. "You don't believe me?"

Jackson rolled his eyes. "Of course I believe you. I mean, I believe *this*. I believe what you're going to give as your deposition so we can press charges. But man, I don't *believe* you!"

Henry relaxed a little. This sounded like the Jackson who would give him shit. He liked that asshole.

"What? What's so hard to believe?"

"You! 'I'm the bad guy, Jackson! I'm the bad guy!' You almost had me fooled, you little turdwhacker. You were never the fucking bad guy, Henry Worrall. You're a goddamned hero."

Henry felt heat wash over his entire body. "No one's a hero for taking it."

"You're a hero for walking away," Jackson said soberly. "You're a hero for pressing charges. You're a hero for dealing with that for eleven years and still believing in the good in people. You'll never fool me again, asshole. I know who I'm dealing with now."

Henry's eyes burned. "Henry Worrall, at your service," he said, embarrassed. "Not much to look at here, sir."

"Just a hero," Jackson said softly, and this time Henry couldn't argue.

THAT NIGHT he waited up for Lance, which had become their ritual in the past month. Lance surprised him by getting there a little earlier with a bag full of ice cream bars, which he put in the freezer as Henry got his dinner ready.

"Ice cream?" Henry grinned. "What'd I do to deserve that?"

"Oh, Henry, there's so very much you could do to deserve that." Lance draped himself over Henry's back then and nuzzled his neck. And then checked his healing face and his knuckles.

"I'm not dead yet," Henry grumbled.

"No, but I've got plans for you," Lance purred, and Henry liked that thing he was doing behind Henry's ear. He would like more of it.

"Plans, I understand." Lance's warmth was seeping in through his bones. "There's a caveat."

"We're gonna get married," Lance said. "I heard that last night. You think I'd forget?"

Henry set down the lettuce wraps he was preparing and turned in Lance's arms. "You think I'd let you?"

"Nope. We're going to have the full happy." Lance's mouth on his was sweet and soft, but it was still driving him up, up, up.

"Really?" Wow. From full misery to full happy in a short time. "I'm impressed. I didn't think guys like me got the full happy."

Lance pulled back and regarded him in all seriousness. "Guys like you should always get your full happy," he said. "I'm just glad I'm part of it."

"I can't imagine a full happy without you." Henry closed his eyes and smiled, tilting his face into the kiss.

Lance moved to trace Henry's jawline with his tongue, and then whispered in his ear, "If I promise to eat later, will you wait for me naked in our bed while I shower?"

Henry swallowed hard. It was *their* bed—that still excited both of them. Nobody could come walking in, nobody could misconstrue Henry's nakedness for them when it was meant for Lance.

Nobody could hear the things they said to each other, the way they talked.

"You promise," he mumbled.

"Swear." Lance took Henry's earlobe between his lips and sucked, and Henry's knees almost buckled. Oh wow. Amazing that this was an erogenous zone. All the shit he'd missed out on and having his ears played with seemed to rank high on the list.

"You're playing dirty," Henry sang.

"I want you bad," Lance sang back, and Henry gave in.

"World's fastest show-*er*!" Henry said as Lance squeezed his package through his shorts.

"I'll set a record," Lance promised, and then he was gone, practically sprinting through the little kitchenette.

Henry put his lettuce wraps back in the fridge and ran toward the bedroom, shedding clothes when he hit the door. He'd gone swimming and showered at the gym after work—his secret places were minty fresh—and he snuggled under the new sheets with a little sigh of decadence and listened to the shower running.

He was hard from anticipation alone.

He stroked himself slowly, not trying to build because he didn't want to come before Lance got out. And he felt it—something he'd thought long dead, something that Malachi had burned out of him forever with that last brutal taking.

He felt a need to be taken.

He reached under the pillow and grabbed the lubricant—Lance's brand, and not some randomly placed lube that everybody shared. Lance had good taste, and the stuff that dripped on his fingers was silky and slick.

Torn between feeling foolish and feeling sexy, he rolled onto his stomach and spread his legs, careful not to get any lube on the red-and-blue striped sheets.

His fingers had warmed the slick up, and his first tentative touch on his rim didn't shock him so much as made him curious. He knew this could feel good—he'd been brought off before with just fucking alone. But how would it feel with some tenderness, some stretching, some of that confident magic Lance had spread around his own asshole when he'd mounted Henry and taken him in all the way?

Henry remembered that night, the way Lance's whole body had shuddered, the way Henry's cock had been everything. Henry wanted that with Lance.

He thrust two fingers in and moaned. *Oh wow. Wow, wow, wow, wow, damn.*

He pulled both legs up to his chest and thrust his bottom out, the sheets falling off as he changed position.

When Lance came out of the shower, still toweling off, Henry was naked, finger-fucking himself without shame. Lance's surprised "oolf" was the reward he never asked for.

"Oh my God," Lance breathed, dropping the towel and coming to the end of the bed to run clean, damp hands over Henry's hips and backside. "That's so sexy."

Henry went to pull out his fingers, but Lance sucked hard on one cheek.

"Ah!" He speared himself deeper and gurgled into the pillow.

"You want that?" Lance asked, reaching in front of him to stroke his cock.

"Yeah," Henry breathed. "I want you there."

Lance let go and moved to stand nearer to Henry's head. "See this?" he asked, stroking his erection and sighing when he got to the end. "That's what seeing you like that did."

Henry opened his mouth and willingly took the end of Lance's cock inside. He swirled his tongue once, twice, and Lance pulled out and bent over, the better to take his mouth.

"I'm gonna fuck you so sweet, your whole body'll feel brand-new."

Henry grinned. "Promise?"

And Lance growled, which should have been hilarious, because he wasn't a caveman, he never had been, but in two quick steps, he was behind Henry, his knees creaking in the mattress as he pulled Henry's fingers away from his opening.

He grabbed the lube and re-upped, and at first Henry opened his mouth to protest, but as Lance placed his cock at Henry's entrance and thrust carefully in, Henry got the gesture for what it was.

Care.

This wasn't a guy who would rip Henry from balls to taint because he wanted to fuck *now*. This was a guy who wanted Henry to love what they were doing as much as he did. And as Lance kept thrusting, slowly enough to bring sweat out along the small of Henry's back, Henry was grateful for every lover, even the ones on set, who had taught Lance how to be as gentle, as careful, as he was being now.

Because when Lance bottomed out, his pubic hair grinding into the skin of Henry's backside, Henry shuddered and smiled.

Glorious.

And then Lance started to move. He started out slow, murmuring, "Let me know if this is good, okay?"

"It's good," Henry told him. "So very good. Don't stop."

"Mm... you're so easy to fuck. Hang on. Going faster."

And he did. God, he did, faster and harder, but never out of control. And every glide of his cock inside Henry's body brought Henry more and more pleasure, closer and closer to an unreachable peak.

"Don't be shy," Lance urged. "Stroke yourself. I told you it was sexy."

Henry reached for his own erection and squeezed, his body so primed that one stroke was all it took. Hot and cold raced up his skin, and he lost himself in the glacial inferno of orgasm, shaking so hard he couldn't fathom words.

As he clenched around Lance's cock, Lance gripped his hips hard and spasmed, crying out and collapsing over Henry's back as his climax rushed out in a hot sticky scald.

Again and again, and Henry fell flat, his cock still twitching in his hand as Lance continued to spurt inside him.

Wow. Oh wow. His synapses were *never* going to stop firing, and Henry was so very overwhelmed, he gave a little moan, rolling to his side and shaking.

"Sh...." Lance soothed him, running gentle hands up and down his arms, nuzzling his neck, as Henry's entire body cut loose. Finally, Lance's touch brought him back to earth, grounded him, and the shivering stopped.

A few more heartbeats and he even managed words.

"Bad news," he mumbled.

"Yeah?" Lance leaned over his back and kissed his cheek.

"I think you have to get your own dinner."

Lance laughed softly. "No, no—I brought you ice cream. You telling me you can't get your shit together for that?"

"Depends. What kind?"

"Coffee crunch."

"You're playing dirty," Henry mumbled. "Give me five more minutes."

"Roll over and kiss me and I'll give you ten."

Well, that was worth it. Henry pulled himself out of the hazy delight of postorgasm and rolled over, kissing Lance and putting all his heart into the kiss.

Lance took him up on it, and the kiss went on, not building, just... just there. The two of them, their hearts in every touch, being kind together after making body magic on the bed.

Eventually they managed to get up and make it to the kitchen in their briefs alone. Henry thought watching Lance eat lettuce wraps over the sink in his underwear was one of the most endearingly sexy things he'd ever seen.

They began to talk over ice cream—Lance eating an Icee in company, of course—and Henry got to talk about his morning, about telling Ellery and Jackson, and later Galen, about pressing charges, and about how well his new boss had his back.

Lance asked him if Malachi would see any jail time, and Henry sighed. "If anyone can make it happen, it's Ellery Cramer. But life's not perfect, and the system isn't either. At least *I* know I tried."

"I know too," Lance said, taking an unexpected lick of Henry's Drumstick. "Wow. Wow, that was a mistake." He looked mournfully at his cherry Icee. "How's that going to measure up now?"

Henry offered him another bit of his ice cream, and Lance took it, smiling shyly. "This is good," Henry said, biting his lip. "We have to do this always."

Lance leaned in and gave him a messy kiss. "Talk about our days? Be honest about how we feel? Do things together? I think that's how we keep this going."

"This is why we need to keep talking to the porn kids," Henry said in all seriousness. "Galen told me John sent two new kids there today. We need to visit tomorrow before you go work out. These kids, they need to see what a relationship is. I don't think some of them know." He paused. "I didn't."

Lance smiled, his eyes glinting wickedly. "The relationship they can see," he said. "The sex...."

"That's all ours." Henry finished off the ice cream cone and then kissed him again, savoring the cherry ice with his chocolate and vanilla. Lance returned the kiss, until the ice cream and the ice was all gone, and together they washed up and went back to bed, to sleep this time.

Before he closed his eyes, Henry took a moment to appreciate being in Lance's arms, the sun seeming to light their way into the future.

Every hard-earned moment of hope, of happiness, was theirs to savor, and every good moment lay in front of them with Henry's new bright future.

A few months ago, he'd been at the end of everything—his career, his relationship, his family.

Who knew the end was only the beginning?

Choose your Lane to love!

Orange

Amy's Dark Contemporary Romance

AMY LANE lives in a crumbling crapmansion with a couple of growing children, a passel of furbabies, and a bemused spouse. She's been a finalist in the RITAs™ twice, has won honorable mention for an Indiefab, and has a couple of Rainbow Awards to her name. She also has too damned much yarn, a penchant for action-adventure movies, and a need to know that somewhere in all the pain is a story of Wuv, Twu Wuv, which she continues to believe in to this day! She writes fantasy, urban fantasy, and gay romance—and if you accidentally make eye contact, she'll bore you to tears with why those three genres go together. She'll also tell you that sacrifices, large and small, are worth the urge to write.

Website: www.greenshill.com
Blog: www.writerslane.blogspot.com
Email: amylane@greenshill.com
Facebook: www.facebook.com/amy.lane.167
Twitter: @amymaclane

AMY LANE
STRING
BOYS

Seth Arnold learned at an early age that two things in life could make his soul soar—his violin and Kelly Cruz. In Seth's uncertain childhood, the kindness of the Cruz family, especially Kelly and his brother, Matty, gave Seth the stability to make his violin sing with the purest sound and opened a world of possibility beyond his home in Sacramento.

Kelly Cruz has loved Seth forever, but he knows Seth's talents shouldn't be hidden, not when the world is waiting. Encouraging Seth to follow his music might break Kelly's heart, but he is determined to see the violin set Seth's soul free. When their world is devastated by a violent sexual assault and Matty's prejudices turn him from a brother to an enemy, Seth and Kelly's future becomes uncertain.

Seth can't come home and Kelly can't leave, but they are held together by a love that they clutch with both hands.

Seth and Kelly are young and the world is wide—the only thing they know for certain is they'll follow their heartstrings to each other's arms whenever time and fate allow. And pray that one day they can follow that string to forever… before it slices their hearts in two.

www.dreamspinnerpress.com

FOR **MORE** OF THE **BEST GAY ROMANCE**

dreamspinnerpress.com

www.ingramcontent.com/pod-product-compliance
Lightning Source LLC
Chambersburg PA
CBHW070112260626
47160CB00004B/1440